Candice F. Ransom

SCHOLASTIC INC.
New York Toronto London Auckland Sydney Tokyo

ISBN 0-590-32774-7

12 11 10 9 8 7 6 5 4 3 2 1   1   4 5 6 7 8/8

Printed in the U.S.A.   06

A Scholastic Publication

A *SUNFIRE* Book

SUNFIRE

For Frank,
who did all the cooking

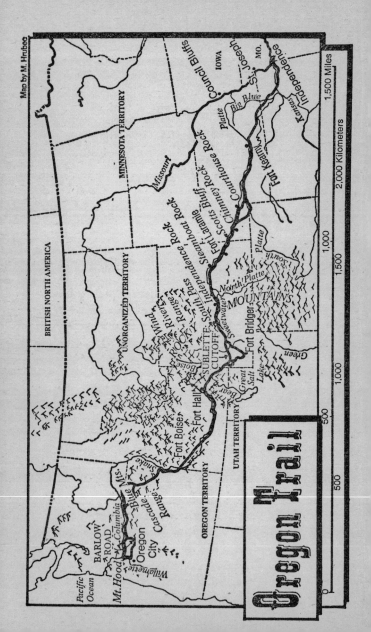

Chapter One

IT had been raining forever, endless rain that dripped down the windowpanes. Amanda Bentley could not stand the cramped hotel room another minute. The instant she saw sunshine breaking through the leaden skies, she grabbed her black, fringed shawl, stumbling over Mrs. Longman's brassbound trunk in her haste to get to the door.

Penitence Longman looked up from her book, her pale eyes blinking like a barn owl's. "Where are you going?"

"Out," Amanda replied shortly. "Just out."

"You can't go out without a chaperon, Amanda, dear," Mrs. Longman said from across the tiny room where she was mending stockings. "It isn't proper."

"I don't care." Amanda put on her shawl and tied it into a defiant knot. "My father doesn't care, either. He traipses around all day long. Why shouldn't I?"

"Because —" Mrs. Longman began.

"— it isn't proper," Amanda finished for her.

Penitence slipped a leather marker to hold her place in the book and closed it carefully. That was the way she did everything, Amanda observed. Penitence suited her name. Amanda could hardly believe that she and the other girl were the same age: sixteen, almost seventeen. With her obedient, meek manners, Penitence acted more like a middle-aged woman.

Placing her hand on the doorknob, Amanda declared firmly, "I'll be back later."

Penitence's great-aunt Minerva looked up from the quilt square she was piecing and pursed her lips into a thin line. She said nothing, but disapproval radiated from her.

"But Amanda," Penitence protested. "You can't go out with your hair unbound!"

Stooping slightly, Amanda caught her wavy reflection in the looking glass hanging over the heavy maple bureau. She noted automatically her smooth, pale skin and her eyes, golden-green and fringed with long black lashes. But her hair! Dark brown, waist-length, and naturally curly, it had always been heavy and unmanageable. Sometimes it took her half the morning to coax it into the required chignon. Ivory side-combs or tortoiseshell hairpins did little to prevent tendrils from escaping and surrounding her

2

head like a halo. In the hotel room, Amanda wore her hair loose, and it hung like a dark cloud.

"It takes too long to put up," Amanda said now. "And with all this rain, it wouldn't do any good. Besides, who cares *how* I look, out here in the middle of nowhere." She opened the door and swept out, slamming it behind her with great satisfaction.

It was true, she reflected, as she walked quickly down the corridor and down the stairs into the lobby. The town of Independence, clinging to the western edge of Missouri, was so uncivilized that if she suddenly turned green no one would notice. Her father told her that, for a frontier town in 1846, Independence was actually quite advanced, due to the Santa Fe trade, which had been going on for years. Amanda found it difficult to believe. For one thing, all anyone ever did here was talk about Oregon: going to Oregon, packing for Oregon, building wagons and bidding on ox teams and buying supplies — all for Oregon. *How I hate that word,* she thought, pushing her way through the crowded lobby.

At the door, a buckskinned trapper, his long hair bound with a strap of greasy rawhide, stepped aside to let her by, giving her a big smile.

The nerve of him, she thought hotly, her face burning with embarrassment. Only in Independence would a man act that way. That was another reason she wore her hair loose. With it hanging down her back, she knew she looked younger than sixteen. She had no desire to attract attention in a town of so few women. All she wanted was to get out of the stuffy hotel room and breathe a little fresh air. And, after passing the trapper, who obviously had not set foot near bathwater for months, she wondered if such a thing as fresh air existed, inside or out.

Colonel Noland's Merchants Hotel, recently rebuilt after burning to the ground the year before, proudly proclaimed itself to be "the westernmost hotel in America, the last one this side of the Sandwich Islands," with accommodations for up to four hundred guests. With steamboats chugging down the Missouri, and wagons pounding into town daily, Amanda was certain there were more than four hundred people in the inn now. Although she and her father had arrived in April, more than four weeks ago, they had had to share their rooms with strangers every night.

"You don't know what it's like," Amanda complained to him once. "Mrs. Longman and Penitence are all right, I guess, but that Aunt Minerva makes the most dreadful noises in her sleep. And Penitence usually winds up with most of the covers!"

"You ought to be in *my* room," Thaddeus Bentley said with a wry smile. "Most nights I can't even get near the bed, much less sleep in it. And every one of the five or six men I share with sleeps with a rifle loaded and cocked, and a Bowie knife unsheathed. I'm *afraid* to snore!"

At the hotel doorway, Amanda stopped. The street that ran the length of the town, forming one side of the square, was swimming in a sea of mud. Men slogged by, up to their knees in red Missouri clay.

Then she noticed a few people walking close to the buildings. Even though their boots were quite muddy, it was obviously nothing like the swamp in the middle of the street. She had on her old riding boots, which were so worn after months of travel, a little mud couldn't hurt. Stepping down, she edged along the porch of the hotel. After a minute, she stopped creeping along, absorbed in the sights.

Independence was an amazing town, she had to admit, in spite of all its crudeness. Never would she have seen so many different kinds of people in Boston.

There were Mexicans, dark-eyed and dark-haired, wearing bright-colored pantaloons and tiny, tinkling silver bells, smoking shuck-rolled cigarettes. Swarthy mountain men dressed in smelly buckskins swaggered down the street, heading for the taverns. Leather-skinned Santa Fe traders, their eyes permanently sun-crinkled, stalked in mud-caked boots, brandishing Bowie knives and bull-whips. Army soldiers from nearby Fort Leavenworth mingled with riverboat captains, roustabouts, and dockworkers. A few Kansa Indians, garbed in horse blankets, lounged in doorways, dozing in the warm sun with their backs against storefronts, broad-brimmed felt hats pulled down low.

The sun warmed Amanda's back, and a breeze carried the sweet scent of prairie spring. In spite of the noise, the confusion of so many people, and the strangeness of the town, it felt good to be outside. Weeks of rain had left the air smelling newly washed and unbelievably fresh. The Missouri sky was higher and bluer than she had ever imagined.

As she neared the edge of town, two Indians mounted on shaggy brown-and-white ponies clopped down the macadam road leading to the steamboat landing. They stared at her with their unblinking black gaze. Amanda should have dropped her eyes to the ground in the ladylike manner which she had been taught, but instead she stared back, openly curious.

She guessed they were around her age, but their faces were so quiet and set, they seemed older. Both wore their long black hair elaborately dressed with golden feathers; their pierced earlobes were looped with strings of beads and more beads; and necklaces of teeth and claws hung around their necks. They rode their ponies bareback with great dignity, as though they had been born in the saddle.

How Joseph would love to see this, Amanda thought.

Joseph!

She stopped to lean weakly against a tree. How many months had she dreamed his name? Was it only last October, her last night in Boston, that he'd told her to wait for him? *Will I ever see him again?* she thought.

During those six months of unrelenting travel, Amanda rode numbly with her father, trying not to think about her uncertain future. Instead, her thoughts turned yearningly toward Boston — and Joseph — even as every mile took her farther away from him.

"We have to push on to Independence," her father said whenever she complained she was tired. "That's the jumping-off point for all trains heading West. We'll have to hurry to get our wagon built and be ready to leave with the others."

I don't care, Amanda thought wearily, time and again. *I hope we get there late and miss all the trains going West. If I never see another foot of road, it'll be too soon.* She only wanted to go back to her house in Louisburg Square, back to Joseph White.

Another white-topped wagon churned mud as it drew up the hill, but Amanda didn't see it. She was a thousand miles away, on that last morning in October, entering the formal sitting room of Joseph's house on Beacon Hill to answer a summons from his mother.

Drucilla White sat in her favorite high-backed chair like a queen on a throne, unsmiling, as always. She pointed a fat finger, indicating that Amanda take the stool at her feet. Amanda obeyed, though she hated sitting at Drucilla's feet like a wayward child.

"Your dress is ready," Drucilla said, taking shallow breaths between each word. "My seamstress delivered it late yesterday. You may pick it up on your way out."

"Thank you, Aunt Drucilla," Amanda replied dutifully.

"It's a lovely gown — almost as pretty as Hester's. Wear it in good health." She narrowed her sharp black eyes at Amanda. "You know I've always treated you like my own daughter since your mother died. It was my responsibility, but I *wanted* to do it. Your mother and I grew up together, went to Miss Finch's together."

Amanda nodded absently; she had heard all this many times before.

"So when Hester was ready to go to Miss Finch's, I didn't hesitate to send you, too, because I knew that's what your mother would have wanted. And besides, it didn't seem right, sending Hester away to school and leaving you here."

There was a pause and Amanda realized she was expected to say something.

"I appreciate all you and Mr. White have done for me, Aunt Drucilla."

"I should certainly hope so. If it weren't for me, well, goodness knows what would have become of you."

"My father —" Amanda began.

"Oh, your father!" Drucilla waved a hand airily. "What Thaddeus Bentley knows about raising children could be written on the head of a pin."

"He's very good to me."

"Of course he's good to you. But fathers don't always know what's *proper* for their daughters."

Amanda wondered why they were going into this at all. As far as she was concerned, this was much-trampled territory. Drucilla was forever pointing out to Amanda how lucky she was to have the Whites — an *important* family — to take care of her, rather than being left to the uncertain fate of being raised by a father who had been an orphan. She half listened to Drucilla's ramblings. If only the woman would get to the *point*. She wanted to go home and try on her new dress. Joseph was coming over tonight, and she had to fix her hair. . . .

At the mention of Joseph's name, Amanda sat up, instantly alert.

". . . know you've been seeing a lot of my son when he's home from school. Hester's told me how you blush whenever he walks into a room, not that I couldn't see it for myself. I do hope that you and Joseph aren't becoming . . . well, too involved. You realize that Joseph graduates next year and will begin work in his father's bank. He'll be in line for the family business, and he'll need a wife who can hold her own in society. Someone from a good —"

"— family! Yes, I *know*." Amanda stood up abruptly. "Why don't you come out and say it, Aunt Drucilla? You don't want Joseph to see me because I'm not good enough! Isn't that it? Have you mentioned this to him? He may have different ideas on the subject, you know."

She swept out of the room, without waiting to be dismissed. Snatching the dressmaker's box off the mahogany table, she ran outside and into the waiting carriage, fuming all the way to Louisburg Square. When the driver pulled up before the entrance to Number 15, she jumped down before he could help her. Not until she was inside the small brownstone did she realize that the beautiful dress was a bribe: Drucilla White had the dress made to keep Amanda from seeing her son.

She ran her hands over the smooth dress box, and an idea stirred within her. Untying the cords, she lifted the lid. Gleaming folds of gray-green silk glinted in the late-morning light.

A feeling of new resolve curved her lips into a small smile. She would wear the new dress tonight. Joseph would not break a promise, no matter what his mother said. And Amanda would be waiting for him, wearing the very dress Drucilla White had tried to bribe her with.

At a little before seven, Amanda stood at the bowfront window, peeping anxiously through the ivory lace curtains. She had been ready since five-thirty. Thaddeus Bentley was not home yet, but he was seldom in before midnight these days. *Everything is going perfectly*, Amanda thought.

She shook her head, delighted to feel the bunches of side curls dance over her ears. She had worked all afternoon on her hair, pinning up the sides, then wrapping the dampened ends around her forefinger, releasing sausagelike curls. The rest of her hair was caught in a gold net, worn higher than fashionable to show off her neck and small ears.

"That hairstyle is much too old for a girl your age," Mrs. Garrity said when Amanda came downstairs for dinner.

"You're not my mother," Amanda told the housekeeper, gliding into the dining room.

The older woman frowned her disapproval when Amanda tied a gold ribbon around her slender throat, which drew attention to her perfect complexion.

After eating three bites of the lamb stew Mrs. Garrity had prepared, Amanda pushed back her plate, declaring she was full. The housekeeper cleared the table, shaking her head, then took her needlepoint into the adjoining parlor.

Between nervous peeks out the window, Amanda turned slowly before the heavy gilt-framed mirror in the entryway, admiring her new gown. It was beautiful, made from chameleon silk, a magical fabric that changed from gray to green to topaz, depending on how the light fell. The dress, like her eyes, was always changing color. The tight-fitting bodice pointed toward a low waist, then belled out into a full skirt that gathered into deep ruffles about the hem. Lamplight glanced off the gold net, giving her dark hair sparkling highlights, and enhancing the green and topaz of her skirt. She knew the ever-changing colors in her dress and eyes would dazzle Joseph.

The French clock on the mantel delicately chimed seven o'clock just as the heavy brass door knocker fell once, twice. Amanda whirled away from the mirror, giving her hair a final pat, and flew into the hall to answer the door ahead of Mrs. Garrity.

"Go on!" she snapped. "I can get it. And don't interrupt us."

The housekeeper retreated into the parlor, muttering to herself about the insolence of today's youth.

Amanda opened the door, smiling.

Joseph White stood on the stoop, with a backdrop of the hazy October evening, his felt hat in his hand.

"Joseph," Amanda said easily, as if she had not been tensely coiled for hours, awaiting his arrival. "Please come in. Cold tonight, isn't it?"

"You're looking wonderful this evening," Joseph said, setting his hat on the table in the hall.

I should hope so, Amanda thought, still smiling. "Thank you. Come in by the fire."

As she led the way into the drawing room,

where a blazing fire chased away autumn chills, Amanda was aware how handsome Joseph looked. His light red hair, worn side-parted and curled under at the neckline, looked darker in the dim light. He had dressed for the evening with care, she observed, noting the high-collared frock coat over a creamy satin stock skewered with a gold stickpin. Because he was tall and thin, Joseph's clothes always seemed to fit well.

"Please sit down." She beckoned to the sofa. What had Drucilla told him? she wondered. Joseph was over eighteen, but Drucilla ruled her children with an iron hand.

Amanda arranged her silk skirts so only the toes of her gold slippers showed, without any idea that in a few short hours her whole life would turn upside-down.

Chapter Two

OUTSIDE, darkness had fallen, and the branches of the maple trees tossed restlessly in the wind. The great orange moon that had risen earlier like a wheel of cheese arrowed shafts of silver-gold light through the bay window. Amanda got up once to light more lamps.

"I know you'll be glad to get out of school next summer," she said, settling back on the sofa. "I know I was."

Joseph laughed. "Hester said you two had the time of your life at Miss Finch's. Didn't you enjoy it?"

"Oh, yes. Well, not everything. Some of the classes, like Latin, I could've managed without. But two years is a long time to be away from home, don't you think?" She gave him a sidelong glance through her lashes. "What are you going to do when you graduate, Joseph?"

He leaned back, stretching his long legs before him. "Oh, go to work in Father's bank, I suppose. In fact, he wants me to start while I'm home on break. I don't mind, really. After all, I have to do something with my life."

Amanda smiled secretively. "Is that all? I mean, aren't you thinking about doing anything else?"

"Like what?"

"Like . . . courting a girl and, well, getting married."

Now Joseph was smiling, the same big, careless grin he always gave Amanda when he was about to tease her. "You have somebody in mind?"

"Surely, there must be *some* girl you're getting serious about."

He heaved an elaborate sigh. "Well, you found me out. It's time you knew, Amanda, I've been seeing Sarah Peabody."

"*Sa*-rah *Pea*-body!" Amanda leaped to her feet, abandoning her ladylike manners. "You never told me —"

Joseph burst out laughing and grasped her wrists, pulling her back down. "You ought to see yourself! Flying up like a scalded cat. Calm down, I'm not really seeing Sarah. I hardly even know her, to tell you the truth."

Amanda folded her arms, still angry. "I wish you wouldn't tease me about things like that, Joseph. I don't like it."

"Don't take everything so seriously. Anyway, we both know a certain little skater won my heart last year."

Amanda sat back, pleased that Joseph remembered a night that was so special to her.

"You had on a silvery cape," he was saying, "and your hair streamed down your back. I thought you looked like . . . like a snow fairy. Like something not quite real. And the night was cold and frosty with the ice sparkling under the stars . . ."

He recalled it almost as well as she did. It was during Christmas, when she and Hester were home from Miss Finch's Finishing School for Young Ladies. The December night was crisp and clear. Stars glimmered in the velvet black sky, and bonfires crackled cheerily on the bank, throwing fitful shadows across the ice.

Amanda wore her hair down and a cherry wool scarf tucked under her chin. Her hands were snug in a fox muff, her cheeks rosy from the cold. As she glided out onto the ice, passing Hester, who skated in awkward starts and stops, Amanda knew she was the prettiest girl there. Joseph thought so, too, since he skated with her the whole evening. From then on, Joseph went with Amanda to parties and lectures whenever he was home. Amanda's memories of last summer consisted of long twilight walks across the Common, pleasant afternoons at the Old Corner Bookstore, and Sunday picnics just outside the city.

Joseph's thoughts must have been traveling the same avenue, for he leaned forward now with an intent expression on his face.

Amanda was certain he was going to kiss her. Should she let him? What would he think of her if she did?

But then the moment passed and he pulled back, as if he had suddenly changed his mind. Clearing his throat, Joseph said, in a voice a shade too loud, "Will you play the piano for me?"

Amanda's heart fell. Why did he have to ask that? "I — can't. I'd like to play for you, but I can't."

"Why not? You mean you don't think you play that well?" He grinned maddeningly.

"No, of course not. I mean, well — the piano's not here."

Joseph looked around the room for the first time. "You're right. How come I didn't notice that before? I must have had my eyes on other things. What on earth happened to it? Wasn't it your mother's?"

Amanda nodded, taking a deep breath. "I think . . . Papa had it sent out to be tuned."

Joseph threw back his head, laughing. "Piano tuners come to the house, Amanda! Had it sent out . . . I swear, Amanda, you're a card." He sobered and asked, "Seriously, where is it?"

"I . . . Papa sold it."

"Sold it? Your mother's piano? Why?"

She plucked at the lace cuff of her sleeve, avoiding his eyes. "I'm not sure."

"Didn't you ask him?" Joseph's gray eyes were serious.

"Well, he's not home much. You know, I've

hardly seen him since I got home from school."

He considered this. "Probably busy at the office. Sometimes attorneys can be awfully absentminded. But still, he ought to have told you."

"I suppose." Amanda gratefully dropped the subject, glancing at the clock on the mantel. "I haven't offered you anything. Would you care for something to drink?"

He stood. "No, thanks, really. I must be going. Mrs. Garrity probably wants to get to bed."

Amanda followed him into the entryway. "I'm so glad you came. When will I see you again?"

In the shadowed hall, Joseph grabbed her hands with an urgency that made her gasp. "Listen," he whispered. "Stop worrying about Mother. I know what she told you."

"You do? Then you know what she thinks of me. Joseph, she made me feel so —"

He squeezed her hands. "I mean it, Amanda. Forget it. She can run my life only up to a certain point. And this"— he gave her hands a little shake — "is where I draw the line. As far as I'm concerned, I can see anyone I please."

"Joseph, are you proposing to me? After all, I'm only sixteen and you have to speak to my father —"

"Who said anything about proposing?" The famous grin flashed again. "You certainly jump to conclusions."

Amanda snatched away her hands. "Stop teasing me, Joseph White. It's not funny."

"Am I laughing at you? I wouldn't dare. You get madder than any girl I ever knew. All right, I'll be serious. Amanda Bentley, will you wait for me until I get out of school? It's only until summer . . . and then we'll talk some more." He shook his finger at her with mock sternness. "I'll be home again at Christmas, so don't go skating with anyone else!"

Before she knew what was happening, he bent down and brushed her lips lightly, then he was out the door with a wave of his hat. She watched him mount his horse, then trot away with moonlight on his hair.

Slowly she closed the door and leaned against it, hugging herself with joy. He had told her to wait! He had kissed her!

Mrs. Garrity came out of the sitting room carrying her rolled-up needlework. "Did you have a nice visit with Mr. Joseph?"

Amanda twirled, her skirts spinning, revealing a froth of petticoats. "It was wonderful! The most wonderful night of my life!"

Mrs. Garrity frowned. "I hope Mr. Joseph behaved properly. You two were awful quiet out here."

"Oh, don't be such a fussbudget," Amanda said as she glided up the stairs. "Joseph did *exactly* what I wanted him to."

In her room, Amanda took off the chameleon silk dress, hung it up carefully, and changed into her nightgown and a light wool wrapper. Sitting before her vanity, she dreamily brushed her hair and wove it into a single braid.

It was still too early to go to bed. She knew she couldn't sleep now if her life depended on it. Maybe if she read a little while . . .

Downstairs in the sitting room, she chose *Oliver Twist* from her father's bookshelf and sat in the green wing chair. But only part of her mind concentrated on the adventures of the orphan; the other part was off imagining what life would be like as Mrs. Joseph White.

The mantel clock had chimed half past eleven when the front door opened with a bang. Thaddeus Bentley burst into the room.

Amanda jumped up, dropping the book. "Papa!"

She had never seen her father look so disheveled. His paisley cravat was loosened, his pointed collar knocked awry. But it was his face that startled her. His normally mild brown eyes were rolling wildly, like those of a frightened horse, and his face was mottled an unhealthy red.

"Papa, are you sick?"

Thaddeus grabbed her by the shoulders. "Listen to me, because I only have time to say this once. Go upstairs and put on your riding clothes —"

"At this hour?"

"Don't interrupt!" he ordered. "I said we haven't much time. Pack a small bag. No more than two dresses. You've got exactly fifteen minutes."

Amanda stared, her brown eyes pools of

disbelief. "Have you lost your *senses?* What're you *talking* about? Where are we going?"

"Amanda, don't stand there asking foolish questions!" he thundered. "Now hurry! Do as I say." He thrust her toward the door. "Get Mrs. Garrity up. I need to talk to her."

Amanda stood rooted in the doorway. Her father turned toward the gold-framed portrait of her mother over the marble fireplace. Behind the portrait was a small wall safe where valuables and cash were kept.

"Papa, what is this about?"

Thaddeus whirled on her. "Haven't you heard a *thing* I've said? Get upstairs, girl. Hurry! If you're not down here in ten minutes, I'm leaving without you."

"I'm not budging until you explain what's going on!" Amanda fired back. "I have a right to know!"

Thaddeus's face was purple as he stormed toward her. "You don't need to know anything! You're still my daughter and you'll do as I say. Now *move!*"

She was stunned. Her father seldom, if ever, raised his voice to her, and tonight he was yelling like a wild man. Frightened into action, she bolted up the stairs.

Mrs. Garrity was already up, standing at the top of the stairs with her guttering candle, holding her wrapper close to her throat.

"Papa wants to see you," Amanda threw at her, tearing into her own room. Standing in the middle of the floor, she turned uncertainly in circles.

Put on riding clothes, he'd said. Flinging open the door to her wardrobe, she pulled out the heavy wool skirt and jacket. Minutes later, she was dressed and had her leather satchel opened on the bed. Two dresses — why only two? Perhaps that meant they were not going very far. Amanda glanced at the chameleon silk hanging on the wardrobe door. The sight of it brought Joseph to mind. Had this sudden trip been engineered by Drucilla in a desperate effort to keep her son away from Amanda? But even Drucilla wouldn't go that far, Amanda reasoned. No, whatever it was, it had to do with her father.

Impulsively, she snatched the green-gold gown off its hanger and stuffed it into the carpetbag. She packed another silk dress, her best crinoline, an extra chemise, a black lace shawl, and her kid dancing slippers. Before snapping the bag closed, she turned to the velvet jewelry case on her dressing table.

The box, with its contents, had belonged to her mother. Eleanor Bentley had died when Amanda was only twelve, too young to wear jewelry. Last year, Thaddeus presented the jewelry to Amanda, a sign to her that she had grown up — in his eyes, at least.

She opened the box now and was not surprised to see only an enameled gold watchpin lying in the bottom. On each trip home from school, Amanda had noticed pieces missing. The heavy, square-cut aquamarine

earrings and matching bracelet were the first
to go, then the pearl necklace, the star sapphire ring set in platinum, the amethyst
pendant, and the onyx pin. When she questioned her father, he said he'd put them in
the wall safe, that the jewelry was too valu-
able to leave sitting on a dressing table. At
the time she had believed him, but now her
thoughts raced like a runaway horse. Did he
sell her jewelry just as he had sold the
piano? What for?

She plucked the watch-pin out of the box
and fastened it to her jacket. Grabbing a fox-
tipped cape and her satchel, she ran out of
her room and down the stairs.

At the bottom, her father was talking earnestly to Mrs. Garrity, who was wide-eyed and
unusually silent. He appeared to be giving
last-minute instructions.

". . . tell them you haven't seen me or my
daughter for several days. You have no idea
where we went."

"But I don't know where you and Miss
Amanda *are* going," the housekeeper wailed.
"Won't you at least tell me that?"

"I can't," Thaddeus said abruptly. "Don't
worry, it's not you they're after."

"It's not her *who's* after? Amanda asked,
setting down her bag.

"Never mind. Make your good-byes to Mrs.
Garrity brief. I'll be waiting outside." Thaddeus snatched up her bag and slammed out.

Mrs. Garrity kissed Amanda through her
tears.

Amanda felt a rush of guilt; she had treated the housekeeper indifferently and now she might never see her again.

"Good-bye," Amanda said. "I'll be back ... as soon as I can." Then she ran out the door.

Standing quietly by the curb were two saddled horses, blowing silvery puffs of chilled autumn air through their nostrils.

Thaddeus had tied Amanda's bag to her saddle and now he helped her mount. Mrs. Garrity stood framed in the carved doorway clutching a handkerchief. Amanda waved at her, wondering if she would see her home or the housekeeper again, as she nudged her horse into a canter to catch up with her father.

They rode through the sleepy Boston streets quickly. It was well after midnight and they did not meet anyone. When they were finally on the Boston Post Road heading out of town, they slowed their horses to a walk. Amanda breathed in night air heavily spiced with the pungent scent of crabapples from a nearby grove.

The moon had risen to its zenith, bathing the tops of the trees along the road and creating dappled shadows. As they rested the horses, she stared at her father, whose face, half-hidden by shifting shadows, made him look sinister. Amanda sat numbly in the saddle. Had it only been a few hours ago that she was laughing with Joseph, preening in her new silk dress? Maneuvering her horse closer to her father's, she asked, "Papa, you *must* tell me what this is all about. Where are we going?"

"South."

"South? Where? To see your friend in Quincy?"

"Not Quincy," he snapped.

"New York? Oh, Papa, I've always wanted to go to New York City, but why'd you pick such a strange time —"

"We're not going there, either."

"Well, *where*?" She drew in a deep breath. "You mean *South* south, don't you?"

"Virginia," Thaddeus replied. "Or one of the Carolinas. Haven't made up my mind yet."

"But *why* . . . why are we leaving? Papa, don't turn away. Please tell me what's going on!"

But Thaddeus had wheeled his horse around. "I can't waste any more time, Missy. We're not out of town yet. We've got a lot of ground to cover before morning." He dug his heels into his horse's side. The animal leaped forward, galloping down the moon-spangled road. Amanda stared after him for a second, then spurred her own horse.

As they made their way south in the cool autumn days that followed, Amanda was able to piece together the circumstances leading up to that last night in Boston. When she had the whole story, she realized that part of her had suspected the truth for some time.

Thaddeus owed money to a great many men because of his gambling, and they were tired of waiting for it. On the night Joseph White declared his feelings for Amanda, the sands in the hourglass had run out for Thaddeus Bentley.

He had been warned by a friend that a couple of thugs would probably beat him up that evening. But Thaddeus suspected they would not stop at a simple beating. Afraid for his life and his daughter's, he bought two horses out of the money remaining from the sale of his wife's jewelry, deciding it was time to leave town altogether.

Amanda refused to accept that they were never going back to Boston. When her father told her, she stopped her horse dead in its tracks. "Never going back!" she screamed. "What do you mean? I thought we were going South for a little while. I have to go back — Joseph and I are getting married!"

Thaddeus reined in his own horse. "Did he ask you to marry him?" he demanded.

"Not exactly, but he was going to, just as soon as he got things settled with Aunt Drucilla."

Thaddeus snorted. "That dragon of a woman! If she doesn't want her precious Joseph to have anything to do with you, you can bet he won't be back. You haven't lost a thing, Missy. We're going on to a new life, you and I. Weren't you tired of Boston?"

"How could I be? It's the only place I've ever known. Papa, how can you *do* this to me? Joseph and I could work things out. He loves me, I just know it. You have to let me go back."

Thaddeus grabbed Amanda's wrist. "We *can't* go back. That's what I've been trying to tell you. Our lives aren't worth a twist of tobacco back there."

Amanda felt tears running down her face. "Why didn't I listen when Aunt Drucilla talked about you. . . ." She raised her head sharply. "She said all along you couldn't resist the cards."

Now Thaddeus gazed down the road, his attention fastened on a mule-drawn cart. He sighed. "I don't know how you got to be so perfect, Missy. Maybe one of these days you'll understand a thing or two about life." He pulled up the reins. "We'd better get moving."

As the days dragged by, Amanda alternated crying bouts with unreasonable arguments, but Thaddeus remained immovable. Many times as she lay awake in a strange bed in a strange inn, Amanda contemplated saddling up her horse and heading back to Boston herself, but after a few weeks, she began to adjust to the idea of moving down South. Perhaps life in Virginia or North Carolina wouldn't be so bad. As soon as they were settled, she would write to Joseph, feeling certain he would come to her. If her father was going to set up a new law practice, he would need a partner, and Joseph would be perfect. All these things were decided in her mind when Thaddeus met a wagon-load of people heading for the Oregon territory, and her whole life changed.

Oregon. No sooner had the strangers mentioned their destination than Thaddeus turned excitedly to Amanda with a new light in his eyes and declared, "Forget Virginia, Missy. We're going West!"

The months that followed blurred into one continuous nightmare for Amanda. Through the coldest winter she had ever endured, they traveled west on horseback through Pennsylvania. A blinding snowstorm in the Cumberland Mountains forced them to stay in a dreary inn that scarcely had enough heat. Over a bowl of cornmeal mush that passed as breakfast one morning, Amanda appealed to her father for what seemed the thousandth time.

"Papa, this is *folly*. We'll never get to this town you keep talking about."

"Independence. In Missouri. Doesn't it have a wonderful ring? It sounds so free. The snow will let up and we'll be on our way in no time."

Amanda threw down her pewter spoon. "I don't *want* to go on! I want to go *home*. I'm tired of riding in the rain and cold . . . sleeping in strange, lumpy beds . . . eating horrible food. I'm fed *up*." She pushed back her chair so quickly, it fell backward with a clatter. "I'm going home and don't try to stop me."

She ran out into the swirling snow, her heavy skirt hampered by drifts that covered the walkway to the shed where their horses were stabled. With freezing fingers, she tried to saddle her horse, but her hands were too numb to work the straps and fittings.

Her father found her sobbing helplessly against the neck of her horse.

"Amanda," he said. "Come back to the inn before you catch cold. It'll be all right. You'll see."

Feeling defeated, Amanda followed her father back to the inn, then went silently to her room. Pulling a scrap of paper from her satchel, Amanda penned a tearful letter to Joseph, begging him to come after her, to take her back to Boston.

The snow did stop as Amanda and her father made their way through the mountains. At the Ohio River, they traded their horses for passage on a flatboat to the Mississippi River. From there it was up the Mississippi, then down the muddy Missouri River on the steamboat *General Brooks* to Independence, where all wagon trains heading West were formed and outfitted.

Although the journey was unbearably long — from October to April — Thaddeus remained enthusiastic, while Amanda was resigned and despondent.

In Independence, Thaddeus registered them at Colonel Noland's Merchants Hotel, then flew about town during the rainy days that followed, buying supplies and having a wagon built to take them over the plains to Oregon, while Amanda paced the tiny bedroom like a caged jungle cat.

Her memories having come full circle, she faced east now, even though she could not see anything but the road leading down the steep hill to Independence Landing on the Missouri. Joseph was a thousand miles away. Even if he had gotten her letter, it would be months before he could get out here. By then she would be gone again.

Face facts, she told herself. *I'll never see him again. My life is over.*

She turned away, blinded by tears. At that moment, a wagon rumbled by, narrowly missing her. She jumped back as the huge wheels churned a spray of mud on her dress. The driver never noticed her, but a young man riding a gray pony behind the wagon yelled, "Get out of the road! You want to get killed?"

Flashing her a wide grin, he was gone. Amanda stared after him, angered by her ruined dress and the boy's rude remarks. Joseph White would never say anything so uncouth. Joseph would have stopped and inquired to see if she was all right. The boy was probably one of those wild Missourians, she decided, heading back toward the hotel. But she couldn't help thinking, *Would Joseph ever have looked so carefree and handsome on a shaggy gray pony?*

Chapter Three

AMANDA heard someone calling her name, and turned to see her father shouldering his way through the jostling throng in the hotel lobby. He had traded his travel-worn coat and trousers for "trail" clothes: a coarse hickory shirt and homespun trousers tucked into buckskin boots. He caught up to her, his face wreathed in a wide smile.

"Pack your bag, Missy. We're heading out."

Amanda froze. "What?"

"Our wagon's finally finished, and six of the prettiest Durham oxen you ever saw are yoked and ready to go. All I've got to do is throw in the rest of the supplies, but that won't take long."

"You mean we're leaving for Oregon *now?*"

"Can't wait any longer. Today's the tenth.

Wagons have been pulling out for over a week now. If we dally around too much, all the grass will be gone."

"So what?" Amanda said.

"For the oxen," Thaddeus explained patiently. "If too many trains start out ahead of us, their teams will eat all the grass. Hurry up now, we've got to be at Indian Creek campground before supper." He gave her arm a reassuring pat, then left.

Amanda was not ready for this. In fact, she was not sure she would ever be ready.

When they first arrived in Independence four weeks ago, the first thing Thaddeus did was order a wagon. Every day, he checked on the wagon's progress, bought a few supplies, then spent the rest of his time in Noland's tavern, listening to wild stories about life on the trail. At first Amanda wondered if he played cards, but she supposed he was too busy. The change in her father was amazing. He threw himself into the new role of settler with genuine enthusiasm. Every evening, as they ate supper in the tavern, Thaddeus would pull out his ever-present guidebook, *The Emigrant's Guide to California and Oregon*, written by Mr. Lansford Hastings. "I've been buying trinkets today," he would say. "Hastings's guidebook recommends taking lots of things to trade with the Indians, especially up in Shoshone country."

"What kind of trinkets?" Amanda would ask, not really interested, but to humor him.

"Mirrors, beads, tobacco, handkerchiefs, knives, fishhooks . . . things like that. According to the guidebook, those items don't take up much room, and they'll be invaluable later on the journey."

Amanda always listened with half an ear. In the back of her mind, she knew going to Oregon was as inevitable as the sunrise, yet she hoped that at the last minute Thaddeus would change his mind and take her back to Boston.

But now, watching her father push through the milling crowd in his unfamiliar clothes, she knew time had run out. They were really going. There was nothing for her to do but go up to her room and pack.

"Leaving already!" Mrs. Longman exclaimed when Amanda told her. "My, your father must have spent a lot of money to get his wagon built so quickly."

"I suppose," Amanda said listlessly, stuffing her ragged, stained riding clothes in the bag.

Penitence laid down her knitting to help Amanda pack. "You don't have a single sunbonnet! Or any plain cotton dresses," she exclaimed as Amanda carefully folded her chameleon silk gown.

"I know."

"But what'll you wear?"

"What I have on. And what's in this bag. That's all I have and, anyway, I'd rather die than be seen in those potato sacks you call dresses." Amanda could just imagine what

Hester would say about her wearing a sun-bonnet.

Aunt Minerva shook her head. "Mark my words, child, you'll be glad enough to have one of those potato sacks — as you call 'em — when the sun gets to beatin' down. That fancy thing you're wearin' will cook you alive."

"I don't care," Amanda said, snapping the clasp on her bag. "Just because I have to go to Oregon doesn't mean I have to look like some dowdy farmgirl."

Mrs. Longman pulled a length of yellow calico from her trunk. "Please take this. Perhaps you'll change your mind and then you'll be able to make something."

"No, thanks, Mrs. Longman. You're very kind, but I'm sure I won't need it."

"Well, if you're certain . . ." She put the fabric back into her trunk and came over to embrace Amanda. "Be careful, child. You're so young to be going on such a journey alone."

"I'm not alone. I'm going with my father."

Mrs. Longman smoothed Amanda's hair back from her forehead. "I know, and he's a fine man. But still, it would be nice if there was a woman around to look after you."

"I don't need looking after. I'm almost seventeen and I've made it this far. I guess I can go another two thousand miles," Amanda said firmly. "Well, I guess I've got everything." She hesitated at the door. As much as she hated sharing a room, she had to admit that she would miss Mrs. Longman, who had become almost a mother to her. And although the room was not much, she did have a bed to sleep in and a roof over her head.

Amanda ran down the stairs and pushed her way through the tangle of people in the lobby and out onto the street. Parked in front of the livery stable was the white-covered wagon that would take her and her father to the Promised Land.

Thaddeus strutted around from the other side, peacock-proud, his brown eyes shining. "What do you think? Isn't she a beauty?" He slapped the rear of the bright blue wagon box. "I had it painted your favorite color."

Amanda hated it on sight, but her father's brown eyes sparkled with pride, and she did not want to hurt his feelings.

"It's — it's very nice, Papa." She stood helplessly, staring at their new home on wheels. A bold coat of paint could not hide the rough-sawed edges. It looked nothing like the elegant carriage they once owned back in Boston.

Taking her by the hand, Thaddeus hopped around, pointing out various features. He lifted the lid of a wooden box. "Here's your grub box."

"My *what?*" Amanda asked.

"Grub box. You keep all your cooking utensils and supplies in here. So when we stop and make camp, you can start fixing meals right away."

Amanda stared at him incredulously. "You mean I'm supposed to *cook?* You didn't tell me *that*."

"Well, of course you have to cook. I have to drive the team and take care of the wagon."

Amanda stamped her foot. "I will *not*. I *refuse* to straddle smoky cook-fires like some common —"

Thaddeus grasped her arm firmly, his eyebrows drawn low in sudden anger. "You *will* help out on this journey. Everyone pitches in, even young children, and you are no exception."

In a more gentle mood, he removed his grip and put his arm around her shoulders. "Listen, Missy. This trip won't be like the one we just made. Riding horseback through the States where we could stop overnight and have a nice home-cooked supper was one thing. But out here, things'll be a lot different. We're leaving the States behind. There won't be any towns at all along the way, just a couple of trading forts and those few and far between. We're going to be living in this wagon for the next four months or so."

"Four months! Is that how long it'll take to get to Oregon?" Amanda cried. It was getting worse all the time. "I thought it would only be a month or so."

"The guidebook says four to six months. I'm planning on it taking us four months. Then, too, we're leaving a little late. We'll have to hurry to catch up. I heard about twenty trains have left Indian Creek already."

Amanda's head was spinning. Six months in a wagon! No towns at all for the next two thousand miles. It was too much to take in all at once. To take her mind off those frightening prospects, she peered into the grub box Thaddeus was still holding open. Fitting snugly inside were a cast-iron Dutch kettle, a camp kettle, a frying pan, a coffee pot, a bread pan, a milk can, a coffee mill, tin plates, tin cups, and two sets of tin forks, knives, and spoons. She let the lid slam. How dreary life was going to be.

Amanda passed a hand over her eyes as though banishing the image before her and asked, "Where are we going to sleep?"

"I'm pitching a tent right outside. I'll rig up a mattress, and you can sleep inside the wagon. Here, I'll show you." Thaddeus tugged at the draw-ropes holding the canvas cover closed at the back.

Amanda's eyes grew round at the sight of boxes and barrels piled haphazardly, clear to the top of the arching bows. "Papa! Where'd you get all this stuff?"

"I've been buying supplies all along. I told you that."

"Yes, but I thought you were buying food for the trip. You've got enough here for an army!"

"Not really. According to the guidebook, I had to allow two hundred pounds of flour per person. That's this right here." He tapped a couple of sacks, then pointed to two smaller casks. "Twenty pounds of sugar per person, ten pounds of salt —"

"Twenty pounds of sugar! Why so much?"

"Well, you see, Hastings says we need twice as much of those things than we do normally because we're not going to be able to eat fresh fruit and vegetables. And the trail is so hard, we're going to need everything we've got." He continued taking inventory. "A bushel of dried apples apiece. Keeps away scurvy, you know." Amanda had no idea what scurvy was, but it didn't sound good. Cloth sacks held coffee, tea, and baking powder for biscuits. "In there is side bacon and over there dried beans," Thaddeus finished.

"Papa, where did you get the money to pay for all this? It must have cost a fortune."

Thaddeus led the way to the front of the wagon. "I used money from the sale of your mother's jewelry."

"Then that's why those men you owed money to back in Boston were so upset. You didn't pay them anything."

"Not much, I'm afraid. I knew we'd need the money more than they did."

"But still," Amanda insisted, "we've spent a lot of money getting this far, what with buying horses and steamboat tickets, and food and inns —"

"Well, I managed to save enough to buy this outfit. We don't have a whole lot left, but enough to make a new start once we get to

Oregon. Some men accused the merchants here of price-gouging, but I didn't find things outrageously expensive. For instance, this wagon cost ninety dollars. Flour was cheap — two dollars for a hundred pounds. But bacon was dear — ten dollars for two hundred pounds. Coffee, tea, sugar, lard — all these things came to about fifty dollars. And I got a good deal on the team. Fifty dollars a yoke, plus our horses in trade."

"Our horses!" Amanda wailed. "I can't ride horseback? Why did you sell them?"

"Costs too much to take them. We'd have to carry grain — they can't live off prairie grass. The best draft animal by far is the ox."

Amanda walked over to the oxen and looked at the six great ugly beasts with disgust. They were all brown and white with humped backs and sharp curving horns. They stood patiently in their wooden yokes, humbly staring at the ground.

"Oh, Papa. They're so *homely!*"

"Homely they may be, but they make the difference between life and death on the trail." He slapped the flank of one of the lead oxen. "Well, Missy, climb aboard. Time to go."

It was a beautiful day, Amanda grudgingly admitted. The sky was a sweep of bright blue. Billowy clouds drifted slowly eastward like great ships under full sail.

As they passed through town, people stopped what they were doing to wave.

Thaddeus waved back, but Amanda sat ramrod-straight on the narrow seat, her eyes forward. She refused to wave to strangers, no matter what the occasion. And anyway, she did not feel the least bit happy to be going to Oregon, the other side of the world, as far as she was concerned.

"How long will it take us to get to Indian Creek?" Amanda asked after a while. The sun was still high in the sky, and her silk dress clung to her back in uncomfortable wet patches. She swished a leaf fan back and forth.

"Few hours, I guess," Thaddeus replied. "It's ten miles or so from town."

"What are we supposed to do there?"

"Find a train to join up with, mostly. You can repack the wagon to suit you better, and I'll work with these stubborn critters."

Amanda suppressed a smile. Not two hours ago, Thaddeus was extolling the virtues of those noble oxen, but after five minutes with them, he seemed to have changed his tune. The team plodded along so slowly that when Amanda fixed upon a large tree up ahead, the same tree was in front of them an hour later.

"Are you sure we'll get there tonight?"

"Hope so," Thaddeus called back. "One thing I learned, you can't hurry oxen."

The hours ground by with agonizing slowness. Amanda watched the sights for a while, but then became bored. There was nothing ahead but road and wagons and trees. What would it be like on the prairie where there weren't even trees to look at? She shuddered at the thought.

Other women got out of their wagons to walk beside their husbands, she noticed. Young girls bounded over endless meadows beside the road, their long skirts up around their knees, picking sunflowers and purple-blossomed heal-all. Children chased each other, their shrill cries mingling with the liquid songs of meadowlarks. Amanda would have welcomed the exercise, but the road looked stony and she was wearing her kid slippers. Besides, there was something un-dignified about a young lady walking beside a team of oxen.

As the sun sank below the prairie, Amanda noticed her father's shoulders drooping with fatigue. It was hard work walking so slowly, keeping six huge animals in line, and he was no more used to this kind of life than she was.

She half stood to stretch the kinks out of her own shoulders. From her vantage point, she saw something that chilled her blood.

A wagon had overturned, and a man lay trapped beneath one of the great back wheels. The scene was one of mass confusion as several men attached ropes to the wagon, while others unhitched the team. Because the wagon was blocking the road, traffic slowed to a crawl to detour around the wreckage. Many stopped to gawk or see if they could be of any assistance. As the Bentleys' wagon approached, Amanda shrank back, not wanting to look. A woman began to wail while two little girls dressed in gaily printed cotton shifts clung to her skirts, sobbing uncontrollably.

Amanda watched, horror-stricken, as the wagon was lifted and the injured man was pulled out. Blood trailed behind him as he was dragged to the grass beside the road. An older man claiming to be a doctor pushed through the crowd. Briefly, he searched for the man's pulse, then shook his head at the wailing woman.

He's dead, Amanda realized, turning quickly away. She had never seen a dead man before.

Thaddeus nudged the team into motion again. As the wheels began their slow revolution, Amanda was aware of their life-crushing power. If she were to fall in their path . . .

Behind them, men shouted to clear the wagon and the woman's screaming trailed into broken sobs.

"Cowards don't start and the weak die along the way," Thaddeus intoned solemnly.

And which category do we fall into? Amanda wanted to ask.

She rode in jolting silence for the next few hours. By the time they pulled into Indian Creek, it was dark.

Chapter Four

NOTHING could have prepared Amanda for the campground at Indian Creek. Dimly visible in the gathering gloom was a sea of white-topped wagons, an endless village stretching over the meadows. Hundreds of campfires sent tendrils of purple smoke curling toward the starry sky. Silhouettes moved just beyond leaping flames, and soft laughter and voices punctuated the night.

Thaddeus guided the team between wagons to a small rise, one of the few spaces left, and began unhitching the oxen by the glow of nearby fires. Amanda sat stiffly in the seat, unable to think of what to do next.

But her father did. "How about fixing us a little supper?" he called, hanging the lines and harnesses on a hook just inside the wagon.

Amanda climbed down with difficulty,

hampered by her skirt and sharp pains shooting across her shoulders. "It's too dark. I can't see anything."

Leaning against the wagon box, she wished that all this were a bad dream, that she would soon wake up. A black, wrenching wave of homesickness swept over her. Boston was so far away . . . would she ever be able to go home again? A chilling thought struck her — would she still *have* a home? Perhaps she had dreamed the house in Louisburg Square . . .

Thaddeus clapped his hands loudly and said, "I'll get a fire started. Why don't you get out the things you'll need?"

"I don't know the first thing about cooking over a campfire," Amanda declared angrily.

"Now don't get that stubborn look on your face," her father warned. "I'm too tired to argue. We'll just have bacon and coffee tonight. I'll be right back."

He walked over to the closest wagon, introducing himself to the group around the campfire as gallantly as though he were in a Boston courtroom. Amanda heard a murmur of voices in response. When Thaddeus materialized out of the darkness, he said jovially to Amanda, "Forget cooking tonight, Missy. I was going to borrow a brand to start a fire, but those people said they had more than enough food. Just dig out our plates and cups and I'll bring some back."

Amanda fished out two tin plates and cups and handed them to him. Moments later, he returned with steaming mugs of coffee and plates piled high with cold biscuits and bacon. They ate standing up, using the grub box as a makeshift table. The bacon was too salty for Amanda's taste, and the biscuits were cold, but it had been so long since breakfast, she ate greedily. The strong coffee made her shudder, but it sent new strength coursing through her. Although she found camp life loathsome, she managed to wipe the plates clean and help her father spread his bedroll on the ground.

"I think I'll forget the tent tonight," he said, yawning.

The moon was high when Amanda crawled into the wagon and sagged, with her last fiber of energy, onto the corn-shuck mattress thrown over the boxes. The mattress had nothing to recommend it — merely a muslin sack split down the back, stuffed with dried corn shucks. Beneath the wagon she heard her father grunting as he rolled himself into his blanket. She tried to adjust the mattress, which rattled and rustled with the slightest movement, then gave up, drawing the blanket up over her. She lay, wide-eyed, staring out the hole in the canvas cover in the back of the wagon.

Fires burned low and the rise and fall of voices died as people all around went to bed. From somewhere on the other side of the campground a guitar strummed softly.

Amanda's thoughts invariably turned toward home. She remembered her room, with the pale Aubusson carpet blooming with pink roses. She yearned for the walnut pencil-post bed, canopied with lace hangings, made up with English linen sheets and a goosedown comforter. In her mind, she could almost touch the delicate French dressing table, a present from her father on her sixteenth birthday, which held Amanda's collection of cut-glass cologne bottles. Her room had only one recessed window that looked out over her mother's rose garden. Thaddeus had built a window seat, and her mother had made pink-flowered cushions. Amanda had spent many hours sitting in her cozy corner, dreaming about Joseph. Joseph . . . would she ever see that teasing grin again?

Amanda turned on her side. Hot tears tracked over her temples, wetting the mattress. If this first day was a sample of what the next four months would be, she would never make it to Oregon.

The sun sent welcoming shafts of bright light into her wagon, but Amanda felt anything but refreshed. She was so stiff and sore, she had to hobble out of bed like an old woman. Besides the knotty discomfort of her bed, cattle and oxen had stamped and snorted all night long. When she did sleep, it was in nightmarish fits and starts, waking with her heart pounding as she desperately tried to remember where she was.

She climbed down the side of the wagon, snagging her skirt on the front wheel, just as Thaddeus came around with his blanket neatly rolled.

"Good morning!" he greeted her. "Sleep well?"

Amanda snatched her skirt free. "Sleep isn't the word for it," she snapped.

"You'll get used to it. In no time at all, that old wagon will rock you to sleep like a baby. How about some breakfast?"

Breakfast! Here she stood in wrinkled clothes and sleep-fogged eyes and her hair a rat's nest, while total strangers milled around her not five feet away. And Thaddeus expected her to fix breakfast!

She finger-combed tangled strands of hair away from her face. "Let me get put together first. Where's . . . ?" she asked delicately.

Thaddeus yanked a thumb over his shoulder. "Behind those bushes. And the stream's at the foot of the hill. I'll get a fire going in the meantime, but it'll be your job from now on."

With enormous loathing and disgust, Amanda used the sheet-draped latrine for women and children, then headed down to the willow-lined stream bank. A girl her own age was scrubbing the dirt-streaked faces of three little girls who squirmed and poked each other.

"Mornin'," the older girl said pleasantly, smiling at Amanda. "I'm Helen Jorgenson. You're in the wagon right next to ours, aren't you?"

Amanda knelt and dipped her hands in the

cool water. "I don't know. When we arrived it was so dark, I couldn't see anything."

"Your pa came over after he got your team unhitched to borrow a blaze. And Mama gave you all the rest of our supper," the girl went on, tugging one of the little girls back to wash behind her ears. "Hold still, Martha."

Amanda bathed her own face, noting her reflection with horror. Her hair was alarming, standing up in Medusa-like snarls. She rocked back on her heels. Helen's corn-yellow hair, she observed, hung in a neat pigtail down her back.

"Need some help?" Helen offered, giving the little girls a playful swat to send them back up the hill.

"No." The last thing Amanda wanted this morning was some stranger's sympathy.

Helen pulled a brush from the pocket of her voluminous white apron and, before Amanda could pull away, began brushing the tangles out of Amanda's hair.

Amanda jerked back. "What do you think you're doing?" she said accusingly.

"Look, your hair is a real rat's nest, if you don't mind my sayin' so. Let me help straighten it out."

Sighing, Amanda realized the other girl was right — it was hard to fix her hair alone. She was so frazzled, she submitted without further protest.

"It's hard gettin' used to no privacy," Helen said as she rhythmically stroked Amanda's curls. " 'Specially if it's just you and your pa. There's nine in our family and we've been on the road so long, I forget what it's like to sleep in a real bed or even sit down at the supper table. What's your name?"

"Amanda. Amanda Bentley." *Helen brushes even better than Mrs. Garrity,* she thought. In Boston, the housekeeper brushed Amanda's long hair every morning and helped her put it up. But since Amanda had been on the road, her hair often went neglected. Having Helen unsnarl the tangles with deft hands was like having a servant again.

"You're very good at this," Amanda commented. "Are you a lady's maid?"

Helen laughed. "Sort of. I have to fix my little sisters' hair, so I'm their maid, I guess. I can't remember when I wasn't combin' the knots out of somebody's long hair."

When the tangles had been smoothed, Helen swiftly plaited Amanda's hair into a single braid. "You've got such thick hair," she said, securing the end with a ribbon she fished from her apron pocket. "There. Feel better? It's not beautiful, but it'll keep your hair out of the way."

"Thank you," Amanda said haughtily. "It'll do, I guess."

They walked back up the hill together. Helen was shorter than Amanda and much stockier. She wore a blue gingham dress under her apron and what looked like boy's boots on her large feet. Amanda's thin-soled slippers allowed the smallest stones to bruise her feet and her silk dress was crushed and wrinkled, but even if her shoes fell apart and her dress ripped to threads, she vowed she would never dress like Helen.

Thaddeus had built a smoky fire. A coffee pot dangled from a pole supported by two forked sticks. Since he was deep in conversation with two men from the next wagon, Amanda knew the rest of the meal was up to her.

A tall, handsome woman with faded blond hair skinned into a bun came toward them. One of the little girls Amanda had seen down at the stream clung to the woman's skirts, regarding Amanda with big brown eyes.

"That's my ma," Helen said. "Her name's Lavinia. Mama, this is Amanda Bentley. We met down at the creek."

Mrs. Jorgenson held out a red-knuckled hand. "Nice to meet you, Amanda. Helen was so tickled when she saw you and your father pull up last evening."

Amanda hesitated. Mrs. Jorgenson's hand was still outstretched. Reluctantly, she returned the handshake, barely touching the other woman's fingers.

"A girl my age," Helen broke in, laughing. "Honestly, I get so tired of lookin' at boys."

"You won't say *that* for long," Mrs. Jorgenson teased. "Amanda, this is my baby, Sarah Jane." She pushed the little girl forward. "And over there"— she pointed to where the other two girls and two boys played with a hound dog —"is the rest of my brood. Martha's the one who looks so much like Helen. Ann's the one with the doll. Can't get that thing away from her. The little imp pullin' Martha's braids is Noah and that's Jason struttin' around like his father."

"The dog is named Blue," Helen put in. "My uncle Jeb and Pa are tendin' the animals."

Amanda couldn't believe that she was standing in the middle of a pasture, exchanging introductions with farm women, as though they were at a party in Boston. She nearly laughed out loud, picturing Helen and her mother in Drucilla White's elegant drawing room.

"I'd better get breakfast," she said, hastily excusing herself.

The coffee was ready, and she had a cup while contemplating the enormous bags and barrels in the back of the wagon. What should she fix? Bacon wouldn't be too difficult once she got it sliced, but how did you make bread? *They didn't teach trail cooking at Miss Finch's,* she thought wryly. In fact, she had never so much as fried an egg. She'd never had to.

Rummaging around in the grub box, Amanda pulled out the iron skillet, the bread pan, and a sharp knife. Thaddeus had unwrapped a side of bacon and pulled it forward. Clumsily, she hacked off two thick strips, which she laid lengthwise in the pan, then placed the skillet over the fire. While the bacon sizzled, she scooped out a mugful of flour from the nearest barrel, heaping it into the bread pan.

Now what? She needed milk, but there was none. Water would have to do. She should have brought some back from the creek. Now she would have to make another trip. She snatched up the bucket and stomped back to the river. How she detested this life!

When she came back, she was greeted by an exclamation point of nasty black smoke billowing from the pan — a signal to everyone that the Bentley girl could not cook for beans.

With a small cry, she dropped the pail and ran over to the scorching bacon, jerking the skillet off the fire. The iron handle burned her fingers. Sucking on them, tears smarting her eyes, Amanda stared helplessly at the ruined food on the ground.

"Are you all right?"

She looked up to see Helen running over.

"Is your hand burned bad?" Helen asked, concerned.

"Yes. No. I don't know." She flapped her hand irritably. "My father is really *mean* to make me work so hard."

"Don't worry," Helen reassured her. "Mama cooked way too much, as usual. Here comes your pa. Pour him a cup of coffee and I'll be right back."

Amanda thought her father would be upset, but he merely laughed at what he considered her ineptness. He had made friends with Helen's father, Henry Clay

Jorgenson, a blond-bearded giant of a man, and her uncle Jeb, a homelier version of his brother; and Thaddeus was in high spirits.

After breakfast, Helen came back to help Amanda. She showed Amanda how to build a cook-fire, using a V-shaped framework of sticks. While they scrubbed plates and the scorched pan, Helen offered tips on trail cooking.

"Don't try to make biscuits for breakfast. Takes too long. Mama makes pilot bread the night before and we eat it cold for breakfast and dinner."

"Pilot bread?" Amanda asked, realizing that the "leftover" food the Jorgensons had generously given them was part of their breakfast and dinner.

"It's made with cornmeal and fried like pancakes," Helen said. "Only crispier. If you fry your bacon first, you can use the grease for the cornbread. Mama says it's best to keep everything real simple. Bacon and bread for breakfast, bacon and beans for dinner, dried beef and beans for supper. Maybe a little rice. Startin' tomorrow, she's makin' us eat dried apples at least twice a day."

Amanda wrinkled her nose. "Sounds awfully monotonous." She scraped her knuckles on the stubborn blackened sides of the skillet. If she kept this up, her hands would look as bad as Mrs. Jorgenson's.

Cooking three meals a day, plus extra for the next day . . . filthy, greasy pans to wash . . . Amanda shook her head. Never! She would never do all that, not in a thousand years. Narrowing her eyes, she observed Helen's efficient motions as she swished the tin plates in the water bucket. Helen seemed awfully eager; perhaps she could be persuaded to do Amanda's chores as well.

"The food is monotonous," Helen agreed cheerfully. "But it's for such a good cause. Won't Oregon be wonderful when we get there?" She took the skillet from Amanda and began scouring vigorously with sand.

"No, it *won't*," Amanda said with a vehemence that made Helen look up.

"Don't you want to go?"

"It wasn't *my* idea to go West," Amanda said.

"Pa says in Oregon we can claim whatever land we survey and settle on," Helen said. And it's supposed to be so healthful livin' out there. Mild weather — no more cold, snowy winters. And rich land . . . evergreen forests with game and streams with fish —"

"You sound like a travel guide," Amanda remarked drily.

Helen grinned, making the freckles stretch over her nose. "That's where I got all that from. Pa's guidebook."

"My father has one, too. It's all he reads these days."

Helen wiped her hands on the grass and stood up. "There. Pans all clean. What else you got to do?"

Amanda sighed. "Just repack the whole wagon, that's all."

"You aren't by yourself," Helen said. "Just look around."

She was right. In every campsite, boxes, barrels, cartons, furniture, and other household goods were piled around the wagons and the bewildered emigrants. Humpbacked trunks overflowed with clothes. Medicine chests were crammed with tiny bottles of liniments and bitters.

"Packing is a real art," Helen said as they walked over to Jorgensons' storage wagon. They had a second wagon they slept in. The heaviest and least-used items should be packed first, she instructed. The lightest and most frequently used on top. She lifted a corner of an old quilt, revealing a glimpse of gleaming maple.

"Mama's wedding chest. Been in the family for ages. She told Pa if *it* didn't go, she wasn't goin' neither."

Mrs. Jorgenson's good china, which she also refused to leave behind, was stored in the last flour barrel to keep from getting broken. More pans and tools hung from a chain that stretched from one end of the wagon to the other.

"What's that?" Amanda pointed to a stoneware jug suspended from one of the bows, from which leafy vines trailed.

"More of Mama's foolishness, accordin' to Pa. Sweetbrier vines from our place in Ohio. Pa declares there won't be enough water for a plant once we hit the plains. But Mama says she'll keep her vine alive if she has to do without herself."

Although Amanda never verbally accepted Helen's offer to help, the other girl began taking boxes out of Amanda's wagon. Amanda moved slowly enough so that Helen hauled out four items to one of hers. After a while she sat on the wagon tongue, fanning herself, while she directed Helen.

By suppertime, the Bentley wagon was shipshape, and outside a pot of beans was shimmering cozily over the fire.

Thaddeus came back in the early evening, his face etched with exhaustion, his clothes grimy after working with the team all day. He sank gratefully to the ground, watching Amanda slice bacon to put in the beans.

"Smells good. Tired, Missy?"

"Yes! So are you from the looks of your clothes."

"It's hard work, there's no denying it. I've been talking to Henry Clay Jorgenson. He says they're moving out at first light tomorrow. Got thirty-six wagons ready to leave. He asked us to join them and I accepted."

"We're leaving tomorrow, too?" She nearly dropped the spoon.

"Yep. I see the wagon's been straightened out. You do that by yourself?"

Amanda did not reply.

Thaddeus gave her a knowing glance. "You knew we had to leave for Oregon sometime."

"But I didn't think it would be so *soon!*" Amanda cried.

"The sooner the better," Thaddeus said. "We're leaving at daybreak, so get used to the idea."

Without another word, Amanda headed out of the camp. Her father did not try to stop her. There was no place to go but the stream. Helen was there, washing a stack of pans. She jumped up when she caught sight of Amanda.

"I'm so glad you're comin' with us! Pa told us."

Amanda drew back. "Why do you care whether I come or not? You never set eyes on me before today."

Helen looked as if she had been slapped. "I thought we could be friends," she said haltingly. "I never met a girl like you before. You look so different from anybody else I've seen, with your fancy dress and your little shoes. . . ."

Amanda was only half listening, suddenly aware of the number of women who had stopped talking to look at her. One girl in particular stared at Amanda before turning back to her dishwashing.

Amanda nudged Helen. "Who's that?"

"Her name's Serena Hawkins. Her family will be travelin' with us, too."

Amanda stole a sidelong glance at the new girl, who had pale, almost white, blond hair worn demurely over her ears. Spotless white cuffs and collar were the only decorations on her gray cotton dress, and the apron over the dress was immaculate. The girl scrubbed the pile of plates at her side efficiently, as though she liked nothing better than to wash dishes.

"She's going with Ben Compton," Helen whispered, as if reading Amanda's mind.

"Who's he?"

"Oh, you'll meet him. His father organized our company. Most likely, his father will be elected captain. Serena's and Ben's families were neighbors back in Illinois, so they've come all this way together."

"How do you know so much?" Amanda asked with annoyance.

Helen gave her a spritely smile. "Oh, I listen to *everything* anyone talks about."

By the time the sun had gone down, campfires twinkled all over the field as they had the night before. A fiddler and banjo player struck up a lively tune and soon young girls and boys were dancing over the meadow.

"Looks like fun. Why don't you go join them?" Thaddeus urged Amanda. "You need to be around young people more."

Amanda was still angry at him. "I have no intention of dancing with some sweaty-palmed bumpkin out in a pasture," she declared. "I'm going to bed."

She arranged herself on the mattress, tucking the blanket around her. The wind carried strains of the music, making her look out the open wagon cover to where she could observe the dancers.

As she watched, a slim, blond girl stepped into the circle. Serena Hawkins. She was claimed by a tall young man who grinned affectionately down at her. There was something familiar about him. Amanda strained to see better. That must be the Ben Compton Helen was talking about.

The music switched to a lively reel. The last time Amanda heard that song was at Hester's birthday last August. Paper lanterns imported from the Far East had transformed the Whites' garden into a fairyland. Amanda had worn a peppermint-striped taffeta gown with wide, graceful sleeves and a satin sash. Even though it was Hester's special day, Amanda knew she had taken the eye of every boy there. When the band struck up a reel, Joseph grasped her hands and whirled her off into the magic night.

Outside on the green, the couple laughed as they executed a series of quick steps. Why did Ben Compton look familiar? Amanda wondered. And why, at the sight of Ben and Serena dancing, did she feel so sad?

Chapter Five

THE next morning brought bright sun and pandemonium in the camp.

Amanda woke to shouting voices, bellowing cattle, the clatter of pans, and the jingle of harnesses. Tucking wisps of hair behind her ears, she climbed out of the wagon.

"What's going on?" Amanda asked her father, smoothing the worst of the wrinkles from her skirt.

"We're moving out this morning. I told you that last night. Ira Compton wants to be on the trail by seven."

"What time is it now?" Although Amanda still wore her mother's gold-enameled watch-pin fastened to her collar, the watch had stopped running some time ago.

Thaddeus consulted his pocket watch. "Twenty after seven. Looks like we'll be leaving a little late. I have to hurry and get the team hitched. Put my things in the wagon, will you?"

"What about breakfast? I'm starving!"

"If there's anything left from last night, that'll be fine. If not, forget it." Snatching the harness from the hook just inside the wagon, he was off.

Amanda stood there, fuming. He could not take an extra five minutes to fix them something to eat. No, he had to leave everything to her. She was still exhausted, even though she had gone to bed early last night, but obviously her father didn't care. She had lain awake, listening to the men talking earnestly around low-burning fires. She knew they were talking of trail dangers, the trackless plains, the lack of grass and water, the threat of Indians. When she finally fell asleep, those images troubled her dreams.

At the stream, she half expected to see Helen, but the only person there was Serena Hawkins. This time the blond girl smiled coolly at Amanda, then extended a slim, white hand.

"I'm Serena Hawkins," she said in a soft, restful voice that reminded Amanda of murmuring pines. "I believe we'll be traveling together."

Amanda introduced herself stiffly, then bent to wash her face and hands. Her reflection was less startling this morning, for the braid had tamed her hair, but there were dark smudges under her green-gold eyes.

It was well after ten o'clock by the time

everyone had sorted out their stock and hitched up their teams. Amanda learned that two other trains had formed yesterday and were preparing to leave also. At last, the thirty-seven wagons forming the Compton party, as it was already being called, were lined up along the road.

From the leading wagon at the far end of the train, a man mounted on a sorrel mare rode down the column, checking the teams, and barking out commands.

"That's Ira Compton," Thaddeus said, handing Amanda a dipper of water. "He's the one who organized the train. There's talk of electing him captain tonight."

"Does he have a son?" Amanda said, and nearly bit her tongue for asking.

Thaddeus lifted an eyebrow. "Yes, why?"

"No particular reason. Just wondering." The image of Ben and Serena dancing flashed through her mind. She still could not place where she had seen him. The memory hovered close to the edge but veered off every time she tried to pin it down.

As the wagons began to roll, Amanda counted them. Their wagon was the twenty-fifth in line, behind the Jorgensons' two wagons and in front of the Lightfoots'. Amanda had seen Sam Lightfoot, his wife Polly, and the older man traveling with them, Frank Grafius. They would probably remain in this position, Thaddeus informed her, for the duration of the journey. At last the Jorgenson wagon wheels creaked forward and Thaddeus hollered, "Git-yup!" to his own team, tugging the lines.

Everyone, it seemed, was caught up in the spirit of the trail. The white-covered wagons were filled with shouting, waving children; the ox teams plodded steadily as the drivers walked alongside hollering commands and cracking whips. Cattle and horses were herded in a parallel column beside the wagon train. Helen and her younger brother, Jason, were in charge of the ten cows brought from Ohio, so Amanda saw little of the other girl. She really did not like Helen and did not want her hanging around all the time, unless, of course, Amanda had a chore for her.

Although the train started out bravely, it began deteriorating almost from the first. Oxen still not broken in to wagon loads balked and lay down in the road, halting the entire train, while red-faced drivers worked to get them moving again. Cattle strayed and had to be brought back. Just off the trail, a hunting party quarreled over which direction they would take.

Ira Compton was everywhere, spurring his horse from one crisis to another. Amanda wondered who was driving the lead wagon. Probably his son, Ben. He looked as though he could handle an ox team alone.

The countryside they traveled through was lush and fragrant. The rains had brought more wild flowers than Amanda had ever seen in any one place: Masses of yellow, white, blue, and purple bloomed against a rich green backdrop of thick, high grass. Bored with riding in bumpy wagons, children raced over the fields, gathering armloads of blossoms as they called to each other in thin, piping voices.

For Amanda, "riding the boards" was even more uncomfortable than riding horseback across half the country. The springless wagon jolted her helter-skelter on the hard wooden seat. After one particularly nasty bump, she rubbed her bottom ruefully, wondering if becoming black-and-blue was part of the much-touted "trail experience." After a few miles, the road became less rocky, but the sun had swung around and she knew her face was getting burned. All the women, even little girls, wore bonnets of heavy calico stretched over wire frames to shield their faces. Amanda decided she would rather perish of heatstroke than wear one. She leaned back into the wagon, though this position hurt her shoulders. She was wearing the "second-best" silk dress she had packed so hastily that night in Boston. Sitting in the full sun, she realized how hot and unsuitable the fabric was.

With nothing to do but sit, and no one close by to talk to, the afternoon dragged. A wagon broke down and the train stopped once more while men worked like demons to repair it and still make camp before nightfall.

When the train moved out again, Amanda clung to her perch, her face clammy, her head spinning. She crawled back into the wagon under the stifling canvas cover to lie on her mattress. The rolling, jouncing motion of the wagon made her more nauseous than ever, and now she gripped the side of her bed, unable to move. She closed her eyes. Bright red-and-yellow swirls flashed behind her eyelids and her head pounded with nightmarish images. She dropped into a feverish sleep.

When the wagon lurched to a stop, she awoke with a start.

Where am I? she thought, fuzzily focusing on a pan swinging from the hickory bow overhead. Lavender light stole through the opening in the wagon cover. She sat up. They must have finally stopped for the night.

"You okay, Missy?" Thaddeus called from outside.

"I — I guess so."

"I'm unhitching the team now. Do you think you could get supper?"

She put a hand to her head. The thought of food brought another wave of nausea. The last thing she wanted to do was cook, but she was too weak to argue. "I'll try," she promised halfheartedly. She managed to get as far as the front of the wagon before collapsing weakly against the frame, perspiration beading her forehead.

The campsite proved to be a disappointment. Every tree for more than a quarter of a mile had been cut for firewood, undoubtedly by thousands of emigrants over the past few years. Wagons rolled off the road in a continuous stream. Around the Bentley wagon, the Lightfoots were busy making a fire, and on the other side, Lavinia Jorgenson was already setting up a tripod over her fire.

Helen's family is always so organized, Amanda thought, gingerly stepping down. *Even with six children.*

She stood a few moments, grateful for the cool breeze and the feel of firm ground beneath her feet. Soon the queasiness that had clenched her stomach for the past several hours disappeared, leaving only her throbbing headache.

Helen ran over. "How'd you like the first day on the trail?"

Amanda opened the grub box, without even sparing Helen a glance. "It was dreadful. I was sick the whole afternoon."

"Really?" Helen's china-blue eyes were wide. "I walked with the cattle all day. My feet hurt but not too bad. Pa says we made twelve miles in spite of the delays."

"That's supposed to be good?" Amanda snapped, setting the skillet on the ground. With all the work she had to do bending over, it would be a wonder if she didn't get to Oregon as stoop-shouldered as an old crone. Grabbing the knife, she sawed off two slices of bacon. "Bacon, bacon, bacon. If I don't turn into a pig on this trip, I never will!"

Helen took Amanda by the arm. "Listen, why don't we go down to the stream? You're going to need firewood and water, anyway. If you wash your face, you might feel better."

Helen reminded Amanda of an over-eager puppy. But she hated going to the stream alone, where other women stared at her. By the time they reached the brook, Helen had gathered enough wood for Amanda's fire.

Running her hands through cool, clear water, Amanda had to admit grudgingly that Helen was right again. She did feel better, and her headache faded to a dull throb.

"You ought to get out of the wagon and walk tomorrow," Helen advised as they headed back. "Riding all the time would make a buzzard sick, Mama says. It's like some kind of seasickness."

"I refuse to walk to Oregon," Amanda declared, sloshing half the water out of her bucket. "I don't want to go as it is, and I won't ruin my shoes by taking one step there."

Helen busied herself, expertly arranging the wood and striking a flint for Amanda's fire. Amanda watched through narrow eyes. Much as she hated the chores associated with trail life, having Helen around only pointed up how incompetent she was.

"I can manage by myself," she said curtly, taking the pointed sticks from Helen.

Helen stepped back, her face openly displaying hurt. "I'm sure you can. It's just that I thought you were sick —"

"Well, I'm better now. I don't want anybody around here thinking I don't do my share."

Helen turned and walked quietly back to her own camp.

Now maybe she'll get the message,

Amanda said to herself as she scooped out flour and soda for biscuits.

Thaddeus returned, his face sweaty and beet-red. Amanda took one look at him and said, "You'd better cool off before you get heatstroke. You're no more used to this climate than I am."

He sank down into the soft, fragrant grass, pulling a grimy handkerchief out of his pocket, which he dipped into the pail of water.

"That's my cooking water!" Amanda cried.

"Sorry, Missy." Thaddeus wrung out the wet cloth and pressed it to his forehead. "I didn't think I could make it all the way down to the stream. It looks so far."

"But not too far for me to fetch water all night!" Snatching the bucket by the wire bail, Amanda stomped down the hill.

The women had left, undoubtedly preparing the evening meal. Only dusty, tired men lined the muddy banks, splashing water over their heads. Having an all-male audience did not appeal to Amanda, so she cut through a grove of willow trees, arriving at a secluded section of the stream where the water cut deeply into stony banks.

She scrambled over the rocks, holding her skirt with one hand and the bucket with the other, silently cursing the thinness of her kid slippers. The sharp edges of the ledge cut into her tender feet, and climbing down the rock face required all of her concentration. She never noticed the coiled snake, ringed with broad copper bands, until she nearly stepped on it.

With a cry, she jerked away, losing the bucket and her balance, and tumbled backward into the rushing stream. Water frothed around her, ballooning her dress. Her braid hung down her back, heavy and wet as a muskrat. The water was only about six inches deep but the fall had knocked the breath from her, and she had scraped her hands on the rocky bottom.

"Well, now *that* was an interesting maneuver!" came a wry male voice.

Pushing her dripping hair out of her eyes, Amanda saw Ben Compton standing on the ledge above her, his hands arrogantly on his hips.

"Look out!" she cried. "The snake!"

With great exaggeration he looked around. "What snake? I don't see any snake."

"There was one right there," Amanda insisted. "Instead of standing up there like a statue, why don't you help?"

"Because this is more fun," he said, grinning. In that instant, Amanda remembered where she had seen him.

Struggling to her feet, she sputtered, "You're the boy who yelled at me when that wagon nearly ran me down."

Ben raised a questioning eyebrow. "I'm afraid I don't —"

"You do too! It was only two days ago, on the road out of Independence. Stop looking at me like I've lost my mind!" She sloshed to the bank, realizing she must have made quite a picture with her lank hair and soaked dress. The fact that the late-setting sun made Ben's hair glint like gold and that he was much taller than she had recalled did not help matters any.

"You know," he began conversationally, as though they were on a street corner instead of the wilds of Indian territory, "you need somebody to look after you — to keep you from falling into creeks and out of the paths of wagons. And you ought to get some better shoes, girl. Those flimsy things aren't the least bit suitable for the trail."

"If it's all the same to you," Amanda fumed. "My feet are none of your concern."

Ben lifted his hat in a mocking gesture. "Whatever you say, Yankee girl."

"And don't call me that!"

"What is your name, then?"

"None of your business!" Amanda retrieved her bucket and stalked by him in as dignified a manner as she could considering her condition.

"And another thing," he called after her. "Don't go exploring by yourself unless you carry a gun. The next copperhead might not be so polite."

So, she thought with a strange sense of triumph. *There was a snake.*

It was not until she got back to camp that her knees turned to water. Copperheads were poisonous. If that snake had bitten her, she would have died a horrible death.

Chapter Six

AFTER the first disastrous day on the trail, Ira Compton established a routine that would carry them to Oregon.

He maintained strict order. Since they were definitely in Indian territory now, the wagons were locked in a tight circle every night, with wagon tongues overlapping and the rear hub of one wagon chained to the front hub of the wagon behind. In the middle of the huge corral, horses and oxen were picketed to prevent Indians from taking them in the night. Guards were posted all night, four standing watch at each compass point, to be relieved every four hours. Because guard duty was assigned alphabetically, Thaddeus drew the first shift.

"Those four hours are like a thousand years," he declared to Amanda the next morning, his eyes red-rimmed. "I don't know why we need guards. Haven't seen an Indian since we left Independence. Hard as I work all day, I need sleep."

"Who can sleep, anyway?" Amanda grumbled over the morning fire. "The wind practically blew the cover off the wagon. And with the horses and cows chomping and snorting all night long, a dead man couldn't rest."

Thaddeus warmed his hands around the mug of coffee Amanda gave him. Although the days were hot, the nights and early mornings were quite cool. "Ahhh. Coffee tastes better every day, Missy. I believe you're finally getting the hang of trail cooking."

"I hope not."

On the second morning after Ira was elected captain, Helen ran up to Amanda's wagon. "We're at the junction of the trail!" she reported breathlessly. "Fellas up ahead said they saw the sign."

"What sign?" Amanda asked.

"The one pointin' the way to Oregon."

Feverish excitement raced through the train like a brush fire as each wagon came in view of the sign and made the gradual turn due west, leaving the Santa Fe Trail. Guns were fired, hats were tossed up with wild abandon, and children cheered.

It certainly isn't worth all that fanfare, Amanda thought, staring at the crude wooden post that read "Road to Oregon," as her wagon came abreast of it. For such a long, arduous journey, someone could have at least put up a bigger sign.

The sun bore down, and sunbonnets were fished off wagon hooks. When they crossed the rock-based ford of Bull Creek, Amanda gazed longingly at the cool water sliding over moss-covered stones. The Jorgenson children, having shed their boots and black stockings and wearing only simple smocks, squealed with delight as they splashed and played.

"You ought to get off that perch and walk with me," Polly Lightfoot said one afternoon.

"No . . . I like riding," Amanda replied, even though it was far from true. She shifted on the uncomfortable wagon seat.

"Suit yourself." The other woman went back to her own wagon directly behind the Bentleys'.

Polly Lightfoot was a pretty, dark-haired young woman in her early thirties, and almost as chatty as Helen. In no time Amanda learned that she and her husband Samuel were both from Woodstock, Virginia, and that shortly after the couple was married, they decided to give up their rocky, unproductive farm and head West.

"It's the only way we'll ever have anything," Polly had confided to Amanda. "Sam and me are both the youngest of nine. The oldest always gets the home place and all the land, leaving crumbs for the younger ones. In Oregon, we won't have to fight over nothin' with our families."

"But don't you miss them?" Amanda had inquired. Scarcely a day went by that she did not long for Boston.

Polly had gazed eastward, an automatic reaction, Amanda thought, before answering in a soft voice, "Yes, I do miss Virginia and my family. I think about them, but I try not to dwell in the past. When Sam asked me to go, I said yes and I haven't regretted it a minute. I'm goin' to Oregon because I want to."

Which is more than I can say, Amanda added to herself.

Samuel Lightfoot was a small man, also in his thirties, with bright blue eyes and an infectious laugh. Frank Grafius was traveling with the Lightfoots as a "hired" hand. He was a grizzled old man with long, gray-brown hair parted in the middle and curled up on the ends, reminding Amanda of a picture of a water buffalo she had once seen. But the gray eyes above the ragged mustache were level and kind.

By the time they crossed the Wakarusa River, Amanda felt she knew most of the people in the party by sight. Besides Ben and his father, she had also met Ben's mother, Rose — a small, tired-looking woman — and his twelve-year-old sister, Eliza, who was dark like her mother and who shamelessly adored her big brother. Eliza became a familiar sight, riding on the back of Ben's pony, her black hair streaming behind her sunbonnet, as Ben rode up and down the length of the column, checking for potential problems.

The Hawkins family rode directly behind the lead wagon. In camp, Amanda often saw Serena helping her mother care for her younger brother and sisters. Serena had a demure, feminine look that set her apart, whether she was scrubbing pans down at the stream, quietly reading by the fire, or dancing on the green in Ben Compton's arms.

Amanda found herself watching Serena at every chance, but she was not certain why. Was it because the other girl was supposed to be engaged to Ben? If Ben and Serena were going to be married, they did not act like it. In fact, Amanda observed, he treated Serena more like a sister. Thinking about Ben and the others gave Amanda something to occupy her mind during long, monotonous afternoons.

Usually, though, her thoughts turned back to Boston, savoring memories of home the way some people savored fine food. Last summer Joseph called on her every Sunday afternoon. Sometimes they rode out of town on a picnic or went rowing on the Charles River. Often they sat in the rose garden in the backyard, sipping tall, cool drinks served by Mrs. Garrity. Amanda wore delicate cotton frocks, festooned with yards of lace and a wide-brimmed hat to keep the sun off her white skin. *Those days are gone forever,* she thought dismally. There was nothing ahead, she felt certain.

There were many streams to cross and at every one, Thaddeus would holler back, "This is nothing compared to the Kansas." The more Amanda heard about the mighty Kansas River, the less she wanted to face crossing it.

When they finally reached the Kansas, they were met by a wedge of white-topped wagons funneling down to a single point, all waiting to cross. A ferry run by two Frenchmen, Joseph and Louis Papin, carried over emigrant wagons and their teams for a small fee.

At dawn on the third day, Josiah Hawkins and Al Albrecht, Ira's second-in-command, ordered everyone to form a line with the teams hitched, ready to go when they were called. Sitting on her wagon perch, Amanda could not understand the rush: The ferry only carried two wagons at a time, and not more than twelve oxen or mules.

"Isn't this exciting?" Helen called, leaning out of her own wagon.

Amanda rolled her eyes heavenward. Helen thought everything was exciting. Getting up at the uncivilized hour of four-thirty usually dampened Amanda's enthusiasm for the day's adventures, but today she sat anxiously, her hands knotted in her lap. She sensed a dangerous, foreboding bite to the crisp morning air.

Who wouldn't be nervous? she thought, after getting a good look at Papin's ferry.

It was a flimsy structure — a platform lashed to three dugout canoes, propelled by men with poles. Maneuvering the wagons up and down the treacherous banks seemed to be the most difficult part of the operation. A rope coiled around a tree on the south bank lowered the wagon down the steep grade and onto the ferry. To get it up the other side, twice the usual number of oxen was hitched to the wagon.

At this particular crossing point, the river was more than six hundred feet wide and wildly turbulent due to a heavy spring runoff. Ira and Ben swam their horses beside the ferry, urging cattle and other loose stock to the other side. The animals pawed their forelegs in clumsy swimming motions, trying frantically to keep their heads above the roiling water. It was dangerous, freezing work for the men. Amanda was not looking forward to her turn at all.

At noon, only a third of the wagons had been ferried across. Unable to start a fire, Amanda handed her father a napkin containing his lunch, a cold biscuit split and filled with bacon leftover from last night. She had finally learned to cook extra food, to save time in the morning and at noon. Taking her share into the wagon, she was grateful to have something to do to break the tedious waiting, if only gnawing a biscuit.

At last it was their turn. Amanda's heart lurched as the wheels rolled slowly. Thaddeus struggled to line up his team to make the harrowing descent down the river bank. Samuel Lightfoot, Henry Clay, and Jeb

Jorgenson helped him anchor the wagon ropes.

The Jorgenson wagon was lowered first, then the Bentleys'. Ahead of her, Amanda heard the squeals of Noah and Martha as their wagon bumped onto the platform. All of the Jorgenson children were piled into the wagon with the covers pulled up. Their supply wagon would come on the next trip, with the Lightfoots'. A few moments later, the Bentley wagon was positioned. Thaddeus stood next to his lead oxen, holding the lines and harnesses slackly. When the oxen started to buck, Ira Compton shouted, "Watch those animals, Bentley!" Thaddeus gripped the lines tighter, trying to quiet his oxen.

With their poles, the ferrymen eased the raft out into the swirling water. The river was foaming, mud-flecked, as though churned by a hundred water mills. Amanda gripped the sides of the seat so tightly, her knuckles whitened, her heart hammering against her ribs. The noise was deafening as men swore, cattle bellowed, and horses whinnied in protest as they were driven into icy water. Above it all, the river roared, drowning out the loudest shouts. For the first time, Amanda realized that each time the men ventured into the river, they were risking their lives. Ira and his son had been working like this all day. Once she caught a glimpse of Ben as he fought to drive part of the Jorgenson cattle ahead of him. His clothes were drenched, his light hair plastered to his head, his face grim with the cold and exhaustion.

About halfway across, the powerful current snatched a pole from one of the ferrymen. The raft wallowed. The man managed to recover his pole, but the river had gained advantage, choosing that moment to tilt the platform at a sickening angle. Amanda screamed as water frothed over the ferry, breaking above the wheels of her wagon, licking at her feet. The wagon slid sideways, heading for the Jorgenson wagon, and Amanda knew she was going to be thrown overboard. She closed her eyes and prepared to be plunged to a watery death.

". . . elp . . . your . . . ather!" a voice called hoarsely in an effort to be heard above rushing water. ". . . elp . . . with . . . team!" The river drowned out most of the words, but Amanda heard enough to know the voice was shouting at her.

She opened her eyes. Benjamin Compton sat astride his lathered pony, his blue eyes shooting sparks as he half stood in the stirrups and waved angrily at her.

Clinging to the wagon seat as the raft dipped again, Amanda gradually became aware of what was going on around her. The ferry had righted itself, but the animals were frightened, their eyes rolling, as they stamped and pulled against their harnesses. Thaddeus was braced against the front wheels of the Jorgenson wagon, trying desperately to get his team in line before they upset the wagon.

Without further hesitation, Amanda climbed down and ran forward, her dress nearly up to her waist, revealing sodden petticoats. She grabbed the yoke of the nearest lead ox and pushed the huge animal back, talking soothingly to it all the while.

"Go back!" her father screamed through clenched teeth. "They might crush you!"

Amanda put her arms around the ox instead and held on until the animal stopped struggling. She leaned against it, feeling the rough, wet hide trembling next to her own soaked skin. Until now, she had been afraid of the huge, ungainly beasts, but now she realized they were as frightened as she.

Miraculously, they reached the far bank. Waiting hands pulled Amanda to high ground and draped a blanket around her shoulders.

"I saw the whole thing," a quiet voice said. "You must have been scared to death."

Through chattering teeth, Amanda replied, "I can't believe I'm standing here now."

She noticed then that her companion was Serena Hawkins, but the other girl wasn't looking at her. Her soft gray gaze was fastened on a small figure plunging his pony back into the river.

"Amanda!" Helen ran up, her apron and dress wet about the hem. "Are you all right? Wasn't it awful? I thought we were done for.

You were just wonderful, helping your pa like that."

Amanda let Helen gush, even though she knew someone else deserved the credit. It was Ben Compton who had galvanized her into action. *If it hadn't been for him. . . .* She shivered at the thought.

Helen followed Serena's gaze out into the river. "Ben is wonderful, too. I think he's the bravest man out there, outside of our fathers."

"They're all brave," Serena said simply, but her tone implied that most of her admiration was reserved for Ben.

Long after the sun had set, wagons continued to be ferried over. Women on the north bank built blazing fires and brewed pot after pot of coffee to fortify men who had been standing or swimming in freezing water since dawn.

Although she was still shaking, Amanda managed to fix a fairly passable supper, but Thaddeus was unable to leave the riverbank, where every available pair of hands was needed now that it was getting dark. When darkness fell, the work didn't stop. Lanterns were lit to guide over the last few wagons.

Still draped in Serena's blanket, Amanda sat huddled by the fire, unable to get warm. She stared into the dancing flames, tears sliding down her cold cheeks. The trail had revealed its dangerous side, and she was more afraid than she let people believe. Her thoughts, like a runaway carriage, skidded toward Joseph. Had he received her letter? Even if he were west of the Missouri, which was most unlikely, would he ever find her? The flames flickered blue and yellow, but her questions went unanswered.

Suddenly, hoarse cries rose from down by the river. Women dropped what they were doing and ran out of the camp. Amanda shed her blanket and followed.

Beyond the leaping lantern light, figures moved with taut purpose as they fought to maneuver a wagon up the bank. There was something odd about the angle of the wagon, half in and half out of the water, the oxen straining in their harnesses.

When her father came up to her, Amanda scarcely recognized him, he looked so weary. "Papa! What's happened?" She put an anxious hand on his arm. "Did anything happen to Ben?"

"Ben? No, it was that Albrecht fellow. His wagon was last and the rope must have been frayed. In the dark, nobody noticed." Thaddeus wiped his sleeve across his eyes as if to erase the memory. "When the wagon broke free and started back for the river, Albrecht jumped in its path. Trying to save his family. The back wheels caught him underneath."

"Is he —?" Amanda couldn't bring herself to say the rest.

"Yes, he's dead. Drowned. In only a few inches of water."

Amanda looked away from the bobbing circle of lanterns where the men were carrying something heavy and limp between them. Instead, she glared at the hateful Kansas, racing smoothly between its banks, blacker than night itself. The river had claimed a victim.

Amanda turned away, unable to take any more. She walked back to the wagon with her father, fixed his plate, then went to bed without even washing the dishes.

In the dark wagon, she kept seeing the gruesome circle of lanterns, the limp form dragged from the clutches of the river. She despised the trail, but, what was worse, knew that in the end the trail would win. They would all die, one by one, before they reached Oregon.

The next morning dawned gray and sober. Ira Compton elected a crew to dig Allen Albrecht's grave, raw as a new wound. Then, with his hat in his hand, Ira preached a brief service. Mrs. Albrecht stared dully into the yawning hole, her children gathered around her skirt as Ben shoveled a spade of freshly turned earth into the grave.

Chapter Seven

THE next few days it rained, and Amanda realized just how miserable trail life could be.

The rain was cold and penetrating, seeping into her bedding and making everything, including the clothes she wore, feel like damp seaweed. Thaddeus plodded along with the team, swathed to the chin in a rubber ground sheet, water dripping off the brim of his felt hat, sometimes slipping in the mire churned up by the heavy wagons.

Everyone cursed the rain.

"We'll probably be hollerin' for it in another week or so," Helen remarked once. "Pa says once we hit Platte River country, we'll be beggin' for a little rain, miserable as it is now."

"I doubt it," Amanda grumbled. "I can't imagine anything more wonderful than being baked dry. Even my hair is mildewing!"

Amanda avoided looking in the mirror that hung from one of the bows. Not only was her hair a mess, but her face was so sunburned from long afternoons of riding into the glaring sun, she hardly recognized herself. The blue silk dress was nearly in shreds, and the soles of her kid slippers had worn through at the heels. In her satchel, she still had her woolen riding habit, which was even more unsuitable to this climate, and her chameleon silk dress, which she did not want to ruin. Knowing that she looked worse than she ever had in her life did little to boost her morale.

A few days later the wagon party arrived, wet and weary, at the prettiest campsite they had seen so far. Ice-cold spring water gushed from a ledge of rocks, falling over the shelf into a basin about twelve feet below. Oak, cottonwood, walnut, beech, and sycamore lined the banks. As if on cue, the rain stopped and the sun came out, bathing the cove in golden light and sketching a faint rainbow over the trees. Everyone's soggy spirits lifted immediately.

Amanda would have loved to explore a branch of the spring and find a quiet place to swim and wash her hair. Instead, following the example of the other women, she busied herself taking supplies out of the wagon to air and dry out. Her bedding smelled so bad, she could not endure another night on the mildewing mattress. Within an hour after their arrival, the clearing bloomed with sheets and clothing spread on cottonwood bushes. Between her chores, Amanda found time for a quick bath, but not enough to wash her hair. Gritting her teeth as she rebraided it and coiled it on top of her head, she consoled herself with the fact that everyone else had dirty hair, too.

The first night after the river crossing, everyone was too exhausted to do more than fall into bed. But on the second night, their spirits refreshed by green grass and timbered hills, people were ready to celebrate. The banjo and fiddle players brought out their instruments and there was dancing on the green.

Helen came over to where Amanda was setting a pan of cornbread to bake over a slow fire.

"Doesn't seem to be any end to it, does there?" she said, referring to the baking. "Come on, let's go join the dancin'. Kick up our heels a little."

Amanda looked over at the couples whirling over the grass. "I'd rather not mingle with strangers. You never know who —"

"Stop bein' such a stick-in-the-mud. We've been on the trail for three weeks now and I haven't hardly seen you smile. Why don't you let yourself have a good time for once?"

Amanda thought this over. She *was* tired of working and being alone. "I'll go sit and watch. But I refuse to dance."

"Well, *I* want to dance. My feet are tappin' already. They can't believe I'm goin' to do something with 'em besides walk behind a cow's tail all day."

Amanda ducked inside the wagon long enough to check her reflection in the mirror. Her hair was passable, but her face was red and peeling. Her dress, without a protective apron, was torn and dirty. If only there was some way to spruce up her appearance.

She stuck her head outside the hole in the back canvas and said, "Give me another minute or two, will you?"

"Don't take too long. My feet are gettin' mighty impatient."

Amanda drew the ropes taut on both ends of the wagon. She tossed her mattress aside, rummaged between some boxes, and came up with her satchel. Opening it, she pulled out the chameleon silk dress. Immediately, memories of that last night in Boston engulfed her. Taking off her filthy dress, she slipped the green-gold gown over her head, delighting in the smooth feel of the fabric and the rustle of the full skirt. She buttoned the bodice with trembling fingers, then loosened the pucker ropes on the canvas cover.

Helen stared with wide blue eyes as Amanda stepped down. "What a beautiful dress! I don't suppose you got another tucked away you could lend me? Forget it, I'd never fit into anything that small in a thousand years."

Amanda smoothed the wrinkled skirt. "Everyone will stare at me, won't they?

Worse than usual, I mean." She half turned, as if to go back into the wagon. "Maybe I should put my old dress back on."

Helen linked her arm through Amanda's. "You leave it on. So what if people stare? I'm staring because it's the prettiest dress I've ever seen. Wear it — give 'em a chance to rest their eyes on something besides cotton and calico."

The music had attracted a large crowd. Not just young people, but children who were avoiding bedtime, and their parents who stood quietly, shoulders touching, enjoying a few moments respite from the endless work.

Amanda hung back at the edge of the circle. *This is a mistake,* she told herself.

Helen plucked at her sleeve. "Come on," she urged, pushing her way through to join the dancers. She began to clap her hands and, before too long, a red-haired boy in a red flannel shirt claimed her for the next dance.

As Amanda made her way to the front, she was aware of a trail of whispers and hard eyes following her. So, she thought, tossing her head, the old biddies *don't* like anyone to dress up.

The girls still wore their modest white aprons over their calico dresses, but the plainness of their clothing didn't prevent them from dancing with as much enthusiasm as if they were at the grandest ball. Several of them came over to Amanda with admiring cries, reaching out to touch the shimmering silk.

Amanda sat down on an upturned keg offered to her. Flickering firelight spilled liquid color down her lap — gold, hints of deep gray. The dress was as magnetic here on the trail as it was in her Boston parlor.

The caller finished barking out the last round, and the winded couples stopped to catch their breath.

Helen towed her partner to where Amanda was sitting. "Amanda, this is Jefferson Bell. Jeff, have you met Amanda Bentley?"

Jefferson gave her a short bow. "Where has a pretty thing like you been hidin'? Why haven't I see you before?" As the fiddle started up again, he asked, "Would you do me the pleasure?"

"No, thanks. I don't care for dancing," Amanda said haughtily.

"Don't like dancin'!" Jeff cried incredulously with popped-out eyes. "I don't believe it. I bet you're jes' shy—"

"Really," Amanda insisted. "I don't want to dance." She shot Helen a sharp look as if to say, *Get rid of this bumpkin.* This was why she had never come to these gatherings before. She knew she would never fit in. She didn't *want* to fit in. And she was furious with Helen for insisting that she come.

A couple swung by and the girl dipped, setting her skirt aswirl. Amanda recognized Serena in Ben Compton's arms. She had not noticed them before.

"Hey, Ben," Jefferson called. "Ever hear

of a girl that don't like to dance? Especially a pretty one like this one here?"

Amanda's eyes met Ben's, and in the gathering darkness it was difficult for her to read his expression.

He called back to Jeff, "Forget it, Bell. The Yankee girl is too good for an Iowa boy."

Jeff laughed and scooped up Helen, sweeping her out onto the green.

Amanda stood abruptly, picked up her ruffled skirts, and fled the clearing, pushing rudely past the crowd. Her cheeks burned as she ran back to her wagon. How dare that Ben Compton talk about her that way in front of everyone! Imagine calling her that rude name! Joseph would never have behaved in such a preposterous manner. Why couldn't Joseph be here now to protect her? she yearned as she climbed into her wagon. She hated the trail and detested her life out here. But at that moment, she despised Ben Compton more than anyone — or anything — else on earth.

As the wagon party neared the Platte River, following the Little Blue, which took them north for 120 miles to its headwaters, they left timbered green hills behind. Beyond, the barren plains stretched like a sandy sea. No wood, only scrubby sagebrush, and no good water until they reached Ash Hollow at the forks of the Platte River, miles away.

The wagons ground up a long slope toward

the Platte, wheels screeching in protest as the land grew increasingly arid.

As the scenery became more alarming, with weird-shaped rocks and bristly vegetation, Amanda became frightened, then angry. Frightened because the land looked so forbidding; afraid she would never live through it; and angry at her father for bringing her here. There was no place to get away from the ceaseless sun, the sand-pelting wind, the loneliness.

In addition, everyone was beset by swarms of mosquitoes, deadlier than snakes, and millions of buffalo gnats, which crawled into their clothing and worried the oxen until they bellowed angrily.

There was also thick, yellow dust churned up by plodding hooves and wagon wheels. In desperation, Thaddeus frequently drove their wagon parallel to the trail, rather than follow the Jorgenson wagons. At times the wagons were fanned out a mile wide to avoid the choking dust. Each day, Ira Compton let a different wagon lead the train to give everyone a chance to be out of the dust.

Amanda rode on the wagon seat, her dress sticking to her shoulder blades and midriff in wet patches. At noon, Thaddeus propped a blanket over sticks to get out of the sun while Amanda sweated over a small cook-fire. During the heat of the afternoon, Amanda sometimes looked back at Helen, walking behind the Jorgenson cattle with her stick, covered from head to toe with dust. And though water was rationed carefully, she never once heard Helen complain.

But Helen worried about her.

"You're gettin' burned up," she said to Amanda one evening after supper.

"So are you," Amanda said defensively, thinking Helen was trying to make her feel bad. She knew she was sunburned and she hated it. She would probably never have milk-white skin again.

"Yes, but your face is worse than mine. Amanda, you've got to start wearin' a bonnet. Here." She untied the strings of the sunbonnet that dangled down her back. "Take this. I can use one of Mama's old ones." She held it out to Amanda. "Take it. Please."

Amanda hesitated, then took the bonnet. "I hate these things. They're so ugly." She plopped the hat on her head and jerkily tied the strings under her chin. "Look at me. You can't even see me the way the brim pokes out over my face."

Helen laughed. "It looks better on you than it did on me. Listen, I'd wear a feed sack over my head to keep from gettin' a bad sunburn. Mama's in the wagon right now with Noah and Ann — those kids are burned to a crisp and they holler all night long, it hurts so bad."

"I suppose you're right." Amanda sighed, untying the bonnet strings. She gave the hat a little slap. "I'll wear it, even though I hate it."

"And that dress you're wearin'," Helen brought up. "It's gettin' a mite ragged and I bet it's hotter than Creation."

"What isn't hot out here in this desert?" Amanda retorted. "We couldn't be any cooler if we ran around in our chemises!"

"Maybe not, but cotton is cooler than silk. Look how it sticks to you. And it's hard to keep clean."

Amanda snorted. "I haven't been able to wash out anything since we left the river. Who wouldn't look grubby?"

"Pa says it's going to be a sight hotter before it's over. Now, I have a dress a woman from Ohio gave me that I think might fit —"

"I don't want one of your hand-me-downs," Amanda said rudely.

"It's not a hand-me-down. It's — it's a loan. I'll lend you the dress till we get over the Divide." Helen gave her a smile. "It's not as ugly as you think — made out of green calico that'll make your eyes look greener."

Amanda's silk dress was filthy with sweat stains. A clean dress, no matter how unstylish, would feel better at least. She remembered the length of yellow calico Mrs. Longman tried to give her back in Independence. Even if she had it now, Amanda knew she was not very good at sewing.

Helen jumped up. "Let me go get it for you. When you see —"

"All right, all right," Amanda gave in. "I don't care what it looks like, just as long as you quit harping at me."

She took the dress, which fit surprisingly well, and rode her wagon perch in slightly more comfort with the bonnet to shield her face and the looser-fitting garment, though she still refused to cover her dress with a huge white apron. *At least the other women won't make those hard eyes at me anymore,* she comforted herself.

The sun bore down unmercifully, turning endless stretches of alkali flats into cool, shimmering lakes that melted into hard salt fields again as they approached. At night, darkness was so intense Amanda felt she could gather it into a ball, like winding yarn. Wolves cried, sending tremors of fear down her spine. Even with her father a few feet away, she never felt more alone.

Finally, they rolled up the last of the grade and looked down upon the Platte River, chewing its way through plains, which were punctuated by stubby grass and the bleached bones and skulls of buffalo. Low, undulating sandhills bordered the river, nearly a mile wide in places, from which a myriad of sungilded branches spun off into golden skeins. "Too shallow for fish, too dirty to bathe in, too thick to drink," was Thaddeus's comment. Amanda thought the river flowed bottom side up, it was so muddy. They would follow the Platte for hundreds of miles, nearly to the Continental Divide.

The valley of the Platte was level and the trail flat except where deep trenches cut across, leading to the water's edge. The wagons had to be eased over these ruts or else break an axle.

"Buffalo tracks," Thaddeus told her. "We're in buffalo country now."

Indeed they were. Although they had not spotted a single bison, the dried, pie-shaped dung, called chips, lay everywhere. When Thaddeus instructed Amanda to gather the chips in the folds of her dress as they rode along the trail, she exploded.

"I will not! I can't imagine anything so undignified! If Mother could see me now —"

"Stop taking on so," Thaddeus interrupted. "You aren't the only undignified lady in this outfit. Everyone had to do it. It's the only thing we have for fuel."

No more timber? What *else* would they have to face? It was then that Amanda discovered that the water of the Platte was unfit to drink. Heavily polluted with alkali, man and beast alike could not drink without suffering from severe stomach cramps, which could be fatal.

They followed the Platte in heat so intense, Amanda could scarcely keep awake through the long afternoons. When the wagon stopped for a noon break, Thaddeus unhitched the team and dropped to the ground, asleep almost immediately.

"Buffalo!" Ben Compton cried one afternoon as he rode his pony furiously down the column.

"Hear that, Missy?" Thaddeus said. "Buffalo at last! We're going to actually see them. Buffalo steaks for supper to-night!"

The entire company halted, whipped to a white heat of excitement to witness this phenomenon. Amanda, who had been walking with her father when Ben tore by, retreated to the wagon. Before she could climb onto the seat, she felt the ground tremble as though split by an earthquake.

To the north she saw a black line on the horizon spreading like an ink stain. As she watched, the line became more defined and she could make out separate buffalo along the edges of the stampede. She sucked in her breath. They were such huge creatures, even viewed at this distance, with great shaggy heads and powerful shoulders. The noise of the stampede was like a cyclone, as hundreds of thousands of animals thundered along.

"Are they going to trample us?" she asked her father.

"No. Look, they're veering to the right. They'll pass us way to the east. Come hold these lines. I'm going to see if anybody is organizing a hunting party."

Reluctantly, Amanda jumped down and took the lines for her father. She leaned against the brown-and-white ox she had named Miss Finch, after the woman who ran the finishing school she had attended, and cast anxious glances toward the herd.

Ten days after sighting the Platte, the wagon company reached the forks where two main branches of the river split. They forded the South Fork at the Upper California crossing. In spite of all rumors about the Platte being a mile wide and a foot deep, which was mostly true, the current in the shallow river was surprisingly strong.

As they went on, they encountered the most rugged terrain yet: a chaotic mass of rocks, hills, chasms, and virtually no trail. Tucked between a thousand-foot wide gateway of high white cliffs was an oasis they all looked forward to — Ash Hollow — a tiny paradise with green grass, cedar trees, and clear, sparkling springs.

"How are we going to get down there?" Amanda asked her father as they stood at the top of the cliff.

Thaddeus pointed to a deep cut in the gorge. "Right down the trail."

"That's what I thought." Her stomach gave an anxious twinge.

Following Ira's instructions, Thaddeus and the other drivers locked and chained the wheels of their wagons, front wheel to back wheel, to prevent the wagon from rolling over the top of the team. Most of the emigrants walked down, with mothers carrying their children, but Amanda stayed stubbornly on her wagon perch.

Ben stopped by on his pony. "Are you *riding* down there?"

"What does it look like?" she shot back at him.

"Oh, I forgot. You don't walk like the

common folk. Might ruin those pretty little slippers of yours."

As her wagon moved out, Amanda thought she detected a hint of admiration in Ben's eyes.

Even with the wheels locked and chained, the wagon flew down the three-hundred yard slope at breakneck speed. Amanda clung to the seat, her heart flattened against her ribcage.

At the bottom, she climbed out of the wagon on unsteady legs, deciding that she would rather walk down the next gorge barefoot over broken glass than take another ride like that one.

Thaddeus, who had strained with the other men to keep the wagon from plummeting to a splintery death below, took a long pull of water from his canteen.

"I don't know," he said more to himself than to Amanda. "I don't know if this going to Oregon was such a good idea after all."

Amanda wanted to beat her fists against his stubborn back. *Why?* she thought in despair. *Why didn't he think about that in Independence? It's too late now to go back.*

Chapter Eight

THE plains curved to the horizon in all directions, with the sun beating down, making them feel as though they were traveling in the bottom of a bowl. The sun flattened the life out of Amanda, filled her eyes with the color of blood, made her feel baked to the bone, her skin as taut as a crudely stitched leather moccasin.

The sun dazzled the endless sea of sand and sagebrush before them, distorting distant objects so that a gopher appeared to be a wolf, a clump of brush a menacing Indian. Occasionally the sun would disappear behind a thick cloud of dust stirred up by southwest ground winds. The winds struck the earth at a downward angle, boiling up great walls of dust that covered the train like a yellow fog and moved with them. Amanda tied a bandanna over her nose and mouth, but the smothering dust filtered through into her nose and lungs, powdered her hair, and gritted her eyes, swelling the lids nearly shut and inflaming the sockets.

Her skin was burned black, peeling to reveal raw flesh beneath; her lips stayed parched and cracked until the corners bled. Although Thaddeus had brought nearly everything else for the trip, he neglected to buy the bare essentials for the medicine chest. Polly Lightfoot lent Amanda glycerine, but it had little effect. Lavinia made a mixture of zinc sulfate, which she gave to Amanda.

During the worst of the heat, Amanda found herself reliving scenes from home: fog rolling in from Boston harbor, skies gray and heavy with unshed snow, green fields outside of town sprinkled with calm, flat ponds like forgotten hand mirrors. And she thought about Joseph. Was he coming for her? And, if he saw her now, would he even recognize her?

Along the level prairie, they often saw other emigrant trains. Sometimes, while she lay sleepless on her mattress, Amanda heard a party passing, traveling at night to rest the teams during the day. There were other signs, too: broken hulks of abandoned wagons like shipwrecks, forlorn pieces of furniture left behind to make the load lighter, putrifying carcasses of cattle killed by the head or drinking poisoned water or both. And there were the wolf-pawed graves of the dead, marked by a pitiful piece of board with hand-lettered inscriptions: "Mary Beth Houser, died this day, June 6, 1846"; "James Pettibone, died from the effects of fever, May 22, 1846."

The ransacked graves upset Thaddeus. He made Amanda promise, if he should die, to have him buried in the road and have the wagon run over his grave till no trace of it showed.

Amanda was horrified. "Don't talk like that! Nobody we know is going to die." As she spoke, a mirage flickered across the plains — a cool stream bordered by shade trees. Amanda was not superstitious, but she wondered if the mirage were an omen. She could almost hear the water gurgling over the rocks. The trail was taking its toll on them both. "We'll get through this," she said with more conviction than she felt. "Nobody else will die."

Thaddeus turned back to the team. "You never can tell."

Courthouse Rock had been visible for the past three days, appearing to float on the shimmering horizon, never seeming to get any closer. When they finally came close to the red sandstone bluff, Amanda was surprised to learn it was still eight miles away. The air was as clear as glass, giving the impression that things were much nearer than they really were. Supposedly named after the county seat in St. Louis, Courthouse Rock was the first of a series of famous landmarks every emigrant armed with a guidebook was anxious to see.

Courthouse Rock marked the beginning of strange rock formations, piled up against each other in the shape of fortresses, cathedrals, and ruined cities. The wagon train passed between towering bluffs in silence, awed in the face of such creations.

Fourteen miles from Courthouse Rock was the celebrated Chimney Rock, standing high above the Platte on its mounded base like a church spire against the blue sky.

"I've been waitin' to see this for almost a year," Polly Lightfoot declared that evening in camp.

"I can't believe it's real," Amanda said, putting away the last of her utensils into the grub box. "We've been in sight of it for so long — almost four days — I'm not even sure it *is* real."

"It did seem to move around, didn't it?" Polly chuckled. "Sam said it must be on wheels. The sun sure does funny things out here."

Amanda joined her father, Frank Grafius, Polly and Samuel Lightfoot, and Martha and Noah Jorgenson on an expedition to the famous rock. Amanda wondered briefly where Helen and her parents were. She had not seen them since they made camp.

At the base of Chimney Rock, members of the wagon party milled around. Some stood on tumbled rocks, heads tilted back to get a better look. The spire was much taller than Amanda had imagined, even after staring at it for nearly four days.

"How high would you say it was?" Thaddeus asked Sam Lightfoot.

Sam rubbed his chin whiskers thoughtfully, then ventured, "Three hundred feet."

Frank Grafius guffawed. "Yer way off, boy. That thing's gotta be at least eight hundred feet, if it's an inch!"

"Oh, I think you're both wrong," Thaddeus disagreed cheerfully. "I believe it's closer to six hundred, six-fifty maybe."

Amanda wandered around to the other side. A pale moon, like a ghost ship, floated above the spire. She came to an outcropping of rock and climbed up, enjoying the panoramic view of the Platte glistening to the west. It was then that she noticed Serena and Ben, hidden from the others by a cleft in the rockface. Ben was posing, one foot on a nearby rock, his hat cocked back on his head, while Serena swiftly sketched in a leatherbound book.

Standing slightly behind and to the right of Serena, Amanda could see the drawing was very lifelike. Serena had managed to capture the confidence in Ben's eyes, as though he had just conquered Chimney Rock.

Because she did not want Serena to think she had been spying, Amanda stepped forward and said quietly, "That's a good likeness."

Serena turned, and, seeing who had

spoken, replied, "Thank you. I enjoy sketching, but this has been the first opportunity I've had since we left Independence." She made a few more lines, then called to Ben, "All done. The light has gone, anyway. You can relax now."

He came over immediately, his blue eyes dancing with amusement. "Well, well," he said to Amanda. "If it isn't the Yankee girl, getting a little local color."

Amanda's face flushed. Why was it she never could think of anything to say back to him?

Serena placed a possessive hand on Ben's arm. "Ben, don't be such a tease. You'll embarrass Amanda."

This made Amanda even angrier, the last thing she wanted was Serena Hawkins defending her. She picked up her skirts and turned.

"Please don't go," Serena said, but Amanda questioned her sincerity. "Ben is sorry for what he said. Aren't you?"

"Don't apologize for your fiancé," Amanda snapped. "It's not your fault he's rude." She scrambled over the rocks, scraping her ankle in her haste, and hurried back to camp.

She found Helen waiting outside of her wagon. Old Blue lay in the dust at her feet, tongue lolling.

"I thought you'd be anxious to see Chimney Rock," Amanda said, intending to brush by her and go to bed.

Helen grabbed her arm. "It's Sarah Jane. She's sick."

Amanda paused. "How bad?"

"She's got a real high fever and red spots. Mama says it's the measles."

Amanda stiffened. Measles was a serious disease, highly contagious.

Helen went on. "Mama's dosing her with laudanum laced with peppermint, but it's not doin' any good." Helen wrung her hands with despair. "Amanda, I don't know what to do."

Amanda didn't know what to do either, but she did know Helen was not helping by acting like this. "Is there anything I can do?"

"I don't know . . . yes. Go tell Captain Compton. He should know there's measles in the camp." Helen turned to go back to her wagon, her shoulders slumped. "Pray he doesn't make us leave the company."

Amanda had never been to the Compton wagon. Ben's sister, Eliza, looked up from a pot of beans she was stirring as Amanda approached. Ben's mother, Rose, was rolling out pie dough on the tailgate of the wagon.

"Amanda, isn't it?" she inquired, frowning slightly. "Thaddeus Bentley's daughter?"

"That's right. I've come for — I've come to tell Captain Compton the youngest Jorgenson child has the measles."

Rose Compton put her hand to her throat. "Lavinia's certain?"

"Helen said she was sure. Will they — Captain Compton won't make them leave the train, will he?"

"I don't know. I guess we'd better tell him. Eliza, where's Poppa?"

Eliza flipped back her black hair. "Out with the cattle."

"Well, go get him. Tell him to come here immediately." She faced Amanda. "Why don't you go back to your wagon? I'll tell my husband and he'll go see the Jorgensons right away."

In the gathering darkness, Amanda tripped over a wagon tongue. Before she fell, a hand shot out and steadied her. It was Ben, returning from his walk with Serena.

"What's wrong, Yankee girl? You still out of sorts?"

Amanda was too upset to give him the sharp response he deserved. "It's the little Jorgenson girl. She has the measles."

Ben's face sobered. "Measles. That's pretty serious."

"Why don't we have a doctor on this train?" Amanda asked.

"We tried, but the only one at Indian Creek when we organized this train had already agreed to go with another party." Ben added, "He shouldn't be no more than a day behind us. I think I'll go look for him." He raced off to where the horses were picketed.

Polly Lightfoot was waiting for Amanda. "That little girl is about as sick as anybody I've ever seen. I offered to help Lavinia by taking Martha and Noah until . . . until this is over. Would you take Ann in with you?"

Amanda wondered if that was such a good

idea, perhaps bringing the dreaded disease into the Bentley wagon. But she did not see how she could refuse.

Some time later she saw Ira Compton as he left the Jorgenson wagon. His expression was grave.

"Are we going to stay here until Sarah Jane gets better?" Amanda wanted to know.

"I've thought about it," Captain Compton replied. "But we've lost so much time already, we can't really afford to lose any more. We'll leave at first light. The Jorgensons can either stay and try to catch up later or move out with us."

"But that little girl is very sick," Amanda said indignantly. "Don't you *care* about her?"

"Of course I care. But I have a wagon train to get over the mountains before the snows trap us. I can't hold up everyone else because of one child. If the Jorgensons leave with us tomorrow, they'll have to ride last. Hopefully, that will contain the disease to one wagon as much as possible."

As Ira Compton promised, they pulled out shortly after daylight with the Jorgenson wagon in the rear. Amanda sat with Ann in the front of her wagon, as they passed a succession of curious mounds and buttes. Amanda averted her eyes when they rolled by a new grave marked with an iron tire arching over the head.

The next day they approached the massive outcropping of rocks called Scott's Bluff. Ben Compton came back, his pony lathered and winded, unable to locate the doctor on the other train.

Amanda saw little of Helen or her mother. Jason herded the cattle as usual, and Henry Clay and Jeb drove the wagons, refusing Frank Grafius's offer of assistance. At noon break, Helen came out of the wagon to get water.

"How is she?" Amanda inquired.

Helen's face was lined with fatigue and worry. "No better, no worse. Mama says there's nothin' we can do but wait."

The evening was strangely quiet in the Jorgenson wagon. Amanda baked extra pilot bread, the only dish she had mastered, and carried it over to Jason. Then, after scrubbing up the dishes, she and Ann sat around the fire. Ann hugged her doll, staring into the flames. An unreal silence enveloped the entire camp, as if everyone were waiting for something to happen.

Just as Amanda had gotten Ann off to sleep in the pallet she had fixed next to her own bed, Helen stumbled out of her wagon, tears streaming down her freckled cheeks.

"She's gone," she sobbed. "Sarah Jane's gone. She died a few minutes ago."

Amanda was stunned, as though the breath had been knocked from her. Someone she had known, had played with and talked to, was dead. A tiny, quiet little girl who had never hurt a soul.

"But she can't be," Amanda said.

"She is," Helen replied slackly.

Amanda remembered the promise she had made to her father. *Nobody we know will die*, she had told him.

Ira Compton held a brief funeral service the next day. At the gravesite, Amanda avoided looking at the sheeted bundle, watching others instead. Lavinia leaned weakly against her husband, sobbing into her apron. Helen stood with the other children gathered around her, her normally sunny face racked with unshed tears.

Helen's face isn't meant for grief, Amanda thought inanely. She met Ben's eyes and held them for a long moment.

After the service, she went back to her wagon. On the ground next to the Jorgenson supply wagon was a shattered stoneware jug. Long green vines were entwined about the broken crockery. Amanda recognized the plant immediately. Mrs. Jorgenson's sweetbrier vine all the way from Pennsylvania. Amanda picked up chunks of pottery and the dying vine, thinking that Lavinia must have finally given up trying to keep it alive.

Chapter Nine

AMANDA straightened up from the cook-fire, reaching skyward in a deep stretch to ease the cramps from her back and shoulders. If she lived to be a hundred, she would never get used to performing all her duties on the ground. She would sell her soul for a table. Or, even better, throw her pan as far as she could. How she hated all this work!

It was evening and the wagon party had circled, putting up camp for the night. Amanda gazed westward. Although the sun had set a short while ago, enough light lingered to point out Laramie Peak, now a purple smudge on the horizon.

They had made nearly eighteen miles that day, struggling up a pass through Scott's Bluffs and then a long, tough pull uphill to the crest of the pass. At the summit, there was a spectacular view of Chimney Rock, some twenty miles back, and ahead, the dark blue shadow of Laramie Peak.

Since Sarah Jane Jorgenson had died, Amanda felt everyone in the company seemed quieter, less enthusiastic. She mentioned this to her father.

"It's just the heat," he remarked. "And the trail. That's all."

But Amanda believed there was more to it than the weather. In the evenings now, Lavinia and Henry Clay and their children went about their business, speaking only when necessary. There was little conversation at meals, Amanda observed from her own campfire. Helen seldom came over to Amanda's wagon to visit.

Amanda was more concerned about her father, though. Thaddeus did not leap to his feet first thing each morning, anxious to begin the day, as he used to. Instead, he lay under the wagon in his blanket until well past dawn, reluctantly getting up long after the other men had. He looked older than his thirty-eight years. Deep lines were firmly trenched on either side of his mouth and beneath his wind-beaten tan his skin was an unhealthy gray.

"Are you ill?" Amanda asked him one morning as he came around the wagon for a mug of coffee.

He swallowed some of the scalding liquid before replying. "I'm fine. At least I will be when we get to Oregon. *If* we get to Oregon."

"We're all tired of this hateful trail," she

said. "You're not alone." She felt like reminding him that this was all *his* fault, bringing them out here.

"Maybe, but I work harder than anyone," Thaddeus complained. "I have to drive the wagon by myself, without even a son to help me."

"I'm sorry I wasn't born a boy," Amanda said curtly. "I guess I'm not much help to you." She turned the bacon with an angry, jerking motion.

Thaddeus put his hand on her arm. "I didn't mean it that way, Missy. You know what I mean. Of course, you're a big help. All the women work hard. In fact, if it weren't for you women, the men would probably starve to death and look like the wrath of God to boot. You keep this train civilized. But," he added, "it's difficult with just the two of us."

Amanda could not argue with him there. It was too late to hire help. Immediately after her husband had been killed at the Kansas River crossing, Mrs. Albrecht had hired the last of the few boys not working for their own families to drive her wagon the rest of the way.

Sometimes Amanda wished she could have the "loan" of a girl or boy to help her with the endless chores. She had everything to do by herself: haul water from as far as a mile away; gather buffalo chips to fill the sack slung beneath the wagon bed, often roving more than a mile off the trail; cook three meals a day; air the beds; wash dishes; do the laundry.

That evening she was so exhausted from the heat and travel, she scarcely knew what she was doing. Her back hurt from the constant stooping as she prepared supper. Then she broke her gaze from faraway Laramie Peak and poked the fire to life with her pointed stick, adding more chips.

She took the bread pan out of the grub box and scooped out a cupful of cornmeal from the crock. The meal was riddled with shiny black bugs. With great disgust, she picked them out one by one, flinging them into the hot fire.

Thaddeus came back from unhitching the team. "Ira's sending somebody around to check our rifles. That man is always thinking up more work. I'll be cleaning my gun so it'll pass inspection. Hold supper for me, Missy."

"It'll be a while, anyway," Amanda said. "I'm making slam-johns for a change. Polly gave me the recipe."

She was tired of soda biscuits and pilot bread, tired of beans and bacon, tired of dried apples and coffee. As she stirred the thin batter for the corncakes her mind wandered, recalling some of the sumptuous dinners she had eaten at the Whites'. A big eater in spite of her ladylike manners, Drucilla believed in plenty of food at every meal. Their dining room table often groaned under the weight of a whole turkey or duckling, a clove-studded ham and a haunch of roast beef, boiled potatoes, onions and carrots, squash sautéed in butter, flaky rolls, cranberries and apple salad, black walnut cake, pumpkin pie and Indian pudding.

With a shock, Amanda realized her mouth was watering. It had been so long since she had eaten delicious food.

The clump of boots on the hard-baked ground caused her to look up. It was Ben Compton.

He tossed her a careless grin. "Hello there, Yankee girl. Fixing some Boston brown bread to have with your beans tomorrow?"

As tired as she was, his comment struck a nerve. He was forever goading her and tonight she was determined not to let him get away with it.

"If you weren't so ignorant," she retorted, "you'd know what I was baking. But like most men, you don't know one end of a frying pan from the other." Actually, she was not all that proficient at cooking herself, but it was the only remark she could think of.

But Ben had walked away and was talking to Thaddeus about his rifle.

Amanda beat the corncake batter with more energy than necessary. *How can he ignore me like that?* she thought. *He treats me like a child. Or a dog that you'd pat on the head as you pass by.*

More upsetting than Ben's behavior was her reaction. Why was she so upset? Ben Compton could not hold a candle to Joseph, so it was not possible that she was attracted to him. And yet . . .

Impatiently, she pushed the notion aside, turned back to her fire. The flames had blazed up higher than ever, fanned by a sudden breeze. She gasped, frightened by the leaping blaze, and caught her foot on a stick. As she stumbled, her skirt swept into the fire. Flames grabbed hold of the thin fabric and began licking greedily upward.

Amanda's screams echoed through the camp. She whirled from side to side, beating her blazing skirt with her bare hands, vaguely aware of people running toward her. Someone yelled, "Get water!"

I'm going to die, she thought desperately. *Burned alive — just another grave along the trail.*

After an eternity, she felt herself being rolled in heavy fabric, which covered her from head to foot. Then she was heaved to the ground with bone-jarring force and a smoky, smoldering darkness engulfed her.

When she opened her eyes again, Amanda saw a flame. It filled her vision. Orange, leaping, and tapered, it sent shadows cringing as it grew. She could feel heat burning against her legs. She cried out.

Helen leaned over her, her blond pigtail brushing the blanket. "Hush, now, it's goin' to be all right."

Amanda stared at the canvas arching overhead, slowly realizing that she was lying on her mattress in her wagon, wearing only a shift. Nearby, a candle in a tin saucer sputtered as the cool night air drifted in through the back opening. She struggled to sit up, then saw that her palms were charred-looking and covered with heavy grease.

Gently, Helen pushed her back. "Lay still. You've had a terrible shock. Try to rest easy."

"What happened? I can't —" The words stuck in her dry throat. All she could recall was heat . . . and burning.

"Your skirt caught fire," Helen told her simply, handing her a cup of water. "I didn't see it happen, but I heard you scream. By the time I got there, Ben had wrapped you in a blanket and was rollin' you on the ground. The blanket smothered the fire."

"Ben?" Amanda frowned as she strained to remember. "I was mad at him for some reason. And I was making something . . . slam-johns . . . the fire had gotten so high —" She sank back on her pillow. "Where is my father?"

Something flicked in Helen's eyes that Amanda could not read. "He's outside. I guess the shock of seein' you like that wore him plumb out."

"Why — ?" Amanda struggled to formulate her ragged thoughts into words. "Why didn't he try to save me?"

Helen replied quickly as she tucked the blanket around Amanda. "I suppose he was rooted to the spot . . . folks get that way when somethin' happens to one of their children."

Amanda was reluctant to accept this. She had the feeling that Helen was not telling her all she knew but was too exhausted to press the issue. When she tried to move her legs, she realized that her right leg was swathed in a thick bandage.

"My leg!" She sat up in terror, straining to feel her leg. Her scorched hands stung and she drew them back.

Helen pushed her back again. "Lay down! It's goin' to be all right. Your hands will be better in a day or so. You got a bad burn on your calf, but that's all. Mama says it's a miracle you got away with just that. Now try to get some sleep." She plumped up Amanda's pillow and smoothed the blanket once more.

Worn out by the effort of moving, Amanda lay back weakly. She looked into Helen's freckled face and gave her a wan smile. "You know that dress you loaned me till we got over the Divide? I don't think you want it back now."

Helen laughed. "Mama always says, 'Never a borrower nor a lender be.' I guess I got what I deserved. It didn't fit me anyhow. Now go to sleep. I'll be over first thing in the mornin'." Blowing out the candle, Helen left the wagon.

Outside, Amanda heard her father's voice raised in question and Helen's murmured reply.

". . . seems fine. Best let her sleep while she can."

Amanda could not catch what her father said, but his tone sounded relieved. Her eyelids sagged and her body seemed to melt into the mattress. She was so tired. . . .

Was it possible, she thought before sleep claimed her, *that Ben Compton did not really hate her, after all?* Why did she care?

Toward morning, her dreams were troubled by images of flames and burning pain. The pain was real enough, she discovered when she awoke. She rolled over onto her side, but that seemed to make it worse. Finally, she took her pillow and propped it under her leg, elevating it, which helped a little. The rest of the night she remained awake, careful to keep her thoughts from straying to Boston and Joseph, or else she would cry.

As she had promised, Helen arrived shortly after the gray light of daybreak began to steal into the wagon. She found Amanda awake, her face contracted with pain.

"Mama said it would be like this," Helen said, her eyes reflecting sympathy. "She'll be over later to change the dressin' and take a look at your leg. Meantime, I'm here to fix breakfast for you and your pa."

"I can't eat," Amanda protested weakly. "I'm not hungry."

"You've got to keep your strength up or else you'll never get better." Helen bustled around the wagon, gathering supplies. "Let me get a fire goin' and some bacon on, and I'll be back to comb your hair and help you wash."

Born with her mother's efficiency, Helen soon had bacon sizzling and had even whipped up a new batch of pilot bread. In no time she had the wagon tidied and had brushed Amanda's hair until it gleamed like satin, then braided it.

When Thaddeus returned from hitching the team, he looked in on Amanda, awkwardly standing over her bed, turning his hat around and around in his hands. "How are you feeling, Missy? Not too chipper, I'll wager."

"My leg hurts," Amanda confessed. "It just about killed me last night. Can't you give me something to make it stop?"

"You know I don't know much about doctoring. Lavinia seems knowledgeable in that area, though. She bandaged your leg. If anyone can ease the pain, she can."

Amanda drew one arm over her eyes, as if she did not want to talk anymore.

Her father sat down on a crate. "When I saw you with your dress on fire, I couldn't move. It was like a ... nightmare. You know, the kind where something awful happens and you can't run? Only this was real. I don't know what came over me, I couldn't even save my own daughter. I guess I went into shock."

"That's what Helen said." Amanda turned to look at her father. He appeared to be so miserable, she patted his hand, saying, "It's all right, Papa."

How funny, she thought. Here she was the one that needed attention, and yet she was comforting *him.*

"If it weren't for that Compton boy . . ." He stood again, unable to finish the sentence.

When Helen called Thaddeus to breakfast, Amanda thought she detected relief in his eyes. "I'll see you in a bit," he promised, stooping to kiss her cheek.

Moments later, Helen was at Amanda's bedside, carrying a plate of bacon, dried apples fried in grease, hot bread, and a mug of steaming coffee. She helped Amanda sit up, then propped a sack of clothes behind her to support her back.

Amanda winced when she moved her leg, but said nothing. She stared wordlessly at the heaped plate.

"Eat," Helen commanded. "I don't want to hear no complaints about my cookin' neither."

Using the tips of her fingers, Amanda picked up the bread and nibbled at it. "It's got to be better than anything I fix. How did you get this bread so crusty?"

"It's a secret. But since you're my best friend, I'll tell you. Sand."

"What? Sand? Oh, you!" Amanda said when Helen started laughing. "Sand is in *everything* we cook!"

"I know. That's what makes the bread so crusty. I'll leave you so you can finish in peace. Be back in a little while."

Amanda picked over her breakfast, pondering Helen's remark. Did Helen really think she was Amanda's best friend? Amanda thought her dearest friend was still in Boston. Or was she? Would Hester White have gotten up at dawn to check on Amanda if she were ill or injured? Would Hester have been willing to take on extra work in addition to her other chores? Amanda doubted it. In fact, any comparison between the two was ridiculous. Hester would rather die than dirty her hands cooking or tending cattle on a hot, dusty trail. And they were made of entirely different substances — Hester mostly air, while Helen was as solid and dependable as the towering rocks that bordered the trail.

At the noon break, Lavinia came into Amanda's wagon to change her bandage.

Amanda had spent a painful morning jouncing along in the hot, springless wagon, assaulted by sand and gnats through the opened ends of the cover. When Lavinia pulled the cotton strips off the oozing wound, Amanda whimpered.

"We have to keep this leg clean," Lavinia said, dabbing the raw flesh with a cotton cloth. "If not, infection will set in. Though I don't know how we can do that, with all the dust and dirt we have to live with." She rebound Amanda's leg with strips cut from a petticoat.

Amanda thanked her. "I feel so helpless. You and Helen have enough to do."

Lavinia smiled down at her. "A pack of

wolves couldn't keep Helen away from here. She thinks the world of you."

Amanda lowered her eyes, plucking the hem of her blanket. "I know. Nobody else has ever been so nice to me. She's . . . well, I think she's . . ." Words could not describe how she felt then.

Lavinia looked surprised and Amanda wondered if she believed her. Amanda realized she had done or said little to prove her sincerity.

Later that afternoon, her father came to see her again. "How soon do you think you'll be up?" he asked. "There's so much to do. I can't do it all."

Amanda was horrified — she was still so sick! But she sat up, gritting her teeth against the pain. "Maybe I can get up tomorrow. Long enough to fix the meals, anyway."

But when Amanda asked Helen if she could borrow a dress and some kind of shoes to wear, Helen was aghast. "Oh, no, you're not!"

"I only need them till I can make another —"

"It's not the dress, Amanda. You know you're welcome to anything I have. You're just not able to get up yet. Why be foolish and rush things?"

But Amanda wore Helen down until she agreed to bring Amanda some clothes.

Early the next morning, Amanda dressed herself in the ill-fitting, coarse cotton dress

Helen brought and the square-toed boots that she was certain must have belonged to Jason. Every movement of her leg brought a new burst of pain. She fought a wave of dizziness, climbing out of the wagon, and hobbled around the campsite. When she tried to set up the coffee pot, she accidentally knocked over a bucket of water.

Lavinia caught sight of her stumbling around and came right over. "Helen told me you were plannin' on gettin' up but I thought you had more sense." She grabbed Amanda by the arm and marched her into the wagon. "Look at you! Face whiter than two sheets. Amanda Bentley, you're as stubborn as the day is long!"

Too exhausted to protest, Amanda allowed Lavinia to put her back to bed. When Lavinia started to pull up the blanket, Amanda kicked it off with her good leg.

"I know it's awful hot, honey, but you have to cover up to keep the dust out. I'll be back later to check the dressin'. Lie still till then, hear?"

Amanda passed the morning in a feverish haze, neither awake nor asleep, caught in a twilight world as her temperature rose. Hours, or maybe years later, she opened her eyes wide but unseeing and said, "Is the river frozen yet? Can we go skating? I have a new fur cape. . . ."

Lavinia put a cool hand on Amanda's forehead. "Burnin' up with fever. Out of her head, too." She stripped Amanda's bandage.

"Helen, run get my medicine chest. I better make a poultice for this leg."

Unaware of the time of day or whether the wagon was moving or still, Amanda tossed on her mattress. Faces floated over her, and hushed voices, taut with concern, spoke in broken sentences. The blurred figures of Helen, Lavinia, and her father mingled with images from the past. She imagined she saw her mother and Joseph. And once, she heard a strange voice.

"How bad off is she?" the voice inquired.

"Right bad," Helen replied, bathing Amanda's forehead with a wet cloth. "Mama's tryin' to get the poison out of her system. Till that happens, though, her fever won't break."

"If only I had moved faster," the stranger said remorsefully. "She wouldn't be in this fix."

"You did the best you could," Helen said. "If it wasn't for you, she probably wouldn't even be alive."

Through the veil of her lashes, Amanda saw her visitor as he turned to leave.

He does care, she thought with a wild conviction. *Benjamin Compton cares about me.*

She slipped over the edge of consciousness into a dream.

She and Joseph were skating on the Charles River. She was wearing her silver fox cape and Joseph had his arm around her waist as he guided her past a ring of featureless faces. The stars were big and bright.

Joseph swung her past a bonfire roaring against the night sky. Suddenly the stars grew larger and brighter as they dropped from the sky. The stars that landed in the snowy bank disappeared with a sizzle, but those that fell into the bonfire caused flames to leap higher. A tongue of fire licked at the river's edge, creeping out onto the ice. Amanda realized with horror that the ice was melting until only the patch they stood on was all that remained. Amanda could not move. In another instant they would be plunged into the murky depths of the dark river. . . .

She awoke with a cry clogging her throat. It was night, but she was not anywhere near the Charles River. She sat up, dimly aware that she was in the wagon, somewhere on the plains. Her nightdress was soaked with sweat and her hair clung wetly down her back.

A figure moved in the shadows. Amanda pinched back a scream.

"Shhhh. It's me. Helen." A candle flared as she approached the bed. "Thank heavens that fever finally broke. Welcome back, we all missed you. Mama will be glad to know her poultices did the trick."

"How long . . . ? What day is it?" Amanda rubbed her eyes.

"Thursday. You've been out of your head for two days. Let's get you out of this gown. I brought one of Mama's, just in case."

With Helen's help, Amanda struggled out

of her wet gown and into the clean one. "Have you been here all night?"

"Mostly. Mama comes over toward mornin' to relieve me." She chuckled. "Actually, it's been kind of restful, except for worryin' about you. Poor Jason has had to drive the cattle by himself."

"I'm sorry to take you away from your work," Amanda murmured. She reached out and grasped Helen's hand. "I know I haven't always been very nice —"

"Hush now. You might have had ruffled feathers when I first met you, but that's because you didn't know nobody. I admit I've been a mite standoffish myself lately, ever since ... since my little sister died. But we're friends, and friends take care of each other. I'll always be here when you need me." She squeezed Amanda's hand.

For the first time in weeks, Amanda slept peacefully.

"Amanda? Feel like company?" Helen called.

Amanda sat up on one elbow. Although the burn on her leg was healing well, she was still weak from her raging fever and had to stay in bed. She couldn't reach the mirror but knew her hair, drawn back and bound with a ribbon, was unruly and her face was sweaty with the heat. Her gown clung to her in uncomfortable wet patches, but there was nothing else to wear.

"Amanda?"

"All right," Amanda called back, thinking Lavinia or maybe Polly was coming to visit. She wiped her forehead with the back of her hand and drew the blanket up. "Come on in."

But the hand that pushed back the canvas cover was very tanned and strong. Amanda's eyes widened with disbelief as Ben Compton climbed into her wagon.

"Hello, Yankee girl. Feeling better?"

She wanted to dive under the blanket. What was he doing here? Why couldn't she have remembered to pack her pretty bed-jacket, or at least have grabbed her black lace shawl to cover the stained gown? Then she realized she had not answered his question.

"Uh, yes. I'm feeling much better," she replied lamely.

"Glad to hear it." He looked around. "Mind if I sit down?"

"No. Of course not."

He is too big, Amanda thought. *He doesn't fit in here.* She watched as he settled on an upturned crate, adjusting his long legs in the narrow aisle. From this close, his shoulders were much wider than she had remembered. Still flustered, she blurted, "I guess I owe you my life. Helen told me what you did the night . . . my skirt caught on fire. I don't know how to thank you."

Ben shrugged. "Anyone could have grabbed a blanket. I was just a little closer, that's all." A teasing light came into his yellow-gold eyes. "After all, we can't have our little Yankee girl hurt, now, can we?"

Amanda was to embarrassed to respond.

He sensed her discomfort and rose, flicking her blanket with the edge of his hat. "I'll let you rest now. You get better, you hear?" He left as suddenly as he had come.

He really does care! she thought, forgetting her ragged appearance.

She was still glowing from Ben's unexpected visit when her father burst into the wagon.

"Buffalo's been sighted! The Captain says any of us low on meat can join the hunt. Will you be all right, Missy, if I leave you?"

"I'll be fine," she reassured him. "Helen and Lavinia are right there. Nothing will happen."

The hunting party saddled up and rode out across the prairie. Amanda lay on her pallet, listening to Helen and Lavinia working outside her wagon. The afternoon turned into another scorcher. Soon the women, tired of working, settled in whatever shade they could find to take a nap.

An unearthly quiet descended. Amanda tossed restlessly on her pallet; she had had too much sleep lately. Suddenly the peacefulness was shattered with unearthly cries and the thundering hooves of many horses. Amanda lay frozen with fear as she realized what the sounds were. Her worst nightmare had finally come true. Indians were raiding the camp . . . and most of the men were gone.

Chapter Ten

Her head reeling, Amanda dragged herself to the opening of her wagon. She clung to the frame, her knuckles pressed against her teeth, paralyzed by the scene before her eyes.

The wagons had been drawn in a loose circle, wagon tongues overlapping, but the wheels had not been locked with chains. Now two wagons had been pushed apart, and leaping over the gap on fleet-footed ponies, were Indians — bare-chested, their black hair streaming out from behind. Their whoops and yells were more terrifying than any wolf Amanda had heard as they poured into the camp, scattering cattle and oxen.

Women fled to their wagons. Children screamed, high-pitched with terror, and ran to hide behind wagon wheels. Amanda saw Helen and Polly lifting Ann and Martha into the Jorgenson wagon. Lavinia was struggling to drag Noah away from his dog as Old Blue barked furiously at the intruders.

The whole scene seemed unreal to Amanda, as she watched young Jason crouch behind a back wheel, poke the muzzle of his rifle through the spokes, then fire. She counted five men, excluding Jason, who was little more than a boy, who had taken refuge under their wagons and were shooting at the attackers.

Through the whirling confusion of horses and people, Amanda noticed that the Indians had established a pattern. Some were driving cattle toward the opening between the wagons, while others leaped off their ponies and ran toward the wagons. They ripped back canvas covers and hauled out sacks of flour, sides of moldy pork, blankets, copper kettles, and whatever else they could grab, flinging the goods to other Indians who swung by to retrieve them. Shots rang out, but no one had been hit as far as Amanda could see. She drew back into her wagon, her heart racing, every nerve in her body quivering with fear.

What if an Indian came into her wagon? What would she do? The thought filled her with such terror, she stumbled in the narrow aisle, scrambling for a knife, a heavy, blunt object, anything to use as a weapon. Thaddeus had taken his rifle and hunting knife with him. She yanked open the nearest box and clutched at something shiny — a tin spatula.

At that instant, the cover of her wagon was thrown back. An Indian leaped up, light as an antelope, balancing on top of the grub box. He froze when he saw Amanda holding the spatula over her head like a tomahawk. Their eyes locked, his bold and black, hers green-gold and wide.

She stared at him, aware that he was tall and lean, not ugly the way she had imagined. His face, under the whorls of red paint, was even-featured with a firm mouth and a strong Roman nose. His long hair was caught up with an upright golden feather. He wore a scrap of deerskin which covered him from the waist to the knees, and fringed moccasins. His bare torso was daubed with more red paint. Around his neck hung a leather pouch and several strands of colored glass beads. He carried no weapon of any kind.

The time they looked at one another could not have been more than a few seconds, though it seemed an eternity to Amanda. The expression she read in his eyes was not hatred or anger, but surprise, as though Amanda was different from what he expected as well.

Then he broke the moment by reaching up. Amanda reared back with her spatula, ready for the blow she was sure would follow. To her everlasting amazement, he lightly touched her hair, which was unbound and cascading down her back in a mass of soft curls. He fingered a curl dangling over her shoulder. With a lightning movement, he snatched the mirror hanging from a bow near the back and jumped out of the wagon.

Amanda's knees buckled. She sank to the floor, burying her face in her hands. She wanted to cry, but no tears came. Sporadic gunshots told her the attackers were finally leaving. She huddled there on the rough boards until the only sounds in the camp were those of sobbing children. A tentative hum of voices swelled and grew as women crept out of their wagons and called to each other.

"Amanda! Amanda!" Helen vaulted through the front of Amanda's wagon, her skirt nearly up to her waist. "Are you all right? I saw that creature sneak in here, but Mama wouldn't let me leave our wagon. Did he hurt you?"

Amanda stood slowly, shaking her head. She could still feel gentle fingers stroking a curl, but she could never tell Helen or anyone else about it. She felt certain no one would understand what she had shared with the Indian — that for an instant they were only two people, curious about one another, not enemies.

"I'm fine," she reassured Helen, smoothing her hair back. "Except that I was scared to death."

"We all were! It happened so fast. You look pale as a ghost. Sit down before you fall down." She pushed Amanda onto the bed. "Did he steal anything?"

"A mirror. That's all." *And a few seconds of my life,* she thought. "Did any of them break into your wagon?"

"No, thank heavens. Old Blue kept on barkin' like the devil. But Jason's checkin' our cattle. I think they took most of our herd." Her eyes dropped to Amanda's hand. "What's that you got?"

Amanda held up her hand, still gripping the spatula. "My weapon. All I could find on short notice." She started to laugh nervously, like a child. "Can you imagine? Fending off a big Indian with a spatula?"

Helen shook her head admiringly. "You were the only one of us completely alone and yet you had sense enough to grab something to protect yourself. Amanda Bentley, you sure are a caution."

"Caution or not, I can't stay in this wagon another *second*. Help me down. I have to get some air." Leaning heavily on Helen, Amanda climbed out of the wagon, using her injured leg as little as possible.

The camp was in chaos. Polly Lightfoot, tears streaking her normally sensible face, was scooping spilled flour into an overturned barrel. Lavinia was comforting her children, handing Ann her doll, holding Noah close, patting Martha on the back.

The men had come out from under the wagons and were running around camp, tending to the oxen and the few cattle left.

On the other side of camp, Amanda saw Serena calmly dispensing coffee to a group of distraught women around her. Amanda wondered if Serena's wagon had been robbed. It seemed unlikely since the girl appeared unruffled, as usual.

"They didn't get any horses," Helen was saying. "Lucky the men had taken 'em all on the hunt."

"Lucky!" Amanda exploded. "Do you think those Indians just happened to be strolling by? I bet they saw our men leaving and planned to raid us, horses or no horses."

"They got plenty besides cattle," Lavinia said, coming toward them. "I saw them grab bags of flour, sugar, coffee —"

"Pans, tools. Anything they could get their fingers on," Helen said.

The image of fingers brushing her hair flashed through Amanda's mind again. "The one that came into my wagon only took a mirror," she put in hastily. "If that was all he wanted, he was welcome to it."

"Amanda!" Helen cried. "How can you *say* that?"

"She's right," Mrs. Jorgenson agreed. "Let them take whatever they want, so long as they don't hurt us." She gathered Amanda and Helen to her. "The thing is, we're all safe."

Lavinia was right. No one had been hurt, although everyone was quite shaken. After the men had gotten the livestock calmed, the party banded together for biscuits and mugs of soothing tea.

Amanda found herself next to Serena, who was efficiently slicing bread. Serena was quiet, one of the few women who had not contributed her comments on the raid.

· "Weren't you scared?" Amanda asked. Ben's girl friend filled her with curiosity — she was so different.

"Of course," Serena replied, piling the crumbly bread on a tin platter. She never looked directly at Amanda.

What did Ben *see* in this girl? Amanda wondered. Aside from her beauty. Serena was so ... so *serene*, it was almost unnatural, as though she lacked basic emotions. She doesn't even *perspire*, Amanda noted with dismay.

"I hear you had a visitor in your wagon," Serena remarked. Somewhat archly, Amanda thought.

"Yes! An Indian broke in, scared me nearly to —"

"I meant Ben," Serena interrupted smoothly, offering the plate to Amanda. "Biscuit?"

Amanda shook her head, confused by the other girl's manner. "Yes," she said slowly. "Ben did come to see me this morning. Just to see how I was feeling. I was glad he did. It was the first time I had a chance to thank him for saving my life."

"Ben is so brave. He always does the right

thing." The corners of Serena's mouth turned up. Amanda wondered what was behind that smile. For all her outward pleasantness, Serena was probably seething inside. After all, the boy she was practically engaged to had visited another girl — alone — in her wagon.

Then it occurred to Amanda that perhaps Serena was telling Amanda that Ben's visit meant nothing, that saving Amanda's life was as significant as Ben saving a drowning kitten or something. For the first time, Amanda wondered if Serena was jealous.

It was nearly sundown when the hunting party came straggling over the plains, carrying freshly killed meat. At the first sight of the hunters, children raced ahead, eager to relate the Indian attack. As news of the raid spread, the men galloped into the corral, dismounting and picketing their horses without unloading the meat tied to their saddles.

Amanda was glad when she saw her father riding in. He brought his horse next to the wagon and jumped down, looping the reins loosely over the front wheel.

"Are you all right, Missy?" he called, running to enfold her in a big hug.

"Oh, Papa! We were so afraid the Indians might come back after dark."

Thaddeus held her out from him, his eyes searching her face. "Jason told me one of them broke into our wagon. He didn't hurt you — If he so much as touched you, I'll —"

"All he took was . . . was a mirror. But you shouldn't have *left* me!" she accused.

Thaddeus sagged with relief. He walked around her, his face contorting with emotion, and pounded his fist on the grub box so hard, the tin plates Amanda had set out danced. "You're right. I should have *been* here. Leaving you so defenseless . . . there was no excuse for it."

The other men felt as strongly as Thaddeus. Ira Compton called an immediate council and listened gravely to the accounts given by the five men who had witnessed the attack. A tally of stolen livestock was made. When the meeting broke, Thaddeus came back to the wagon where Amanda was resting.

"Ira was all for pulling out tonight," he told her. "He's afraid those Indians might come back for the horses after dark."

"Well, are we?" Amanda did not relish the idea of traveling in the dark.

"No. We've got all this fresh meat we can't leave behind. Too many of us are getting low on food." Thaddeus helped himself to bacon and beans simmering over the fire.

"So we're staying?"

"Just the night. Ira's doubling the guards. Most of us will be up, anyway, getting this beef cut up to dry. We're leaving at first light, same as always."

As the fires burned long after dark, Amanda thought about the attack. One thing she understood with startling clarity was that the Indians were more organized than the wagon party. The natives knew every rock and river in this territory, while the emigrants, for all their guns and education, were out of their element, and the last Army installation was Fort Leavenworth, over six hundred miles east. They were all very much alone.

Amanda's thoughts were interrupted by Ben Compton, striding across toward their wagon. He stopped Jason, who was busy helping his father and uncle prepare the buffalo meat, clapping him on the shoulder.

"Heard about how you protected your family today. You're a brave boy, Jason."

Amanda turned slightly away, picking at the hem of the dress Helen had loaned her. She had not seen Ben since he came into her wagon earlier that day. Could it only have been this morning that he visited her? She wondered if Serena had said anything to him.

Now she felt his eyes upon her.

"Hey, Yankee girl," he called cheerfully. "Good evening, Mr. Bentley. You must be mighty proud of your daughter."

"What?" Thaddeus said.

"You mean you haven't heard about your daughter clubbing an Indian with a spoon?"

Thaddeus looked over at Amanda. "What's he talking about?"

Amanda was glad it was dark so no one would see her blush. "When the Indian broke into our wagon, I tried to find a weapon. All

I could find was a spatula. Don't worry, I never got near the Indian. I told Helen and she must have told Jason. Now it's probably all over camp."

Ben waved, saying good night, and moved on. Amanda watched him walk away.

"You stood up to an Indian with a *cooking utensil?*" Thaddeus said unbelievingly.

"It's all I had." She shifted her leg to a more comfortable position. "You know, Papa, I'd like to learn to shoot."

"Shoot a gun?" Thaddeus stared at her with eyes reddened from working over the smoky fire. "You seem to do pretty good with a spatula —"

"No, really, Papa. I feel so defenseless."

"Well," Thaddeus said slowly, remembering Amanda's narrow escape. "We'll see." Amanda felt his reluctance was due to the fact that he did not shoot very well himself, and teaching her would only point this up.

Before the meat-curing fires had been extinguished, Amanda climbed into the wagon and fell into a nervous, twitching sleep, haunted by visions of whooping, red-painted Indians riding into camp. She would awaken with a jerk, only to descend back into the same nightmare.

Sometime later, a roaring sound caused her to sit bolt upright, clutching the blanket. A sudden gust of wind whooshed through the canvas flaps, setting the kettles overhead to swinging. The roar intensified as the sky opened and rain drummed down. Amanda had never seen rain like this before. It poured from the sky in thundering sheets, rippling the canvas top.

The wind rose, and one side of the cover peeled back. Amanda leaped up as wind and water hit her, soaking her from head to foot. She heard Thaddeus under the wagon, sputtering with anger.

"Papa!" she screamed. She grabbed the canvas before the wind tore it completely away. Gasping, she held onto the cover as a curtain of rain streaked her face, plastering her hair to her scalp.

Thaddeus hurried into the wagon and together they pulled the cover back over the wooden bows and lashed it secure.

"This storm is tearing up everything not nailed down out there," he yelled. "Anything loose is *gone*. I've never seen anything like it."

He turned to leave.

"Where are you going?" Amanda shouted, pushing her drenched hair out of her eyes.

"The team!" Above the roar of the storm, they could hear the animals bellowing.

After her father left, Amanda knelt on her soaked mattress, plugging her fingers in her ears. The storm was even more frightening than the Indian attack. The wind rocked the wagon, and hail plummeted to the ground: huge, canvas-ripping chunks of ice the size of hen's eggs.

Worried about her father, Amanda crawled forward to look out. Hailstones bounced like ghosts' marbles on the ground, which was already an oozing mire. Lightning streaked angrily through the purple sky, arrowing to the ground in a blaze of white heat so intense it illuminated everything in the wagon train with electric sparks.

Thaddeus slipped and slid through the mud toward the wagon, shoulders hunched against the pelting ice chunks. Suddenly a gust of wind snatched off the felt hat that had been jammed low on his head. A spear of lightning revealed the scrap of felt sailing an unbelievable fifty feet in the air. Thaddeus climbed back into the wagon, gasping for breath, as water puddled around him.

Amanda prayed the storm would soon end. Thunderstorms back East were usually of short duration — seldom more than twenty minutes or half an hour. But she had forgotten that out West things were played by a different set of rules. It was nearly dawn when the thunder rumbled away and the rain dwindled to a drizzle.

When meager daylight timidly crept across the sky, Amanda saw that the storm had done more damage than the Indians had. Wagon covers had been slashed by hailstones; water buckets and tools not fastened properly had been stripped and carried yards away by the wind, smashed beyond salvage.

Amanda and her father ate a quick, cold breakfast. Then the wagon party pulled out on schedule. Yesterday's buffalo hunt had cost them all dearly: a day's delay, an Indian raid, plus the loss of food supplies and cattle. To add to it, the storm had carried off every strip of buffalo jerky drying on the wagon covers.

The sight of Fort Laramie's whitewashed brick walls lifted their sagging spirits. By noon, only the Laramie River stood between the wagon train and the first outpost of civilization they had seen since leaving Independence forty-four days before.

Laramie Peak rose behind the fort, which Amanda learned was a trading post, not a military installation. The Black Hills marched to the north, and beyond the fort were buttes in all shapes and colors. The fort itself was a hollow square with fifteen-foot-high walls of adobe brick. Two blockhouses guarded opposite corners. Inside the square, storerooms, apartments, and other rooms were sandwiched between another wall. The inner quadrangle was used for grazing horses. Gates at each end barred intruders. Outside the wall was a scattering of Indian lodges — circular huts built of straw and dried mud.

Amanda felt her heart tighten when she first glimpsed the Indian dwellings. But Frank Grafius quickly assured her that they were occupied by Indian women, wives of the French trappers who brought their goods to the fort to trade.

Fort Laramie appeared to be the last emigrant dumping ground. Furniture, barrels of old clothing, anvils, wagon parts, trunks, stoves, and other household items littered the ground surrounding the fort. As the wagon party prepared to strike camp, Indian women stood in the doorways of their lodges, staring shyly at the white women. They wore peculiar combinations of dresses, coats, and jackets scavenged from the discards.

To everyone's relief, Ira Compton declared a stopover at the fort to buy supplies and repair wagons. The battered emigrants were eager for a break in the day-to-day routine. Some wrote letters to families back home, which could be mailed from the fort. In no time, the cottonwoods lining the Laramie River blossomed with laundry. The storerooms were visited as the emigrants stocked up on rice, whiskey, tobacco, leather to repair harnesses, and other goods. Thaddeus bought Amanda a length of blue-flowered calico to make a new dress, and some salve for the burn on her leg. Amanda was delighted with the material. Even though she was not very skillful with a needle, at last she could get rid of the horrible brown dress Helen loaned her after her accident.

Lavinia used the opportunity to bake pies, tantalizing the whole camp with the aroma of cinnamon and apples, while Amanda and Helen unloaded the wagons, spreading supplies on the ground to dry after the drenching rain. Thaddeus was ecstatic when Lavinia gave him a pie.

"After six weeks of bacon, bread, and coffee, this is sheer heaven," he said, gleefully forking into his third piece.

"It feels good just to stop for a day," Amanda said.

"Enjoy it. We won't have too many more stops," Thaddeus said.

"What do you mean?"

He gazed westward. Amanda followed his gaze. The Black Hills humped to the north like shapeless black monsters. Beyond the quiet campground, the plains, muted by moonlight, stretched to meet a star-studded sky. A coyote gave one long, bone-chilling cry.

Home, Amanda thought. *So far away.* The word had no meaning for her anymore, she had been on the road for such a long time. She wondered if she would ever have a home again.

"We're only a couple of weeks from the pass over the Divide, but then we're only halfway to Oregon. If we don't hurry, we'll get caught in early snowstorms."

Not even halfway to Oregon! Amanda's heart sank like a stone.

"We've come such a long way," she said. "And it's been so awful. Will things be better after this?"

Thaddeus sighed. "I'm afraid not. The stretch from the Platte to here was pretty grim, I agree with you. But according to everything I hear, the trail from here to the pass is even worse."

Chapter Eleven

"PETUNIA is limping pretty badly," Amanda warned her father, touching the left hind leg of the ox. "You'd better check her hoof."

Thaddeus stopped hitching the lead oxen and came back to where Amanda was standing. He lifted Petunia's leg. "You're right. It's got a bad crack. I'll heat up some grease and sulphur after supper tonight." He straightened, heaving a huge sigh. "Think they'll hold out, Missy?"

"I hope so. They seem to be strong animals." She patted Petunia's thin flank. *But will* we *hold out?* she refrained from asking. Every day she felt like running back to Boston.

She had affectionately named their team. In addition to Miss Finch and Pansy, the lead oxen, there were Petunia, Fern, Violet, and Buttercup. Fanciful names for plain, deserving beasts.

Everyone in the wagon party was concerned with their team. All of the oxen were weakened by the day-to-day drudgery of pulling heavy wagons up hills and down gulleys, over rough roads or no road, foraging only on poor prairie grass and drinking polluted water, which caused their bellies to swell and gave them cramps.

"Water is a long way off," Thaddeus explained when Amanda complained that they appeared to be on the road longer than usual. "Ira says we've got to make at least fifteen miles a day now. All we've found so far is sulphur water, and it's killing the animals."

In order to keep the train going at such a murderous pace, Thaddeus and the other drivers occasionally unhitched a travel-weary ox and let it roam, even though this overburdened the others in the team.

Earlier that day, one of the Compton oxen had collapsed in the road and refused to get up. Amanda knew that as hardy as these animals were, a downed ox would not get up again. Ira Compton unhitched the ox and left it there to die. Amanda was appalled, leaving that poor creature to the wolves when it had worked so hard for them. Life was so unfair out here.

The trail was lined with grim reminders that this country was not fit for any living creature: dead horses, oxen, mules, and cows in various states of decomposition, usually wolf-gnawed. The odor was so overpowering, Amanda had taken to wearing the bandanna over her nose again to keep from gagging at the stench.

The trail from Fort Laramie proved to be more monotonous than dangerous. Sagebrush, blowing sand, an endless sky empty of even a single cloud most days. As they approached the Red Buttes, a pair of red sandstone towers, the two strands of trail ascending the Platte to the South Pass through the Rockies merged and all wagons going to either California or Oregon came together.

With the additional traffic, the road became littered with more furniture and supplies unloaded by desperate emigrants. Amanda lost count of the sacks of beans, stacks of half-rotted bacon, iron stoves, kegs of nails, and other items, often with a sign reading "Help Yerself" tacked to the pile.

"Trouble is," Thaddeus commented after they had passed a heap of nicely kept furniture, "people wait till their team is worn out before they throw away those things." He kicked at a polished cherrywood desk until the legs broke.

Amanda looked away, a new worry creeping into her mind. People were developing strange quirks in their personalities lately, she noticed. Polly Lightfoot, always ready to laugh, burst into uncontrollable sobs the night before when her tripod collapsed and her kettle fell into the fire. Sam joked less and Frank Grafius seldom spoke except to pass a dour remark. Even Lavinia had become more withdrawn, though Amanda attributed her silence to the death of her little girl. Only Helen remained steadfast and cheerful, trudging behind the wagons, driving the few cattle the Jorgensons had left.

But Amanda's father had changed the most. He sank into deep depressions, surfacing to complain about his aching feet, the slow pace, the rocky trail, the hot sun, the ceaseless wind, guard duty, the monotonous meals — things no one had any control over. But when he began stopping the wagon to talk to every turnaround they met, Amanda's niggling worry grew into alarm.

Turnarounds were a sad, ragtag lot who had had enough and were going back home. Most had lost too many animals to continue; others simply could not endure the hardships any longer. They looked like lost schoolchildren to Amanda, with dazed and bewildered expressions, as though they had no idea how they had gotten out there or what they were doing. She knew just how they felt.

To keep her mind occupied, Amanda began to make a dress out of the blue calico her father had bought in Fort Laramie. She was intently stitching buttonholes one night when a familiar voice drawled, "Kind of late to be sewing. Shouldn't you be sleeping?"

Without waiting for an invitation, Ben Compton sat down on a box next to Amanda.

By now, she was used to his teasing. "Hello, Ben."

"Hello, Yankee girl. That's a pretty dress you're making. Almost as pretty as that shimmery one you wore the night of the dance." So he had noticed her gown that night!

"Is this one for somebody special?" he asked.

"Only myself," she replied. "I'm tired of wearing rags. Borrowed rags, at that." Now she wished she had finished the dress last week — the coarse butternut brown dress Helen had given Amanda after her accident was too big in the waist and was streaked with sweat stains. Amanda was embarrassed to be seen like this.

Ben's blue eyes, glittering in the firelight, followed her every move, making her nervous. She tried to keep her hands steady as she rethreaded her needle and began stitching around another buttonhole.

"Beat any Indians over the head with your spoon lately?"

"It wasn't a spoon," she said. "It was a spatula. And it was the only thing I could find that day. Papa had taken the rifle, not that I could have used it, anyway."

"Why don't you learn? Shooting isn't hard."

"I'd like to. I mentioned it to my father but he didn't exactly jump at the opportunity."

Ben smiled. "He's probably scared. You're

dangerous enough without putting a gun in your hand!"

She glared at him. "And what do you mean by that?"

His eyes danced with amusement. "All you had to do was give that Indian one of your famous tongue-lashings. He would have high-tailed it right back up into the hills!"

"Is that so?" Amanda declared in a haughty tone. "The fact of the matter is, you men are afraid."

"Afraid!"

"Yes, afraid. If you teach us women to shoot, you'll find out that we're better at it than you are."

He hooted. "All right, Miss Yankee Girl. Tell you what . . . I'll put my life on the line and give you a lesson. Tomorrow. How's that?"

"All right," Amanda said, her eyes glittering with the challenge. "What time?"

"At the noon break. After we eat."

"Anything you want me to bring?"

"Just yourself. I'll bring my rifle and ammunition." He patted her on the shoulder as he turned to go. "I certainly hope your aim is as keen as your tongue."

"You just may be surprised!" Amanda snapped.

The next day the wagon party broke at noon near a large rock formation known as Steamboat Rock. The whole company was in high spirits because the best water on the entire trail, the Sweetwater River, was no more than a day away.

"Missy," Thaddeus called after the noon meal. "I need you to —"

"No!" Amanda declared. "No more work! I've got something else to do. Something for me, for a change."

She flounced out of camp, returning Helen's greeting with a brief wave, ignoring the look of surprise on Helen's face at her new blue-flowered dress.

Walking across the dry, barren ground with the sun glaring down, Amanda mentally reviewed her appearance. Finishing the dress cost her a night's sleep, but it was worth the effort to have something new to wear, even though some of the seams were crooked and the stitches were large and clumsy. She had braided her hair this morning and wound the braids around her head. She also deliberatley left her sunbonnet at the wagon.

Why was she feeling so fluttery? After all, he was just teaching her to shoot. Ben was going with another girl and they were going to be married as soon as thcy reached Oregon. And anyway, who ever heard of a romance blossoming over a shooting lesson in the middle of the plains?

Ben had already propped a scrap of board against a rock. "What do you think of our target?" he called to Amanda as she approached.

"It certainly is large enough. Couldn't you find an old barn lying around for me to shoot at?"

That made him laugh, revealing deep dimples on either side of his mouth. Amanda had to remind herself why she was here.

With his rifle crooked under his arm, Ben led her in the opposite direction. "You won't think it's so big from back here."

They walked about fifty yards before he stopped.

Amanda turned and squinted at the target. "Way back there? That's not fair! I can hardly *see* the board!"

"I told you. Now, close your mouth for a minute and listen." He held up the gun. "This is a Hawken half-stock rifle — the best money can buy. My father bought one for each of us in St. Louis. It takes a .54 caliber ball. Now watch how I hold it." He brought the rifle to his shoulder, with his right hand under the wooden stock and his left around the muzzle. Then he handed the gun to her. "You try it. Careful — it's loaded."

Amanda nearly dropped it, surprised at how heavy it was. She raised the butt awkwardly to her right shoulder as he had done, straightening her left arm to support the muzzle.

"Place your other hand on the trigger," Ben instructed. He came behind her and put his arms around her, positioning the gun a little higher. "Now sight along the barrel until you see the board."

Amanda was aware of the nearness of his body but managed to close one eye, raising and lowering the rifle until she thought she saw the board, which seemed to have moved back a hundred miles.

"You see it? Now pull back the hammer."

"That thing sticking up?"

Ben gave a pained expression. "Yes, that thing. Easy . . . don't yank it. Ready? Now squeeze the trigger . . . *gently!*"

Amanda pulled the trigger. The gun fired with a flash of fire from the muzzle and a sharp blast that deafened her. The stock slammed against her shoulder and up, cracking her under the jaw. The recoil sent her reeling backward.

When she could hear again she sputtered, "Why didn't you *tell* me it would hurt like that?" She rubbed her jaw ruefully.

"Because." Ben took the gun and began loading powder and a lead ball into the barrel. "If I had, you'd flinch before you pulled the trigger."

"And now I won't?"

"You'll get used to it. Try again?"

She heaved a sigh. "All right." Was there *anything* in this world that she could learn to do without too much struggle?

"This time hitch the stock up higher and grip it firmer."

Amanda took the gun, lifting it to her shoulder. She hoped Ben would put his arms around her again, but he merely nodded that she was holding it correctly. She sighted carefully, set the hammer, then winced as she released the trigger. Crack! The rifle shoved her back but didn't bruise her jaw this time.

Her arms rubbery, Amanda lowered the gun. "Did I hit the board?"

"Can't tell. Let's walk down and see."

At the target site, Ben picked up the board and examined it. "Look! You did hit." He pointed out the burned edge where her bullet had creased the side. "And only on your second shot!"

"Is that good?"

"I think it's great. Let's go back and try again."

In the blazing sun, Amanda fired shot after shot, her shoulder flaming with pain. She never came close to the board.

"You're tired," Ben said after a while. "Let's call it quits for today."

"Just once more," Amanda begged. Even though she was exhausted, she had to show him she could do it.

He sighed and reloaded the gun.

Mustering the last fiber of strength in her aching arms, Amanda raised the gun, sighted with the first sense of accuracy she had experienced so far, and deftly squeezed the trigger. The board flew apart, shattered by the impact of her bullet.

Ben threw his hat into the air. "You did it, Yankee girl!" He pulled the gun away and gave her a big hug.

Amanda drew back hastily, her face

flushed, confused by her jumbled feelings. She looked up into his face, studying the depths of his blue eyes, trying to read what was behind them.

"We'd better head back," Ben said shortly. "Must be time to move out."

He walked her back to her wagon, promising her another lesson soon. Amanda watched him walk back to his own camp. A figure in a gray dress swooped down upon him. Serena. Had she watched the shooting lesson? Amanda wondered. And what had happened at the end?

In camp that evening, everyone went about their chores with barely contained excitement. Independence Rock, smooth and turtle-backed, dominated the horizon. They would reach the famous landmark sometime tomorrow, a cause for celebration.

Amanda sat by the fire, sipping coffee. A breeze lifted the tendrils of hair that had escaped her braid. The nights were getting colder, even though the days were still scorching.

She looked up when Henry Clay stalked through their camp.

"Bentley," he called to Thaddeus. "We got visitors. Some Mormons bound for California, wantin' to know if they can share our camp."

Thaddeus glanced at the strangers. "Better tell Ira."

"On my way." Henry Clay hurried off.

Soon a number of people had gathered

around the small party. The newcomers had only seven wagons. Amanda stared at the ragged children, the bone-thin women in faded bonnets who stared grimly back. She had never seen Mormons before.

"Just for the night," one of the strangers was saying politely to Ira. "Don't want to intrude, but we fear there might be Indian trouble. They'd likely attack a small group like us."

Ira scratched his head. "Well . . . I'd like to have you, but I have to bring it up before the men. Let them decide."

He called a council. Although Amanda was not invited, she could tell from the tense faces that the idea was not met with enthusiasm. A decision was reached and Ira approached the stranger again, shaking his head.

"I'm sorry. If it were only up to me, I'd be glad to welcome you and your friends, but the majority voted no. I'm truly sorry."

"Don't feel bad," the stranger said. "We get used to bein' treated this way. Thanks, anyway." He walked back to his party with dejected shoulders.

Amanda noticed Ben standing nearby, a small knot of anger twitching in his jaw. She went up to him.

"What's the matter? You look upset."

"Democracy!" He spit out the word. "Some democracy we live in."

"What are you talking about?"

"Just because those people are Mormons

. . . because they think differently than we do, we don't want to have anything to do with them."

"I still don't see —"

"I'm too mad to talk about it now, Mandy. See you tomorrow." He turned on his heel and walked across the camp.

Mandy! He'd called her Mandy. Not Yankee girl. No one else had ever called her Mandy before.

As she headed back to her own wagon, she saw Serena stop Ben. Ben seemed to be shaking his head angrily at something Serena said, then he strode off beyond the wagons. Serena stood there, her hands at her side, looking after him as the darkness swallowed him. Then she half turned toward Amanda. It was too dark for Amanda to read the expression in the other girl's eyes.

Chapter Twelve

INDEPENDENCE Rock drew Amanda like
a magnet. The wagon company had been in
sight of the humpbacked landmark for two
days, and when they camped by the Sweetwater River within walking distance of the
rock, Amanda felt she had to see it closer.

She stood by her wagon, transfixed by the
rock formation, which lay like a beached
whale turned to stone in the crook of the
river.

Helen passed Amanda on her way to the
river with a huge sack of clothes. "Goin' to
wash clothes, Amanda?"

"I'm sick of working," she confessed. "And
I'm not going to. Today, I'm doing as I please,
for once."

Helen shifted her sack. "I know just how
you feel. But as long as we're stopping over
a day to rest the teams, Mama wants me to

get as much washin' done as I can. So I better move. See you later."

As she watched Helen drag the heavy sack down to the riverbank where other women were already at work, Amanda felt a twinge of guilt.

"I don't care!" she said aloud, stamping her foot. "I don't *have* to work like a mule all the time."

No one heard her declaration. Thaddeus was herding the team toward the rich grass that lined the banks of the river. The Lightfoots and the Jorgensons were also busy. From across the camp, Amanda could see Serena Hawkins sitting on a crate with nine or ten children seated cross-legged on the ground around her. Serena had asked Captain Compton if she could start an informal school to be held during the longer breaks. Ira had consented, and Serena's school had begun the very next day. At first the only pupils were Serena's sisters Abigail and Josie and her brother Thomas, along with Ben's sister Eliza. But now Amanda recognized Martha and Ann Jorgenson and the youngest Bell children, as well. As an alternative to trail chores, Serena's school was gaining popularity with the children.

Amanda wondered how Ben felt about the school. It seemed as though Serena and Ben had so little time to be together. When the trail had become too arduous, the evening dances had ceased and opportunities for young lovers to slip away were infrequent.

Amanda had not seen Ben alone with Serena, and she was glad.

But now she was torn, standing beside her wagon. She should be washing clothes like Helen, or baking extra bread, or unloading the bedding to air, or doing any of a dozen tasks. It was work, work, work from morning till night, and for the last couple hundred miles, there had been no time for relaxation or even thinking. If she did not escape right this second, she would go insane.

Without a backward glance, Amanda walked out of the camp. She headed away from the river, toward Independence Rock. Several minutes later she had reached the base, which was surrounded by a drift of rocky rubble. Amanda tilted her head back. High up, there were names etched upon the granitelike surface. She shaded her eyes to see them better.

"I bet you're the first person from our company out here," a voice said behind her.

Amanda was not surprised to see Ben smiling at her. Had he also felt the pull to come see this stone monument, or did he follow her from camp?

"I hope so," she replied. "I'd like to be first at something on this journey."

He grinned, the sun-weathered creases around his eyes crinkling. "Weren't you the first one to stand up to an Indian with a spoon? Or was it a gravy ladle?"

"A spatula. Are you *ever* going to let me forget that?"

"A great story like that? Not a chance." He leaned against a rock, scanning the countryside. "Out sightseeing?"

"Actually, I decided to come up here instead of beating clothes against a rock down at the river."

Ben nodded. "I don't blame you. It probably won't be too long before the others call it quits and walk up here for a look-see. This place is the most famous landmark written about in all the guidebooks, you know. In fact," he added, "we're supposed to try to be here by Independence Day."

"Is that how the rock got its name?"

"I guess so. We didn't make it, though."

"We're only three days late," Amanda pointed out. "That's not so bad. And look — see the names up there? I wish I could get closer to read them."

From out of the corner of her eye, Amanda saw that Ben was not engrossed in the smooth walls of the rock but was staring at her. She was glad her blue-flowered dress was not torn yet and that the long skirt hid her clunky boots. Her hair was piled on top of her head in a jumble of thick curls, while her sunbonnet dangled down her back. Even though her face and hands were hopelessly sunburned, she knew she looked pretty.

Suddenly Ben grasped her hand. "I have an idea! You said you wanted to read those names. Come on, we'll climb up and see them."

"Climb this huge, slippery rock?" Amanda echoed. "Are you crazy?"

"Where's your sense of adventure?" he challenged, tugging her toward a cleft carved in the rock wall.

"I used up what little I had just getting this far," she said. "Ben, I really don't think I can climb up there."

But he was already digging his boots into the scrabbly slope. He offered his hand. "Grab hold. Now hold your skirt up with your other hand. That's it."

Ugly as her boots were, Amanda was grateful for them. The seemingly smooth sides of the rock were actually creased with many cracks and crevices, presenting brief footholds. Ben pulled her up with him in a steady ascent, for there was no place to stop. Ten minutes later, they collapsed on a sun-warmed ledge near the top, both gasping for breath.

The first to recover, Ben stood and looked down. "Mandy, just look at this view! You won't believe it."

Amanda flapped one hand weakly. "I'll take your word for it."

"No, you won't." He bent and hauled her to her feet.

He was right — the climb was worth the effort. Far below, the Sweetwater River snaked through rolling prairie, reflecting the cloudless sky like a sapphire necklace. Nestled in the curve of the river, the white tops of their wagons glistened in the sun.

In the distance Amanda could make out another train, with tiny teams and miniature wagons, toiling up the ribbon of trail.

"How far away are they?" she asked.

"About half a day from us."

"This is wonderful," she told him. "Thanks for bringing me up here." Then she shivered. The wind was quite strong up here, pulling her hair free from its pins until it streamed out behind her, and whipping her dress around her legs.

"You're cold," Ben observed. "That wind is cold. Probably because we're only about a hundred and fifty miles from the Rockies. Come on, we'll drop down some, get out of the wind."

He clambered down to another stone ledge and held out his arms. Amanda leaned forward until he grasped her around the waist, lifting her down easily as though she were weightless. He let go quickly.

"Better?" he asked.

She nodded, aware that he was staring again, this time at her tumbled hair, falling in deep curls over her shoulders. To cover her own confusion she pointed out letters carved in the rockface over her head. "Can you read that?"

Ben climbed a small outcropping and recited, " 'The Oregon Company, arrived here July 26, 1843.' " He twisted to read others. " 'J. W. Nesmith from Maine.' 'F. F. McKee.' "

"It looks like a registry book," Amanda

said with a giggle. "All the best people from society have signed in."

He grinned at her. "Should we add our names for posterity?"

She shook her head. "I don't think I will. You go ahead."

While he unsheathed the knife attached to his belt, Amanda stole a sidelong glance at him. The wind ruffled his thick hair, which had been lightened by the sun and had grown so long it curled over his collar. Hard work on the trail had toughened his body. She could see whipcord muscles tighten in his thighs when he leaned forward to read the names. Although she was dismayed by her own sunburned skin, the incessant sun and wind had bronzed Ben's face, making his blue eyes bluer and his hair even tawnier.

Now he ran his hand over the rock until he found a smooth place, then began scratching his name into the soft surface with the knife point.

Amanda watched as letters emerged, first a *B*, then a *W*. "What's the *W* stand for?"

"Wesley."

She tried the name aloud. "Benjamin Wesley Compton. That's a nice name."

"Thanks. Yours is nice, too. It fits you." He began filling gunpowder into the etched letter to make them stand out.

She leaned back against the sun-warmed stone, clasping her hands around her knees, watching him. When had she last felt this relaxed?

"Your father is doing a good job getting this wagon train to Oregon. He seems made for this kind of work." *More than my own father*, she added to herself.

"He does, doesn't he?" Ben agreed, scraping off excess gunpowder from the *W*. "Sometimes I think he'll almost be disappointed when we get there. The adventure will be over."

"What *will* he do in Oregon?"

"Farm again." Ben sat back on his heels and surveyed his handiwork. "We had a nice place in Illinois, but my father decided to pack up and go West."

"Just like that?" Amanda thought only her father was that impulsive.

"Well, it wasn't exactly an overnight decision. Josiah Hawkins wanted to take his family West, too. We spent last winter building our wagons, and this spring we headed for Missouri."

"Didn't you hate leaving home, leaving all your friends?" But then she thought, *Why would he? Serena was with him.*

"Not really. We had done some traveling down South when I was younger, before my sister was born. So I'm used to moving around."

"Where did you go?" Amanda had never been further south than Maryland.

Ben paused to remember. "Everywhere, it seemed. Virginia. The Carolinas. Georgia. My father did odd jobs here and there, butchering hogs, hauling freight, things like that. He just couldn't find the right place to settle down."

"Was he — what was it Mr. Grafius called it? — fiddle-footed? Just liked to travel from place to place?"

Ben frowned. "Not exactly. He saw . . . things that bothered him."

"What things?"

Ben put his knife away. His mouth tightened and his eyes suddenly became grim, reminding Amanda of the way he looked when the Mormon wagon party had been turned away.

"Ugly things," he finally replied, his voice hoarse with emotion. "Slavery." The word fell heavily between them, dimming the sun-dazzled day for an instant.

"I was real little," he went on. "No more than six, I guess, but I'll never forget the sight of those people working in the fields, men and women, under that hot sun. The sweat rolled off their backs, but they never broke stride. They couldn't, you know, till their work was done."

Absently, Amanda reached up and traced her fingers over Ben's signature. Slavery had been a topic much discussed in Boston. She had seen scathing editorials in the newspapers and the tracts handed out by abolitionists.

Ben continued, "My father hated seeing people treated that way so much, he had to get me and my mother away. We wound up in Illinois, but then discovered later that things really weren't much different there."

"What do you mean? There is no slavery in the northern states."

"No, not slavery. But something nearly as bad. You see, we lived on the banks of the Mississippi, not too far from a place called Nauvoo. A few years back, Mormons bought some swampy land and settled there. Nobody understood their religion. They were too different from everybody else. Then people thought the Mormons were becoming too strong politically." Ben tossed a pebble over the ledge. It skittered down the sloping wall, then was lost from sight. "There was a lot of yelling and fighting and then . . . one night some people were murdered. Mormons."

Amanda listened in shocked silence. Now she understood Ben's reaction when his father had sent away the wagon party.

"And that was when my father decided to come West," he concluded.

"What happened to those people . . . the Mormons?"

"They were finally forced to leave. Last we heard they were building wagons . . . probably heading West, too," Ben added thoughtfully.

Suddenly he asked, "Why are *you* going to Oregon, Mandy?"

The question took her by surprise. Without thinking, she gave her automatic reply. "Papa wanted to go and he made me go with him."

"You really hate this trip that much?"

"I had a wonderful life in Boston. At least, I thought I did. But then Papa got into trouble and . . ." She stopped, reluctant to reveal more.

"That's all right," he reassured her. "I didn't mean to pry." He gazed out over the camp below. "A lot of people are leaving the States to start new lives. I don't blame anyone who doesn't want to drag along his old life, no matter what mistakes he's made."

Amanda smiled. "You sound like a wise old man."

He smiled back and her heart lifted. "Sometimes I feel like an old man, wise or not. Tell me about life in Boston."

Slowly, haltingly, Amanda told him about her mother, who had died, and how the Whites had taken over Amanda's education. She talked about life at Miss Finch's, their house in Louisburg Square, Hester and Drucilla White, the parties and social events she attended. She mentioned Hester had an older brother but never alluded to the fact that she and Joseph had nearly been engaged. That magical evening last October when Joseph visited her was so long ago, Amanda was not sure it had ever taken place.

When she came to a stop, Ben said, "City living sounds all right. But I think I'd get the jim-jams before too long. I prefer wide-open spaces."

"I can tell. You seem to love this country."

"I do. The air out here is so crisp and the sky is so big, I feel like jumping up every day and really *doing* something. Don't you, Mandy?"

"It *is* pretty," Amanda had to agree. "But — I don't know. Life is so harsh. When it rains, it rains buckets. When the sun is out, it beats down endlessly. Nothing is done by halves out here. The wolves cry at night . . . and there are Indians. I wouldn't want to live here."

"Oregon will be different. Better in every way."

Amanda lowered her gaze to her lap. She didn't want to think about getting to Oregon — not just yet. When the wagon party reached Oregon City, their final destination, she and Ben would have to go their separate ways: she with her father, he with Serena. She wanted to bring up their engagement but hated to spoil the day. Then a thought, both frightening and exciting, struck her with the brilliancy of the sun mirrored in the Sweetwater below. *I'm in love with Ben! In love with Ben, not Joseph!* How had it happened . . . and what was she going to do?

"What are you thinking?" Ben said, peering into her face.

Amanda shook her hair back, giving him a tremulous smile. "Nothing . . . really."

"It looks like something important." His eyes met hers, searching for the answer there. "Mandy . . ." He leaned toward her.

Amanda felt herself drawn to him, her eyes half-closed in anticipation of the kiss she was certain would follow.

Just then they heard the whoop of children. They looked down and saw a group of people from their wagon party scrambling up the slope. The moment between them dissolved.

Ben stood. "Well, I guess we'd better head back down. Looks like a passel of sightseers are on their way up."

Amanda was reluctant to leave . . . if only there was some way to recapture the special time they had shared up here. She had an inspiration.

"Can I borrow your knife?"

"My knife? Sure." He unsheathed it and handed it to her.

Although the knife was large and awkward to handle, she managed to scratch a tiny *A.B.* in the rock beneath Ben's name. His name and hers, linked together for as long as this rock stood.

Ben smiled approvingly, then took her hand and they climbed back down. For the first time since she left Boston, Amanda's steps were as light and sure as a mountain goat's. The shadow of a golden eagle caused her to glance up once. The bird looked beautiful and free, soaring against the blue sky. Wistfully, she wished the day never had to end.

Chapter
Thirteen

THE next morning was so cold, Amanda had to chip through ice that had skimmed over the water bucket. She prepared breakfast, shivering in her thin shawl, wondering how they would ever make it through the mountains in September, if it was already this cold in July.

Stopping for a moment to gaze up at Independence Rock looming majestically over the campsite, she realized that yesterday had changed her life. She still yearned for Boston, but now her thoughts were filled with Ben. She strained for glimpses of him in camp, imagined ways to be near him. She suspected he felt the same about her, and if they had not been interrupted yesterday, she was sure he would have kissed her.

After breakfast, she met Helen down at the river, filling water buckets.

"Good morning," Amanda said.

Helen did not return the greeting. Instead she regarded Amanda with wide eyes. "Somethin' is goin' on around here."

"Oh, really? What?"

"You," Helen said. "You look different."

Now Amanda stared at her friend. "What do you mean? I'm wearing the same old dress, these same horrible boots. My face is as sunburned as ever."

"It's not your clothes I'm talkin' about. It's the way you've been actin' lately. This mornin' when I looked over, you were starin' off into space. Somethin' is occupyin' your mind."

Amanda filled her own bucket and hauled it up on the bank. "I don't know what you're talking about, Helen. I don't stare off into space, I'm just tired. Who isn't with all the work we have to do?"

"I know a tired face," Helen said. "Yours is tired but it's somethin' else, too."

"You seem to know so much, you tell *me* what it is, then," Amanda challenged, her hands on her hips.

Helen flipped the wire handle of her bucket back and forth. "When I first met you back at Indian Creek, I said to myself, 'Now here's somebody really pinin' for home.' You were awful homesick, talkin' about Boston all the time. You still mention it now and then, but not as much."

"Well, there's not much point, is there? I can't go back."

"It's pretty obvious that you've gone sweet on Ben Compton," Helen said knowingly.

"I don't have to listen to this!" Amanda snatched up her filled bucket, sloshing half the water, and started up the hill.

"Wait!" Helen ran to catch up to her. She stood in front of Amanda, blocking her path. "People are talkin'. You know how it is, with everybody in each other's pockets, day after day. Nothin' like a romance to speculate on. 'Specially since Ben is supposed to be engaged to Serena."

The heavy bucket was straining Amanda's shoulders, so she eased it to the ground. "Are you saying that people are gossiping about Ben and me?"

Helen looked uncomfortable for the first time since she had started this conversation. "Let's just say it's no secret about the day he gave you a shootin' lesson. Or the hike you two took up Independence Rock yesterday. And Serena must know, too. I'm surprised she hasn't been around to talk to you. I just thought —"

"Don't worry about me," Amanda said abruptly, tired of discussing her personal life. "I can take care of myself." She picked up her bucket once again and climbed the hill to her wagon without another word to Helen.

But as she mindlessly went about packing dishes and burying the remains of her fire from the night before, she thought about Helen's warning. Was Helen only concerned with Amanda's welfare or did she have another motive? Helen had always openly admired Ben....

That's it, Amanda thought. Helen was in love with Ben, too! She was trying to scare Amanda away so she could have a chance at Ben. Amanda knew, however, that Helen was no more attracted to Ben than any other girl on the wagon train.

Her biggest worry, as Helen had pointed out, still remained: Serena and Ben were supposed to be engaged.

In camp a few days later, Amanda was setting out the supper dishes when someone approached her from behind. She was so startled she dropped the plates, which fell with a clatter.

"Serena!" she cried. "You scared me! I didn't hear you walk up."

"Hello, Amanda." Serena stood before her, dignified and graceful as always in her gray dress and immaculate apron. Amanda wondered how Serena managed to avoid the dirt and dust that plagued them all.

"Can I help you with something?" she said now, her heart thudding. Did the gossip about Ben and her finally reach Serena's ears?

Serena did not reply right away. Amanda knew that the other girl was preparing a speech, and the thought made her more uneasy. She stared openly at Serena, taking in the smoothly parted white-blond hair, the pale gray eyes that revealed no emotion. *Her lips are too thin,* she thought inanely.

Serena returned Amanda's gaze. "When I left Illinois with my family," she began in a measured tone, "a young man asked me to be his wife."

Amanda's stomach flip-flopped. Then it was true! Serena was engaged to Ben. Why didn't he *tell* her?

"I accepted on one condition," Serena continued. "You see, this young man had a rather wild reputation. He courted a number of girls besides me. We could have been married before we left Illinois, but I wanted to wait. I felt that a long journey such as this one would give him an opportunity to . . . finish sowing his wild oats. When we reach Oregon, he'll be ready to settle down."

"If you're talking about Ben, why don't you just come right out and say so?" Amanda said angrily.

"I know you and Ben are getting friendly. This isn't the first time he has flirted with another girl. But he always comes back to me." Serena spoke calmly but firmly.

"I don't know what you're talking about," Amanda said stiffly. "Ben showed me how to shoot once, and we took a walk another time. But that's all. I'm spoken for myself," she added. "A Boston boy. He'll be out here any day to come get me. Take me away from this horrible life."

Serena looked mildly surprised, as if she

knew Amanda was lying. "I had no idea. Are you going on to Oregon with him then?"

"No," she replied vehemently. "He's taking me back to Boston. Home. Where I belong. And we'll live in a big house on Beacon Hill, not some lice-infested cabin in Oregon."

Serena was regarding her with pity now; Serena didn't believe her. "Of course. I'm sure you'll be very happy. When are you expecting this young man? Is he on another train?"

"He's riding out here on a Kentucky thoroughbred," Amanda lied. "Wagons are too slow. He wants to come get me as soon as he can."

"Well . . . I just didn't want you to get hurt," Serena said. "I suppose Ben knows about your suitor?"

Amanda's head was reeling from the lies she had just told. "No. Why should he? Like I said, he's nothing to me." She turned back to her dishes, wiping them with shaking hands.

"Good night, then." Serena left for her own wagon.

"Good night!" Amanda thought wildly, *How can it possibly be a good night?* Her dreams had just been shattered.

If Serena had been telling the truth, then Ben did not really care about her . . . he was only flirting.

The wagon train finally reached the mountains and began the slow climb upward. The

landscape became one of greasewood, sagebrush, and coarse grass. Cottonwood and
taller brush traced the routes of creeks leading off the Sweetwater, which had dwindled
to little more than a creek. To the north, the
snowcapped peaks of the Wind River range
rose above clumps of spruce and alpine fir.
The light dusting of snow reminded everyone
how little time they had left.

Amanda trudged beside the team with her
father, scarcely aware of the plume-like rock
formations bordering the trail or the huge
eagles gliding in wide circles overhead. She
had not seen Ben for the past few days. Her
seventeenth birthday had come and gone and,
as usual, Thaddeus had forgotten. Back in
Boston, Drucilla always sent Thaddeus a curt
note of reminder, but out here, she guessed
Thaddeus had lost track of the time. Her
thoughts were as gloomy as the countryside
they traveled through.

Sometime after the noon break on the
second day of ascent, the train halted
abruptly.

"What is it?" Amanda asked her father.

"Judging from the shouting up ahead, I
think we're over the Divide! Halfway to
Oregon." Thaddeus left the team to talk to
Jeb Jorgenson.

Cheers and gunshots marked the long-
awaited crossing. Amanda used the celebration as an opportunity to slip away. She
needed to be alone, even if only for a few
moments. Since she had had that conversa-

tion with Serena, Amanda had been in a mental turmoil. Had Serena told Ben about Joseph? Was that why she had not seen him since that day at Independence Rock?

Stooping, Amanda plucked a blade of tough buffalo grass and began shredding it. When she saw Ben approaching, her heart lurched, then she was filled with despair. She did not really want to talk to him now.

"Mandy!" he called. "How come you're way out here? You should be whooping it up with the others."

"I don't know what there is to celebrate," Amanda said sulkily. "If this is the famous pass, it certainly doesn't look like much."

"What did you expect, a big gold gate with a sign that says 'This Way to the Pacific'?"

"No. I don't know . . . I just thought the pass to the West would be a little more spectacular." She shook her head, wishing he would go away. She came here to be alone, and his presence only made her feel more confused.

Ben moved closer. "What's the matter, Mandy? You look so unhappy. Has something happened?"

She turned her head so he would not see the tears filling her eyes.

"Talk to me," Ben demanded.

When she did not reply, he whirled her around, forcing her to look at him. Her tears spilled, even though she tried desperately not to cry.

With one hand, Ben traced the wet trail down her cheek. "Mandy..."

He bent and kissed her, softly but firmly. Amanda tore away from him and stepped back, her eyes wide.

Serena was right, she realized with growing horror. Ben was just flirting with her, playing with her feelings while he was engaged to someone else.

Unable to deal with her own reaction to the kiss, Amanda fled, scrambling up the slope to the safety of the wagon train. She heard Ben calling her, but she never glanced back.

Chapter Fourteen

AMANDA raced up the hillside like a frightened antelope, snagging her skirt on brush and ripping it free, turning her ankle on loose stones. She did not stop until she reached her wagon, her thoughts as tangled as her hair. Ben's voice calling her echoed in her ears, and the feel of his lips on her burned in her mind. With trembling fingers, she touched her mouth.

It never should have happened. If he had kissed her a few days ago, she would have been overjoyed, but now . . . Serena had changed everything. Making an impossible situation even worse, Amanda realized with a wave of shame, she had responded to Ben's kiss — she *liked* it.

Now she pushed her hair off her damp forehead. The wagon train was ready to pull out. She joined her father beside their team.

Thaddeus cracked the whip somewhat list-lessly and called "Git-yup!"

"How come we're moving out so soon?" Amanda asked. "I thought we would have made camp back there."

"Pacific Springs is a few miles ahead. Everybody is anxious to see water flowing west." Her father sounded noticeably unen-thusiastic and his footsteps dragged, plod-ding slower than the oxen.

"Feeling all right, Papa?"

"I'm just tired. So tired of ... everything." His voice trailed off weakly.

Who isn't? she thought, but aloud she said, "You look pale. Are you sure you're not sick?"

For an answer he left her holding the team while he went back to the wagon, returning with an old jacket, which he put on.

"You can't *possibly* be cold!" Amanda cried in alarm. "It must be a hundred degrees right now. I'm roasting."

"Well, I'm not. I feel chilly. Must be the change in altitude." He lapsed into a sullen silence.

As they trudged down a trail bordered by gray boulders and gray-green sagebrush, Amanda's thoughts turned inward again. Over and over in her mind Ben caught her by the shoulders, forcing her to face him, to look into the depths of his piercing blue eyes as he bent to kiss her.

Pain washed over her in great waves, and her eyes filled with tears, blurring the barren landscape to shades of gray. Why did he have to hurt her this way? The two times in her life she had allowed herself to care for a boy, she had gotten hurt. First she had to leave Joseph; Joseph, who had never tried to come after her, take her back to Boston where they could be happy. And now Ben. She wondered if she would *ever* be happy. Or would she be like her father, restlessly searching from one end of the continent to the other? At least he had known happiness during the years her mother had been alive.

Amanda blinked hard, determined not to shed another tear over Ben, and set her shoulders squarely, resolving to avoid him the rest of the journey as much as possible. It was the only way. She could not afford to be hurt again — surviving the trail was difficult enough. Ben wouldn't miss her; he had his family . . . and Serena. Amanda had no one except her father . . . and a thousand miles of wilderness and desert to cross before she could begin to unravel her life.

When they reached Pacific Springs, Amanda said to her father, "Let's go look at it. See if water running west tastes any different." Most of the emigrants were heading for the famous stream spilling down the hillside.

"No," he replied flatly, unyoking the oxen. "Give me a hand here, will you?"

Disgusted with his attitude, she stomped over to help. She was busy unfastening the leather straps of the lead oxen when suddenly her father pitched facedown without a sound.

Amanda screamed, throwing herself beside his still body. "Papa! Help me, somebody! My father!"

Immediately Henry Clay and Sam came running over.

"What happened?" Henry Clay demanded as he knelt by Thaddeus.

"I don't know! He just fell down. Is he going to be all right? What's the matter with him?"

The two men turned Thaddeus over and set to work reviving him. Amanda gasped at the sight of her father's ashen face, his chest barely rising and falling, like the shallow breathing of a bird, not a full-grown man. Henry Clay shot a meaningful look at Sam, who nodded in agreement.

"Mr. Jorgenson — Sam — please! Tell me what's wrong with Papa?"

"He fainted," Henry Clay said. "But he's coming around now. Sam, let's get him into the wagon."

Amanda waited outside, knowing there was no room for her in the cramped wagon box. Sam climbed down first, followed by Henry Clay.

"We put him to bed —" Sam began.

"Can I see him? Why did he faint like that?" Amanda broke in, her voice quavering with anxiety.

Henry Clay faced her, his light blue eyes mirroring concern. "Your father has mountain fever. He's going to be very sick."

"Mountain fever? What is that?"

"It's pretty serious." Henry Clay hooked his thumbs in his worn belt and stared at the mountains surrounding them. "Caused by the high altitude. We're thousands of feet above sea level now. Notice how hard it is to breathe? Maybe there's something in the air that none of us is used to."

Amanda pressed her fingers to her mouth. "You mean we're all going to get this illness?"

Sam shook his head. "Hard to say. But don't you fret now. I'll send Polly over right away. And Frank will tend to your team." He patted her on the shoulder.

Henry Clay added, "Got any extra blankets?" She nodded. "Better dig them out. Your pa is goin' to need them."

Numb with shock, Amanda stood like a rock in a stream while everyone around her was busy setting up camp. An image of a freshly heaped grave flashed across her mind. No! That would not happen to her father. Gathering her skirts and her courage, she climbed into the wagon.

One look at her father lying on her bed, shivering under her wool blanket, galvanized her into action. She pawed through their supplies until she found two coarse blankets. Laying them gently across her father, she noted the beads of perspiration on his face and how deep-socketed his closed eyes appeared. With the back of her hand, she felt his forehead, the way her mother used to do when Amanda was sick. He was burning up and he did not stir at her touch.

"Amanda?" Polly heaved herself into the wagon, carrying a pail of fresh spring water, a towel thrown over her shoulder.

Amanda stumbled over to her. "I'm so glad you're here. Polly, he's so sick! I don't know what to do."

Polly glanced over at Thaddeus. "You covered him up? Good. Here, take this rag and sponge off his face now and then. And do you have a basin or an old pan?"

"I — I think so." She rummaged around flour sacks, spilling a bag of coffee beans, until she produced a pot that was too scorched to use any longer.

"Sam said he'll be nauseous, so be ready. There really isn't a whole lot you can do, Amanda, till this thing runs its course."

"You're not leaving! Please stay!" Amanda implored the older woman.

"Sorry, hon, but I've got supper to fix for two hungry men . . . It'll be all right. Try not to worry. You might get yourself sick, too."

But Amanda had little time to be concerned with her own welfare, she soon discovered. As her father's temperature soared, he was alternately racked with teeth-chattering chills and bouts of nausea, as Polly had predicted. Amanda stayed by him, wiping his face and holding his head when he was violently sick. Finally he slept, giving her the opportunity to slip out and throw together a hasty, unappetizing supper over a smelly sagebrush fire. Gazing into the leaping flames, an untouched plate of food in her lap, she never saw the man approach until he spoke.

"Amanda Bentley?"

She looked up into the brown-bearded face of Josiah Hawkins, Serena's father and one of Captain Compton's second-in-command. "Mr. Hawkins —" She started to rise.

"Please sit, young lady. You look tuckered out. Ira Compton asked me to come check on your father. How is he?"

"About the same."

"Too bad. Will you be able to travel tomorrow?"

"Me? I'm all right, but my father is too sick to be moved." She remembered how dreadful she felt jolting along in the bumpy wagon after her accident.

"I'm sorry," Josiah said. "Captain Compton can't take the chance of us all getting the sickness. Ten others have come down with the fever. The sooner we head out of these mountains, the better off we'll be. And we have to get grass soon or our teams will die. Now, you need someone to drive your wagon —"

"No, I don't," Amanda said quickly. She could guess what was on his mind. Ben was one of the few young men available to fill in, and she was afraid Josiah would suggest that Ben drive her wagon.

"I can do it myself," she added hastily, ignoring Josiah's look of disbelief.

"Amanda, driving a team of oxen is not easy. I'm sure you've helped your father, but driving by yourself is quite a different matter. And you don't appear very sturdy, if you don't mind my saying so."

"I know I can do it," she said with more confidence than she actually felt. "I'm stronger than I look."

"Well —"

"I'll just have Mr. Grafius or somebody hitch them up for me. I can do the rest."

His eyes still reflected doubt but he admitted, "We are mighty shorthanded. . . . If you think you can handle it —"

She scrambled to her feet, letting her plate slide to the ground, aware that she was not instilling confidence in him.

"I'll be fine, Mr. Hawkins. Don't worry about me."

He tipped his hat. "I hope so. Holler if you need help."

Amanda could scarcely believe what she had done — committed herself to *driving the team*. Alone. True, she had watched her father handle the oxen these past weeks but, as Josiah had said, watching and doing were two different things. She shook her head and gathered up the dirty dishes to wash.

Helen was already at the spring. "How's your pa?"

"No better. Mr. Hawkins told me we're moving out tomorrow, no matter how many get this terrible sickness."

"It's awful. I hear Eliza Compton has it

and so does Jefferson Bell. Mama's so afraid one of us will come down with it, she's watchin' us like a hawk." Helen took a pan and began scouring its blackened sides. "Who's drivin' your team tomorrow?"

"I am."

Helen's eyes widened. "You? Amanda, have you lost your mind? You can't handle six big oxen, over this rough rocky —" She broke off coughing, as though the whole idea of a young girl driving a wagon choked her.

"I can and I will." Amanda stood up abruptly, indicating the issue was closed. *Anything to keep Ben away*, she thought.

"Well, if there's something I can do to help..."

Rubbing her temples, Amanda tried to think. It had been such a long, exhausting day. "Do you have an extra blanket? Papa has all of ours and I'll have to sleep under the wagon tonight."

"You can bunk with us if you want," Helen offered. "We have a little more room now that ... since my sister died."

"Thanks, but I'd better be close in case Papa turns worse."

She spent a restless night rolled in the horse blanket Helen had given her, waking every few hours to check on Thaddeus. He threw up a few times, mumbling unintelligibly. Amanda knew he was delirious and worried that he might become dehydrated. Toward morning Thaddeus opened his eyes, and whispered Amanda's name.

"Missy. Promise me something —"

She bent closer to hear him. "Yes, Papa?"

"If I should die —"

"Don't talk like that!"

"— promise me you'll go on. You can make it, I know. Find someone . . . settle down . . . be happy."

"Please don't say these things. You're going to be fine."

He went on as if he had not heard, his eyes fixed on the canvas overhead. "Oregon will be a great land. You can do anything you want . . . really make something of yourself, not be a failure like me."

She smoothed the covers. "Go back to sleep, Papa. Stop worrying. You need to rest."

Outside again, Amanda leaned against the back wheel. Stars shimmered eerily in the black sky, looming larger than ever, a trick of the thin atmosphere. Her father had to get well. He just *had* to. What would she do in Oregon all alone? How would she even *get* there? The question reminded her that tomorrow she would be driving the wagon. Self-doubt assailed her like a hundred tiny darts. But she would make it — the last thing she wanted was for Ben to learn she needed his help.

If her father should . . . She could not bring herself to think of the word, but she had to face the possibility. *Go on to Oregon*, Thaddeus had said. She did not *want* to go to Oregon, had never wanted to. It was one reason she could not promise him.

Amanda rubbed her temples. Too many decisions. Too much responsibility. All she really wanted was to go home. To go to sleep in her own bed in her own room and wake up when everything was right again.

Picking up her blanket, she wrapped it around her shoulders to ward off the penetrating cold. She stayed awake the rest of the night, listening to the lonely cry of a coyote.

Shortly after daybreak, the camp came to life. Sam brought the Bentley oxen around and maneuvered them into place.

Amanda ran a hand raggedly through her hair, which she had no time to comb and rebraid this morning. Her eyes felt gritty from lack of sleep. "Where's Mr. Grafius?" she asked, knowing that Sam had his own team to hitch.

"Sick."

"Oh, no! Has he got the fever, too?"

" 'Fraid so. Polly's been up half the night with him." He sighed as Amanda handed him the harnesses. "I don't know what'll become of us. Heard this morning three more people took sick last night." Deftly, he yoked Violet and Fern together. "Who's drivin' your wagon till your pa gets on his feet again?"

"Me."

Sam stared at her, his light eyebrows arched with surprise, but he merely said, "Watch out, then. These animals are hungry. Hard tellin' what they're liable to do."

Amanda scratched Buttercup behind the

ear, noting the oxen's jutting hipbones and dull, lusterless coats. How awful, the poor things were going hungry. There had been next to nothing for them to forage on for the past several days. "I'll be careful," she told Sam. "But I trust our team. We've all been through so much together."

She could not handle her father's long bullwhip, but the six oxen, accustomed to the sound of her voice, obeyed her command to move out. She held the reins in both hands, aware that the slender straps were all that enabled her to control the lumbering beasts. The animals stumbled down the rutted trail, tottering in their wooden yokes.

Driving the wagon was more difficult than she had ever dreamed. Her arms ached from straining against the reins and her voice was already hoarse from shouting commands. The sun sweltered down, burning off the morning chill. Before they had traveled a mile, the bodice of Amanda's dress was soaked with sweat. The blue-flowered dress she had worked so hard to make was in tatters already. *The next time I decide to walk across the country*, she thought drily, *I'll be sure to bring at least a dozen dresses.*

At noon, she gratefully turned the team over to Jeb Jorgenson so she could slice stale bread left from supper two nights ago and make a pot of weak tea. She took a mug and a hunk of bread into the wagon.

Thaddeus lay asleep, the covers kicked to the foot of the bed. Had his fever broken?

Anxiously, she felt his forehead. He awakened, shaking his head at the mug she held out.

"Try to drink it, Papa," she urged. "You need liquids."

He rolled away from her like a petulant child. "Don't want it. Don't want anything."

The break was over before Amanda had a chance to eat. The descent became more rugged, but her team limped along, following her orders as she walked beside them. *If any of my friends in Boston could see me now,* she thought, *they'd wonder if this was the same Amanda Bentley who once danced the night away.* Her dainty feet, she recalled, had never even stepped in a mud puddle, much less hiked along dusty, stony roads.

Her feet began to swell, and the ill-fitting boots raised a blister on the back of one heel. The blister rubbed with each step until she felt a rush of warm stickiness — the blister had broken open, exposing raw flesh. But she could not stop, bleeding foot or not.

"Need some help?" Helen called later that afternoon. "You look played out."

"Could you check on my father? See if he'll drink that tea I left?" Amanda made a futile attempt to wipe the thick yellow dust off her face.

"Sure." When Helen came back, she was smiling. "I think he's getting better, Amanda. He drank the tea and even ate a bite of bread I dunked for him." Peering at Amanda's sweat-streaked face, she inquired, "When did *you* eat last?"

"I can't remember. I didn't have time today. You know, Helen? I don't think I'm cut out for this line of work." The oxen seemed to hesitate. She prodded Petunia with a blunt-ended stick. "Come on, what's going on up there?"

"Oh, my Lord!" Helen gasped. "One of your animals just dropped!"

An ox in the middle yoke had collapsed suddenly in the road, dragging its yoke-mate down as well. Amanda yanked back on the reins, halting the lead oxen.

"Helen, run quick and get your father!" She knelt next to the entangled animals, fumbling with the yoke that bound them together. If she did not hurry, the rest of the team might panic and trample her and the struggling ox.

Then Henry Clay and Jeb were there, skill-fully separating the animals. Stricken, Amanda watched as Jeb raised Violet to her feet, but the other ox lay with its nose buried in the dust, sides not moving.

"This one's gone," Henry Clay declared, briefly feeling for a pulse in the throat.

Fern — dead? Amanda could not take it all in. How could one of her oxen have dropped dead in the harness like that?

"Sorry, Amanda. I know how rough it is to lose one," Henry Clay said.

"What killed her? She seemed fine this morning —"

Henry Clay shrugged. "Starved, from the looks of her. I'll lend you one of my cows to fill in."

The men dragged Fern's body to the side of the trail, while Amanda looked on, heartsick and helpless. The animals worked so hard, for so little, only to die out in the middle of nowhere. *They deserve better,* she thought. Fern should have had a happy life, plowing some farmer's fields, with plenty of green grass to eat, instead of hauling a heavy wagon a thousand miles with no food or water or rest.

Overcome by guilt, she turned away from the sight of the ox's bony body where flies had already begun to cluster. Before tomorrow, she knew, the carcass would be stripped clean by wolves, leaving only the bones to bleach in the sun.

Jeb brought back a sharp-flanked black-and-white cow. When he harnessed and yoked the cow in Fern's place, Amanda was ready to move on.

The afternoon march was long and dry. Her throat was so parched, she did not have enough saliva to lick her cracked lips and the sun dazed her. *If only I could be granted three wishes,* she thought inanely. First, she would ask for water. Buckets of it, for her and for the poor animals who trooped along at her command, tongues lolling. And then she would ask for good spring grass for them and some fried chicken for herself. Forget those things . . . she wanted to go *home.* But if she could not be magically sent home then perhaps . . . But no, she would not think of Ben. Resolutely, she brushed aside the image of his blue eyes, his burnished hair.

The train stopped again and she looked in on her father. When she saw him sitting up, she almost cried with relief.

"Papa! You're feeling better. Can I get you anything?"

"No." His color had returned, but his eyes were empty, expressionless.

Amanda sank onto the box near the bed. "Fern died."

"So that's what all the commotion was."

"Helen's father gave us one of their cows. A lot of oxen are dying, I hear. It's so hot!"

"We're all better off dead," he said tonelessly. "We're never going to make it."

"Don't say that!" Though she was exhausted, she was not defeated, not ready to lie down and give up like one of the animals. "Henry Clay said we need to lighten our wagon. What can we get rid of?"

"I don't know —"

"*Well, think!*" She was losing patience with her father. "What can go?"

Raising up on one elbow, Thaddeus pointed to a pile of blacksmith tools. "Toss those."

"These things? They look useful. Are you sure —"

"You asked me to get rid of something and I told you. Don't give me any argument. Throw them out." He slumped back onto the pillow.

As Amanda heaved the heavy iron tools out of the back, she saw Jason and Helen lifting down their mother's beautiful hand-rubbed wedding chest. Lavinia stood by, watching with tightly set lips, as the chest was reverently set down by the trailside.

So, Amanda thought bitterly, *it has come to this*. Everything that meant so much to Lavinia — her youngest child, her plant cuttings, her family's wedding chest — she had to sacrifice. *Where will it all end?* Amanda thought.

But later that evening, Amanda was amazed to see Mrs. Jorgenson holding Noah in her lap, with Ann and Martha leaning comfortably against her, while she told them a story. No matter what hardships the Jorgensons suffered, they remained a family. Helen and Lavinia exhibited a strength of will that left no doubt in Amanda's mind that they would make it to Oregon. And her father? He did not have the same spirit.

She sighed. Her arms ached from holding the reins all day, and her feet were so swollen she could hardly stand. The blister on her heel needed tending, but she lacked the energy.

"Mandy."

Her name was spoken softly, but her heart jumped as though a cannon had been fired.

Ben approached her fire, his eyes shadowed in the semidarkness. "I heard about your father. How is he?"

"Getting better, I think." She turned away,

remembering her resolve to avoid him. But she could not very well walk away.

"I also heard that you drove the team by yourself today. How'd you do?"

"I managed."

"So it seems. Lost an ox, too, didn't you?"

"Is nothing sacred around here? Or do the people at your end of the train have nothing better to do than talk about me?"

"I know you're angry with me, Mandy. I'm sorry about . . . the other day. I didn't really mean for that to happen."

She tossed a twig into the fire, watched it ignite and curl with the heat. "According to what *I* hear, you do that sort of thing all the time."

His face tightened. "Who have you been talking to?"

"Never mind. I also heard you are engaged to Serena, but I suppose that must have slipped your mind those times we've been alone."

"Who do you believe?" he demanded. "Me . . . or this other person?"

"I don't know and I don't really care. As far as I'm concerned the subject is closed. Now I want to put out my fire and go to bed."

"All right, Mandy. If that's the way you want it. I won't bother you again." He looked at her coldly, turned on his heel, and marched out of her camp.

As it turned out, Amanda did not go to bed right away. She sat staring into a dying fire most of the night, unable to get warm.

Chapter Fifteen

"WHAT happened at the meeting?" Thaddeus asked, plumping his pillow so he could sit up. He looked much better, though he claimed he was still weak.

Amanda handed him his breakfast plate and watched as he took a bite of hard bread, the first solid food he had accepted in two days. Satisfied that he would keep it down, she sat beside the bed and answered his question. "They decided to take the Greenwood cutoff."

"And not go on to Fort Bridger?" Surprised, Thaddeus stopped with his tin mug halfway to his mouth.

"That's right. The cutoff is supposed to save time."

"If we live through it," he muttered.

"What's so bad about it?"

Thaddeus sipped his coffee. "Well, I don't

know much about the route myself, other than what I've heard. It's pretty rough territory. The worst part is that there's no water. At Fort Bridger, we can buy supplies. Good water all the way down after that. The teams can rest. What is our illustrious leader thinking of?"

Amanda shook her head. "All I know is what Sam told me when he came back from the meeting. They had to decide whether to take the trail south to the fort or cut straight across to the Green River. According to Sam, we can save seven whole days by going this way."

"But there's *no water!*"

Amanda shrugged. "Tell me the last time we had a lot of water, except when we followed the Sweetwater?"

"If you think it was bad before, you haven't seen anything yet," Thaddeus stated wryly.

But Amanda did not hear him. She was suddenly back on Independence Rock with Ben, gazing down on the Sweetwater sparkling in the sun. Such a bright, wonderful day, filled with the promise of better days to come. And now that promise was shattered. Remembering hurt too much, so she busied herself straightening the wagon until she heard Jeb and Frank Grafius yoking her team.

"Time to leave. Keep your plate, Papa. I don't have time to wash the dishes. I'll have to do them tonight." *That and everything else besides,* she added wearily to herself.

As she turned to leave, Thaddeus asked, "Can you manage, Missy?"

"I've been managing on my own for two days now, Papa."

Had it only been two days since she took over driving the team? It seemed like forever. Her feet stayed swollen and red, like balloons, and her arms felt as stretched and flimsy as the worn leather reins she gripped all day. Her strength had been drained from her as thoroughly as a bucket of water tipped over into the sand, and yet she still had to keep going.

"I'll be up soon. Tomorrow, maybe." Thaddeus promised halfheartedly.

"Don't worry about it, Papa. Just rest till you get well."

Of the fifteen members in the company who had come down with the mysterious illness, Thaddeus had taken the longest to recover.

Faker. The word surfaced from out of nowhere. *He truly could be sick,* she argued with herself. *Maybe he had a worse case than the others.* But as she nodded her thanks to Jeb, taking the reins of her team, she wondered if she was excusing Thaddeus simply because he was her father.

"We'll come to the Little Sandy River first," Jeb was telling her. "After we cross it we'll hit the Big Sandy and stop to load up on water. Got all that? Good." He smiled at her. Amanda hoped that a nice woman in Oregon would see past Jeb's homeliness and appreciate his gentle ways. "I was talkin' to Henry Clay last night. You've done real good drivin' this rig these past few days. A lot of people didn't think you could do it."

One of Mrs. Garrity's favorite sayings slipped off her tongue. "It just goes to show what a body can do when it has to."

Mrs. Garrity! Amanda had never treated the housekeeper very well, and now she would give her eyeteeth to be with Mrs. Garrity in her cozy house in Louisburg Square. Autumn was coming soon — Amanda's favorite time of year. The fall scarlets and yellows set Boston off to perfection, the way a ruby necklace enhanced a green ball gown. But she did not have time to daydream now; she had work to do.

Commanding her team to move out, Amanda mentally went over Jeb's directions. Ben must be out scouting again, passing on information about the trail ahead. When mountain sickness struck the team, she knew he had given up scouting to drive wagons or herd cattle on horseback.

Amanda had not seen him since the night he dropped by her camp. Why did he come that night? She never learned the reason — not that it mattered now. And he never really denied that he and Serena were engaged, a realization that hit Amanda later with the impact of being kicked in the stomach. She had been too busy driving, tending to her father, and doing her regular chores to think about that evening. In a way, the backbreaking work helped keep her numb, too tired to feel anything.

They reached the Little Sandy in good time. Clear water rippled over fine, yellowish sand. Willows bending in the breeze lined the banks. Around the trees, the grass was close-cropped and trampled with hoofprints, signs that other trains had been there before them. Rolling away on the other side of the river was a flat, barren tableland, relieved only by occasional clumps of dried sagebrush and rocks.

At sight of water, Miss Finch and Petunia, the lead oxen, picked up their feet, almost running toward the river. Amanda dug her boots into the sand, straining to hold the animals back, shouting, "Halt!" They finally obeyed her, but not before Amanda thought her arms would be pulled from her shoulder sockets.

"I'll get yer wagon across, little lady. No need for you to try."

Amanda turned to see Frank Grafius tugging on his whiskers. "Thanks, Mr. Grafius. The river looks shallow, but I'm not sure I could get the team to cross."

"Oh, they're ornery critters all right. Nine times outta ten, they git halfway over, then double back. No trick to swimmin' stock — jes' a lot of cussin'!"

Amanda smiled. The older man was as coarse as burlap, but he could always be counted on to help. Since Thaddeus had been ill, she found out that most everyone was quick to pitch in — apparently an unwritten law of the trail her father preferred to overlook.

Frank took the reins. "That man oughta be horsewhipped, lettin' a schoolgirl drive the wagon while he lays in bed!"

Her cheeks flamed. She knew that few people in the train had a favorable opinion of her father. He had done little to earn one so far.

Once across the Little Sandy, Amanda took control over her team again. By nightfall, they reached the larger river called the Big Sandy. Amanda surrendered the reins to Frank, who unhitched the team and led the animals down the steep riverbank while she set up camp.

The coffee had barely come to a boil when Thaddeus climbed out of the wagon, buttoning his threadbare shirt.

"Hi there. Feeling better?" she asked.

He sat down by the fire. "Thought it was time to get up. I don't think I could stand another day bouncing around that wagon."

"I know. It's terrible." Guiltily, she mixed flour and water in the bread pan. Did he overhear Frank's earlier remark? And the silence that followed when she did not disagree? "I'm glad you're up again," she said, kneading biscuit dough. "Hungry?"

He sighed, pouring himself some coffee. "I am — but not for beans and biscuits."

"Well, I don't know what I can do about that," she said crossly. "Cornmeal, flour, beans, and apples are all we have. And since we haven't passed any good inns lately, I guess we're stuck."

"I don't care. I'm tired of the same old thing, day after day."

Disgusted, she rolled out the dough and placed the pan to bake over the fire. What did he expect her to do? Create a miracle out of four ingredients? She hadn't asked to come out here. Why take it out on her? And instead of sitting there, he should be checking on the team, not leaving his work to others.

Slamming the lid on the pot of beans, Amanda announced, "Supper won't be ready for a while. I'm going for a walk."

Thaddeus never looked up but sipped his coffee and stared morosely into the fire.

Though her father had warned her, Amanda could never have been prepared for the nightmare of the Greenwood cutoff.

Before leaving the Big Sandy, every pan, barrel, cask, and bottle — anything that would hold water — was filled. Captain Compton had instructed them to carry as much water as possible, for there were more than fifty dry miles to the Green River without so much as a trickle between.

The wagons traveled in a straggly line across the desert, through gravelly ravines, past alkali lakes that shimmered in the sun with blinding whiteness. Not a stalk of vegetation grew except the inevitable sagebrush. And since buffalo did not roam this far west, there were no fuel-providing buffalo chips. Amanda despised the greasy, smelly fires they had to make from brush.

After the first day during which they marched seventeen miles through ankle-deep sand, Amanda wished fervently that Ira Compton had been voted down and they were taking the longer route to Fort Bridger. Wheels screeched in earsplitting protest as exhausted oxen dragged the wagons. In addition to the noon break, Ira designated two water stops. Amanda carried water to their team, hating herself when she had to pull the bucket away before the poor ox had done little more than wet its tongue.

"Not too much," Thaddeus cautioned. "We have to conserve water."

"But it's so mean to give them a swallow, then snatch the bucket away!"

"We need the water for ourselves. They are only animals. Why do you think they call them 'dumb ox'?"

Amanda's temper flared. "How can you say that? Our oxen have risked their lives to get us to Oregon. Fern *died* giving us her very last step —"

"It's their job. Like it's my job to make them work." With a crack of his whip, Thaddeus urged the team to move on again.

To take her mind off her own dry throat and parched lips, Amanda wondered when her father had lost his compassion and become so selfish, so unfeeling. The journey was changing them all. *What will he be like in another five hundred miles, by the time we reach the end? And what kind of person will I be? As sour and bitter as a persimmon, probably.*

On the second day, everyone's water supply was dangerously low, in spite of their conservation efforts. Amanda walked beside the team, the hem of her skirt dragging in the sand, one hand on Petunia's harness, trying not to remember the sparkling cut-glass goblets brimming with spring water that Mrs. Garrity used to set on the supper table every night. She was so thirsty, she was certain she would go insane. Like the oxen, her mouth was too dry to even produce saliva.

"Here." Frank Grafius came up and handed her a smooth white pebble.

"What's that for?"

"Put it in yer mouth and suck on it. It'll help you make spit. I picked up a pocketful back at the river. Had a feelin' we'd be needin' 'em." He left to distribute pebbles among the Jorgensons.

Amanda placed the round stone under her tongue with a smile. What would Drucilla White say if she knew Amanda was talking to a man about "making spit"? Most unladylike!

On the third day, they passed another train that had stopped to bury a woman and a young boy who had died from exhaustion. A tremor of apprehension coursed through Amanda as the sheeted bundles were rolled into a shallow grave. Only the other evening she had asked Helen half-jokingly if anyone could die from tiredness. Now she had her answer. No one in their wagon party had died since Sarah Jane Jorgenson, even during the mountain sickness.

It was difficult to keep her thoughts from traveling in a morbid direction, as Thaddeus maneuvered their wagon around the rotting bodies of horses, mules, and cattle that lined the road. It seemed as though they were taking a shortcut to death.

"How much farther *is* that blasted river?" Thaddeus grumbled later that afternoon. "We've made better than sixteen miles for the past three days. What if we're going in the wrong direction?"

"I don't know," Amanda replied, stopping to empty sand out of her boot. She had to do that so often, she just left the boots unbuttoned, so they flapped with every step. "I guess we ought to have faith in Captain Compton. He only wants to get us to Oregon."

"Maybe it's high time somebody questioned his competence —"

Suddenly the wagon sagged; a tire had slipped off the back wheel.

"Damn! That's all we need right now. It must be a hundred and ten out here, and now I have to get that wheel fixed!"

Amanda picked up the heavy iron circlet, leaning it against the wheel. "What if we left it off?"

"Can't do that. A wheel wouldn't last two

miles in this sand without a tire. And if we lose a wheel we're really in trouble. No, we'll have to have it repaired."

The Lightfoot wagon approached, and Thaddeus flagged Sam's attention. "Need some help. Can you spare Frank? I lost a tire."

Frank Grafius assessed the situation with a grunt. "Got any extry wood?"

"I think so." Thaddeus turned to Amanda. "Bring me the crate next to your bed."

When Amanda brought the crate Frank began breaking it into long pieces. "Git a fire goin', man. Block these wheels," Frank ordered her father. "And git me yer smithy tools."

Thaddeus hesitated. "Blacksmith tools? I had my daughter throw them out to lighten the wagon."

Frank stared at Thaddeus, his gray eyes incredulous. "You did *what?* Why'd you do a durn-fool thing like that for?"

"I'll borrow Henry Clay's," Thaddeus said quickly, hurrying away.

When he returned, Jeb was with him, carrying a jack, among other tools. Jeb and Frank cranked up the wagon so the wheel cleared the ground. Thaddeus placed wooden blocks behind the two front wheels, braking the wagon. While Jeb set about building a fire, Frank whittled a number of flexible wedges. It was slow, hard work. Amanda watched for a while, then went over to her father who was sitting in the meager shade of the wagon, mopping his brow with his bandanna.

"Why aren't you helping those men?"

"I don't know anything about repairing a wheel."

"How can you say that, Papa? We've watched a dozen wheels being fixed."

"I'd probably just be in the way."

But Thaddeus did not get to rest long. "Bentley!" Frank growled. "Git some rawhide and a bucket of water!"

"Water!" Thaddeus cried, as if Frank had asked him to bring back a bucket of diamonds. "Who has water to spare?"

"Jes' git some. Else you'll burn yer rig down when we slap that hot tire back on."

Some time later Thaddeus came back with a pail of water generously donated by several members of the train. Amanda hoped he thanked them.

"What's the delay here?" Ben rode up on his pony. He spoke to Thaddeus, never looking in Amanda's direction.

Amanda looked quickly away, before her face could betray her feelings.

"What does it *look* like?" Thaddeus snapped, eyeing Ben impatiently.

"My father asked me to see what was holding you up." Ben's tone was polite but frosty.

"You can tell the *Captain* I didn't plan to break down, if that's what you're implying.

Whenever somebody throws a tire, the train stops so it can be repaired. Why should it be any different now?"

"Because we have to get to water! The teams are dying. And we will, too, if we don't get to the Green River by nightfall."

Thaddeus waved a hand. "I don't want to hear about it. I didn't vote to come this way and wouldn't have, if I had been consulted. And I can't move with three wheels. Why don't you pitch in instead of whining?"

Amanda saw the muscle twitching in Ben's jaw as he dismounted, tossing the reins loosely over the wagon tongue. She knew he was angry and she didn't blame him. Her father's attitude was inexcusable.

Ben took the tongs from Jeb and held the tire over the blazing fire until the iron glowed orange. Sweat ran in rivulets down his tanned face and in no time his hair and thin cotton shirt were soaked. Amanda could not imagine a worse torture than standing over a fire in the suffocating heat.

The wedges Frank whittled were tied on the outer rim with rawhide strips. When the tire was hot enough, Ben and Frank slammed the glowing iron ring over the built-up wheel. Jeb doused the whole apparatus with water to prevent the wooden parts from catching fire. Frank uncranked the jack, lowering the wagon.

"Good," Thaddeus said crisply, as if he had done it all himself. "Now we can get going again." He ran up to remove the blocks from the front wheels.

As if in a dream, Amanda saw the wagon, parked on a slight incline, begin to roll slowly. "Look out! It's moving!" she screamed.

Frank leaped forward, pushing Thaddeus out of the path of the heavy wagon. But Ben, who had been examining the tire on the other side, had no time to move. Amanda's heart froze in her throat as the wagon crushed Ben, trapping him between the big front wheel and the rear yoke of oxen.

Chapter Sixteen

As long as she lived, Amanda knew she would never forget the sight of Ben pinned between the oxen and the wagon, crumbled over the wheel, his arms dangling and his head lolling like a broken doll. The soles of Amanda's boots seemed melted into the sand; she could not move.

But Jeb and Frank sprang into action. Frank slammed the wooden blocks beneath the wheels to halt the wagon while Jeb slapped the rumps of Buttercup and Pansy, forcing the oxen to move away.

"Don't jes' stand there! Git help!" Frank yelled as they dragged Ben's limp body off the wheel, laying him on the ground.

Thaddeus remained sprawled in the dust where Frank had pushed him out of danger. But all Amanda needed was one look at Ben's pinched white face. She fled down the trail toward the Jorgenson wagons.

Lavinia knew instantly that something had happened. "Who is it?" she demanded.

"Ben Comp — Compton . . . the wagon rolled —" Between words Amanda caught her breath in huge gulping swallows.

Lavinia did not wait for further explanation. Shouting at Martha to watch out for the younger children, she climbed into the wagon, reappearing almost instantly with her wooden medicine chest.

They hurried back, stumbling in sand that filled their shoes and tugged at their long skirts, hindering their every step. Amanda was reminded of a recurring nightmare she had had after her mother died. Her mother was very sick and calling for someone to help her. Amanda tried to go to her but found she could not run. The ground slid backward, carrying her farther away from her mother. She felt that way now, as if she would never get to Ben.

By the time she and Lavinia arrived at the Bentley wagon, Ben had regained consciousness and was speaking to Frank, who leaned over him.

Lavinia dropped to her knees beside Ben. "Tell me exactly what happened, Frank."

"Glad you could come, ma'am. The wagon started rollin' while Ben was in front. He got mashed between the wheel and the team. I brung him over here but other'n that he ain't been moved a hair. He come around a minute ago on his own." Amanda sent a silent thanks to Frank for not mentioning that the accident had been her father's fault.

"How are you feeling, Ben?" Lavinia asked. "Where does it hurt?"

His voice was weak but audible enough for Amanda to hear his reply. "Like a hundred knives sticking in my chest. Hurts most when I breathe." His chest barely moved, he was breathing so lightly.

Lavinia prodded his chest and ribs. He winced when her fingers probed his right side. "Fractured ribs," she pronounced. "Your arm's not broken. Jeb, take Ben's horse and ride to the head of the column. Tell Captain Compton what happened. Ben should be moved as little as possible, so get him to bring his wagon back here. When Ben is settled, I'll treat him."

Jeb took off and Lavinia continued to examine Ben for further injuries.

Amanda anxiously waited to one side. She felt half-responsible for Ben's accident. She should have spoken up before he ever got off his pony, told him not to help her father, that Thaddeus had plenty of assistance.

Her father came up, dusting off his trousers. "I hope you don't think it was my fault. Do you think I would have let the wagon roll if I had seen the boy?"

Amanda could not bear to look at him. "I don't know what to think, Papa."

"Don't blame me, Missy. I didn't do it on purpose."

His eyes were genuinely sincere, but all Amanda knew was that Ben was seriously hurt due to his carelessness. "We'll talk later," she told him. "Right now I think you'd better move our wagon. Captain Compton will be here soon."

The Compton wagon arrived with a grim-faced Ira at the reins. Eliza raced ahead of the team, tattered skirts and black braids flying, while Mrs. Compton sat rigidly on the wagon seat.

"Oh, Ben!" Rose cried, leaping down and running to her son's side. "My poor boy!"

"Oh, Ma. Stop crying. I'm just fine." He smiled at his mother.

He won't say a word to me, Amanda thought in despair. *I've been here the whole time, and he's never even looked at me!*

While the men slid a plank under the injured man and carried him into the wagon with Lavinia, Eliza, and Rose trailing, Amanda wondered if she would ever get a chance to tell Ben how sorry she was. She was kicking dirt over the fire Thaddeus had left burning, when Lavinia called to her from the back of the wagon.

Amanda went over. "What is it?"

Lavinia leaned down, lowering her voice. "It's Rose. I can't do a thing with her. Acts crazy as a June bug! Just sits, wringin' her hands and cryin' like Ben's been killed or something. I can't work with her like that. So I told Eliza to take her to my wagon.

"What do you need me for?"

"Help me bind Ben's ribs. Ira is off checkin'

the rest of the train, and anyway, he thinks doctorin' is women's work. Come on."

Bind Ben's ribs! Amanda could scarcely believe her ears. He was not even *speaking* to her — how would he react to her touching him? She opened her mouth to protest, but Lavinia was offering her hand and pulling Amanda into the wagon.

"I'm making a plaster," Lavinia said as Amanda maneuvered around half-empty sacks of coffee and bundles of clothing lying helter-skelter. The Compton wagon was not the least bit organized.

"Go sit with Ben till I'm ready," Lavinia said. "Then we'll tape the plaster on him." She indicated a cot at the front end and resumed taking supplies out of her chest.

Ben was lying in the wooden bunk. His blue eyes followed her through the clutter. She noted his face was still very pale, and dark rings underscored his eyes, but she was filled with relief when he summoned a shaky smile. At least he didn't object to her presence. She sat down next to the bed.

"Mandy." There was a world of emotion in that single word.

For Amanda, the hot, dusty plains disappeared, and the anguish of the past few days dissolved. This was the Ben she had come to know and care for that day on Independence Rock.

"Oh, Ben," she whispered, hoping Lavinia would not overhear. "This shouldn't have happened. I'm so sorry."

He put his hand on hers. "Now, Mandy. Don't cry."

She nearly laughed. How typical of him. He was the one hurt and yet he was comforting her! She found a bucket half-filled with tepid water and poured him a mugful.

"You must be in awful pain," she said. "Rest easy. Lavinia will fix you up. That woman can perform miracles."

"Not always," Lavinia said, approaching the bed with a wet, peculiar-smelling cloth. "I couldn't do a thing for my own daughter." She spoke without bitterness, but Ben and Amanda exchanged a glance. "Broken ribs hurt right much, but they aren't too serious. You'll be on your feet in no time, a big, healthy man like you. Amanda, help me get him up."

When Ben was in a sitting position, Lavinia removed his shirt and placed the plaster on his bruised ribs.

"Phew!" Ben exclaimed, wrinkling his nose. "What's *in* that thing?"

"You don't want to know. Amanda, rip this old petticoat into strips, will you?"

Blushing, Amanda tried not to stare at Ben's wide shoulders and well-developed arms while she tore the garment. His skin was smooth and bronzed to a V at his neck where his shirt had been unbuttoned. Ben winced, but never uttered a sound as Lavinia and Amanda tightly bound the cloth strips around his torso.

Tying the ends into a secure knot, Lavinia

instructed him, "Keep your arm still, that'll help your ribs heal faster. This plaster ought to draw the pain out. Try not to move any more than you have to. Or take deep breaths." She repacked her medicine chest, adding, "A cup of tea will sure taste dandy right now."

"I'll fix you one," Amanda offered, wanting to stay near Ben as long as possible.

"No, thanks, hon. Helen should have some waiting. Will you keep our patient company till Rose gets back?"

Lavinia must have read her mind. It was not very proper for Amanda to be alone with Ben even if he was injured, but Lavinia never seemed to be dictated by convention. Eagerly, she watched the older woman leave.

"Mandy —"

"Ben —"

They spoke at the same time, then laughed, easing the tension between them.

"We only have a few minutes before my mother comes back," he said. He reached for her hand, enclosing it in his strong fingers. "I just want to say how sorry I am for all the trouble I've caused you."

"Oh, Ben, you're hurt and it never —"

"Please, Mandy. Let me talk. Everything — this misunderstanding — has been all my fault and I want to apologize." The words were punctuated with shallow gasps. Amanda was afraid he was overtaxing his strength, but when would they ever have another opportunity to be alone?

"Ben, I've been so *confused*."

"I know. I have, too. Mandy, I don't want you to spend another second doubting how I feel about you.

Her heart turned over. She had waited so long to hear this!

"The day we crossed the Divide . . . when I kissed you. I just couldn't help myself that day . . . you looked so sad. I couldn't bear to see you unhappy. And then I wound up making you feel even worse." He squeezed her hand.

"Oh, Ben, it wasn't you . . . not entirely. It's —" She lowered her gaze, hating to bring up Serena's name, knowing that to do so would break the special feeling they were building.

"You were going to say 'Serena,' weren't you?" He sighed, and the effort caused him to wince again.

"Maybe you should be resting. We can talk some other time. Your mother will be furious if she thinks I've been upsetting you." She started to rise, but Ben pulled her back.

"Listen to me, Mandy. I know you think Serena and I are engaged."

"Well, aren't you?"

He replied, "It's not what it seems. I realize that doesn't make much sense and it's asking a lot of you to believe this. But the fact is, I can't marry Serena. Not now. Not ever."

Amanda's pulse thundered in her throat. "I don't understand."

"It's a long story." He passed a weary hand over his eyes.

"But Serena said —"

"I know what she told you. At least I think I do. But *I'm* telling you that I can only marry a girl I truly care for."

She stared at him. "You don't love Serena?"

"No. I don't," he replied softly. Although he did not say it, Amanda knew that he cared for her very much. "Serena and I have made a big mistake and I think we both know it."

"What are you going to do?"

"I'm not sure. I don't want to hurt her. But don't worry. I'll figure out something."

Outside, voices announced the return of Ben's mother and sister.

"I've got to go." She stood up reluctantly. They had so much to discuss, so much time to make up.

He released her hand with a final squeeze. "We'll talk again. Soon."

Eliza burst into the wagon, rudely shoving past Amanda in her haste to see her beloved brother. Over Eliza's head, Ben gave Amanda a long wink.

On the way back to her own wagon, Amanda felt happier than she could ever remember, even that night when Joseph White asked her to wait for him. Ben loved her! She was certain of it. Perhaps there was a chance for happiness, after all.

The feeling of hope was so new and delicate, Amanda found she was walking lighter, holding herself carefully, as though the slightest pressure would destroy it, like popping a soap bubble. But what would Serena do when she found out that Ben wasn't going to marry her?

The wagon train moved out without further delay. The teams staggered through the sand and rocks for the next five hours. Just before sundown, a line of stunted timber was sighted with whoops of joy. Trees only grew where there was enough water. The Green River at last! The long, dry march had finally ended.

Emigrants and animals alike needed little encouragement. Soon the swift-running stream was filled with splashing children and thirsty livestock. Women were dragging bundles of dirty laundry out of their wagons.

Kicking off her shabby boots, Amanda tucked her ragged skirt between her legs, fastened the end around her waist, and waded out. The water felt so cool and delicious, she felt she could stay in it forever. The river flowed just below her knees. Her toes flexed, digging into the gravelly bottom. Suddenly a sheet of water rained over Amanda's head, the sunlight turning droplets into tiny rainbows. Amanda spun around, thoroughly drenched.

"Helen! Was that you!" Amanda hit the water with the flat of her hand, spraying her friend until she was as wet as Amanda.

Doubled over with laughter, Helen called,

"Enough! I give up!" They waded back to the bank and sat down to dry in the sun, Helen still giggling.

"I thought we'd *never* get to this river," Amanda declared. "I didn't have so much as a swallow of water all day."

"Me neither. It's been awful walkin' behind the wagons in all that dust. I tried to call Jason once, and all that came out was a little puff of dust."

Amanda giggled, but broke off as a spasm of coughing drowned out her laughter. Violent, racking coughs shook Helen's shoulders, leaving her winded. She pulled a handkerchief from her sleeve and touched it to her lips. Amanda blanched when she saw the scrap of white cloth come away blood-flecked.

"Helen! Oh, my God! What's *wrong?*"

Hastily Helen put the handkerchief away.

"How long have you been like this?" Amanda asked, her eyes wide with concern.

"The last two months, more or less." Helen gripped Amanda's arm. "Promise you won't tell anyone. I've managed to hide it this long from Mama. If she finds out, Lord knows what it'll do to her after losin' Sarah Jane."

Amanda had seen those symptoms before. Hester's grandmother and aunt both had died from it. Consumption. How could Helen have gotten this dreadful illness? Was anything ever fair in life?

They sat in silence, each occupied with her own thoughts, while the sun set, staining the sky blood red.

Chapter Seventeen

THE misty August morning had given way to another stifling day. On a brief halt, Amanda stood at the back of her wagon, one hand resting on the grub box, gazing eastward. She stared beyond the last straggling wagons bumping along in the dust, beyond the rutted trail winding down the craggy mountain they had descended, beyond the gray peaks rising to meet a gray sky.

She was remembering a Sunday afternoon the summer before, riding out of the city on a picnic with Joseph. The memory returned in a series of half-formed, disjointed pictures. The Whites' elegant brass-trimmed carriage with red leather seats. Joseph's soft, fawn-colored coat and his lazy smile as he flicked the reins, setting the pair of matched grays into a snappy trot. The road bordered with blue-flowered chicory and a trail of Queen Anne's lace like a bridal veil. Green meadows spangled with dandelions like scattered gold pieces. Cows and sheep grazing contentedly. Cool ponds turning to silver in the late afternoon light.

But then the picture faded and Amanda was left standing by the wagon, wearing the stained blue calico dress patched in several places, the memory leaving a cloudy residue, like soapsuds in a bathtub. Whatever happened to that carefree girl in the frilly peach gown, shading her delicate skin with a parasol, laughing and talking to an attentive boy about nothing in particular?

Now her shoulders seemed bowed under the burden of responsibilities, of surviving from one day to the next. On the plains there was no leisure time, no idle chitchat. Activities and conversations revolved around food, water, the heat, the teams, the wagons — and their destination.

Oregon. Amanda sounded the word silently, noting how it filled her mouth with full, round syllables. Oregon — the answer to everyone's dreams. But miles of endless desolation and hardship crumbled the enthusiasm of even the most optimistic emigrant. They were all so tired, they scarcely remembered what life was like back home or why they left in the first place.

At least Amanda had found Ben. Knowing he was there helped make the trip bearable. She rubbed her hand across the rough lid of the grub box, as she recalled the talk they'd had two nights before.

Ben's broken ribs healed quickly in spite of his being bumped along the rocky trail. The first day he was up and around he sent a message to Amanda to meet him outside the corral after supper.

Amanda waited just beyond the circle of wagons, clutching her black shawl in a futile attempt to keep warm, until Ben materialized out of the gathering darkness.

He touched her arm. "Let's walk a little," he said.

"Do you think you should? I mean, today being your first day up and all."

"The exercise will do me good. And I want to make sure we have privacy."

He struck a path out across the prairie, between tumbled rocks and ankle-twisting chuck holes. The sharp wind bit through Amanda's thin shawl. He noticed her shivering and put an arm around her shoulders.

"You're cold."

"I'm fine. Just being with you is enough."

"I'm glad you feel that way, Mandy, but I'd hate for you to catch cold. Do you want to go back?"

"No."

They found a boulder among the stunted sagebrush and sat down. It was a moonless night but the stars created a glimmer of light. The silhouettes of the crooked bushes appeared sinister somehow. Amanda imagined all kinds of nameless creatures lurking behind them.

"It's time you knew about Serena," Ben began.

A wolf howled in the distance. Amanda suppressed another shiver.

"I think I told you my family's farm was close to the Hawkins place back in Illinois." She nodded. "Serena and I went to school together. We got to be pretty good friends."

Amanda wondered when the friendship blossomed into an engagement but said nothing.

"I guess those early years of traveling from state to state left me kind of restless. I couldn't seem to settle down." His voice became lower, as if he were about to confess something he had never admitted before now. "I courted a lot of girls, but none really special. I wasn't really looking for a special girl. Finally, my father got fed up. He took me aside and told me to stop acting like a gadfly and settle down. I walked over to the schoolhouse — Serena was teaching by then — and told her what he said. She said, 'You know, Ben, if you started courting me, your father would think you were settling down and it would solve my problem, too.' Serena didn't want to get married yet, because she'd have to quit teaching, but her parents were worried about her. So we decided to have an arrangement — meet every so often and talk, like we were courting."

"Just to satisfy your folks?" Amanda asked.

"That's right. Pretty stupid, wasn't it? Anyway, soon after we started seeing each other, our parents decided to move to Oregon. That was last fall. And what with the preparations and building the wagons, I got too busy to talk to Serena much."

"She told me that she refused to marry you before you left Illinois. That she wanted to wait. Were you really going to get married if you hadn't moved to Oregon?"

Ben sighed unhappily. "I don't know. Except for that day at the schoolhouse, we never talked about marriage. It wasn't in either of our minds to get married, but our parents seemed happy, so we just let the arrangement slide. And it never bothered me that much because I figured by the time we got to Oregon, Serena would have met someone else. That would have been a way out. But as it happened, I met you," he added, putting his arm around her again.

Amanda's mind was whirling. Ben had never been truly engaged — not if he never intended to marry Serena.

"What are you going to do?" she asked.

"I'll have to talk to her. Tell her that this engagement business is off — not that I ever felt it was on." He tightened his arm around her shoulder. "And I have to tell her about us."

Us. What a wonderful word that was,

Amanda thought. Only two letters, but filled with a world of possibilities.

"How do you think she'll take it?"

"I'll just say that it's time we faced facts ... that the engagement had never been real and it was time we stopped pretending. She may be relieved. After all, this pretense must be just as hard on her as it is on me. Don't worry," he added, "I don't want to hurt her. She has always been a good friend."

"Maybe you can go on being friends," Amanda suggested, though secretly she doubted it. Serena seemed far too proud to be friends with anyone who rejected her.

"Maybe."

"Ben, what are we going to do when we get to Oregon?"

He stood. "First things first. We have plenty of time to talk about that. Right now it's getting late. And you're just about frozen. I'd better get you back to camp before your father comes after me with a shotgun."

Ben kissed her gently and they walked back to camp.

Since that night, Amanda had seen little of Ben or Helen or anyone else as the terrain became more rugged. To get the exhausted team to tackle the mountains required both Amanda's and her father's full-time efforts. And there were many more mountains to cross before it was all over. Now she wished she could lie down right where she was, in the shadow of the mountain, and not have to take another step.

* * *

As she stood in the wagon the next morning, clad in only a chemise, she felt her sharp collarbone and protruding hipbones. She covered her face with her hands. What must she look like to Ben? The monotonous trail food combined with hard work had caused her to lose weight. And whenever she brushed her hair the bristles of her silver-backed brush were packed with lusterless hair — more evidence of poor diet. She felt so grubby . . . would she ever soak in a hot tub again? The scar on her calf was not as red and glaring as it had been at first, but she knew some mark would probably always remain. At least her skirts covered it.

Problems were getting the best of her. Her father, Ben, Serena, Helen's illness, the trail. If she wrote them all down on slips of paper, tossed them in a hat, and drew out only one — no matter which one it was — it would still be too much for her to handle.

Chapter Eighteen

JUST when Amanda thought she could not abide one more day of rationed water or barren countryside, they crossed the Bear River, entering the lush Bear River Valley.

"I can't believe this!" she said to her father. The sparkling river coursed between grassy banks; beyond that, lush, flowered meadows rolled away like a rich Persian carpet.

"It is kind of unexpected after all that dust and brush," Thaddeus grudgingly agreed. "I was beginning to think we weren't going to come in contact with another blade of grass till we got to Oregon."

Captain Compton ordered a three-day lay-over to rest the animals and let them fatten up a bit. *Three whole days in this paradise,* Amanda thought eagerly as she helped unhitch the team. She could wash her hair, rinse out her dress, mend a pair of stockings, take a long bath . . . Hanging up the harnesses, she deliberated on what wonderful thing to do first.

Amanda headed for the river, and as she cut across the meadow, she met Helen and her younger sisters carrying towels, brushes, and soap.

"We're goin' up to those hot springs. There's supposed to be a bunch of them not too far from here. Mama gave us the rest of the afternoon off to wash our clothes." Helen reached out and ruffled Ann's thick brown curls. "And maybe do a little hair washin'. Want to tag along?"

"*Hot* springs? Really? Just let me get my things." Amanda rushed to locate a coarse towel of English hemp, her comb and brush, and the very last piece of soap Polly had given her.

The day took on a holiday atmosphere. Morning clouds that had threatened rain parted and revealed an azure sky. Mountains marching in the distance had shed their cloaking mists, standing as white and sharp as church steeples. Yellow-throated meadowlarks tossed gay songs into the air. Amanda swung Ann's hand, following Helen, who apparently knew where she was going.

"Pa says we can't miss them. See those mounds?" Helen pointed to dome-shaped heaps of earth about a mile away. "The guidebook said to look for them — that's where the water shoots out of the ground. Can you imagine such a thing?"

"Just so we have privacy," Amanda said. "I'm planning on taking a *long* soak. I have a thousand miles of dirt to get off."

"Me, too. And Mama says the hot water may help my cough —" Helen broke off, giving Amanda a meaningful glance over her sisters' heads.

So, Amanda thought, *she couldn't hide her illness from her mother after all.* Today Helen looked the picture of health — pink-cheeked, bright-eyed, her pace crisp, as though she had spent the morning lolling in bed instead of helping her parents with the oxen. And she had not coughed once. Amanda wondered if Helen felt as good as she appeared.

"Is that wild onion over there?" Helen asked her sisters. "Mercy me, I bet it is. Martha, why don't you and Ann run over and dig enough for supper. Get some for Amanda's too. We'll chop some up in our beans, make 'em taste like a hundred dollars."

"I doubt it," Amanda said, watching the two girls skip through the tall grass. "But I suppose any change would taste better. Did you ask them to leave for a purpose, or are you just craving onions?"

"Both. But mostly I wanted to tell you something. Mama cornered me the other night. She said she knew I was sick, probably with consumption. She's done a lot of doctorin' in her time, you know, and she's seen many a case."

"Oh, Helen. What did she think?"

"Well, she talked it over with Pa and Uncle Jeb, and they decided not to tell anybody else. Not yet. There's no point, really. Nothing nobody can do. But Pa asked around and found out that there's a doctor at Fort Hall and he's goin' to have him take a look at me."

"How do you feel? I mean, you aren't coughing today."

"Some days it's worse than others. Sometimes I wake up in the night, all hot and sweaty, even as cold as it's been lately. And my chest feels heavy, as though something is sittin' on it. And if I get up too fast, I get light-headed."

Amanda couldn't think of anything to say, so they walked along in silence, slowly so the two girls could catch up when they had filled their skirts with onions. She realized how serious Helen's illness was — good days were only a temporary situation.

The small mound they were making for proved to be more than two miles away and was twenty feet high, with water issuing from the top, gushing into the air and down the sides. The water was persimmon-colored and delightfully warm. Amanda wanted to settle right there, but Helen pointed out that they could be seen from the trail. Another mile down the road, they found a stand of cedar enclosing a number of springs that tumbled from cones. The water temperature ranged from warm to very hot. The trees made a perfect dressing room. In no time, the girls shed their clothes.

Amanda eased into a warm, bubbly spring until the water was up to her chin. She closed her eyes in sheer bliss.

She watched Ann and Martha splashing downriver a moment before Amanda said, "Helen, I'm worried about my father."

Helen nodded, her unbound hair swirling in the foaming water behind her. "I know. He does seem . . . different than he was when we first met at Indian Creek. Why do you suppose that is?"

"He says he's tired, but it's more than that. He's discouraged, doesn't seem to care whether we get to Oregon or not. He never talks about setting up a new law practice the way he used to. It's like he's given up. He drives the wagon like a puppet, just gets through the day and that's about it."

"Maybe when you actually get to Oregon, he'll perk up," Helen suggested. "Does your pa know about you and Ben?"

"He must know I'm seeing Ben, but he hasn't even asked me. I don't think he likes any of the Comptons, but he's never said a word. He just doesn't seem like my father these days."

"Wait till we get to Oregon. He'll probably snap right out of it. My folks don't act as hepped up as they did at first either. Everybody is just bone-tired, that's all."

They soaked for a while, shoulder-deep in the warm, bubbling water. Then Helen took her sisters back to camp, leaving Amanda to dress and doze in the sun.

When she woke up, she took her brush and comb, climbed on a flattish boulder, and dreamily brushed her still-damp hair till it gleamed. The day had been so perfect, she wanted to cherish it, the way she used to save the first flower of spring by pressing it between the pages of her father's leather-bound Shakespeare.

"Are you a wood sprite or are you real?"

Amanda tossed her head so that her waist-length hair rippled. "A wood sprite. Any second I'll vanish before your astonished eyes, leaving only a ghostly memory."

Ben hoisted himself onto the rock, then presented her with a bouquet of just-picked lupine. "Well, if you're going to disappear, I'd better give you these quick."

She buried her face in the pink and scarlet blossoms. "Ben, they're beautiful. The flowers seem prettier out here, don't they? More colorful or something."

"You look pretty good yourself." His blue eyes appraised her. He twisted a silky curl around his forefinger. "The sun brings out red highlights in your hair, did you know that? Fiery, just like you are."

"Do you really think I'm fiery?" Amanda giggled as she added, "Aunt Drucilla would faint if she knew how unladylike I've become."

He released the curl tenderly. "Oh, you're every inch a lady when you have to be. But you don't get carried away with fussy manners. When you get angry, you let it show and that's good." His voice took on a teasing tone. "Tell me, Miss Bentley, when you get married, are you going to throw skillets at your husband?"

"If he doesn't behave, I may have to." At the mention of marriage, Amanda wondered if he had talked to Serena yet.

"I know what you're thinking."

"You do? I didn't know you were clairvoyant."

"I talked to Serena. This morning."

Amanda's eyebrows rose in surprise. "You *do* read minds. Well? What did she say? She couldn't have been too mad; you're still in one piece."

Ben smiled ruefully. "Have you ever known Serena to fly off the handle? No, she was as cool as an iceberg when she told me, 'I know, Ben. I couldn't marry you either. When I get married, it'll be to someone who loves me.' "

"Did you — did you tell her about us?"

"Yes, I did. I told her I cared for you very much."

Amanda was aware that he had moved closer to her. "How did she take it?"

"All she said was, 'I'll hope you'll be very happy.' But I think she's right. I know I'm going to be happy with you."

He was so close, she was forced to look into his eyes. "Ben . . ."

The kiss was as soft as a rainy afternoon, as sweet as a field of white violets, and then he kissed her again, harder and longer.

When Ben pulled back he said, "You are so pretty sitting here, with your hair down. Will you always wear it down for me?"

"When I can. However, when I'm helping to throw an ox so you can grease its feet I'd rather have my hair up!"

He laughed. "Just think of all the wonderful experience you're getting on this trip. You'll be ready for anything in Oregon."

"I'd rather not think about that. Do me a favor? Let's not talk about work today in any shape or form." She added self-consciously, "I don't know how you can say I'm pretty. My hands are as tough as shoe leather. And my face is so sunburned —"

He took her hand, turning the palm up. "What's wrong with a few calluses, Mandy? They prove you've worked hard — I know, I'm not supposed to mention that word. In my eyes, you're a lot prettier now than that first day I saw you in Independence. You wear your calluses like a badge."

"But my skin —"

"How many compliments do you want in a single afternoon? All right, one more." Placing his hands on her shoulders, he turned her toward him again. "If you must know, your brown skin sets off those green-gold eyes of yours like jewels. How's that?"

This time Amanda met him more than halfway when they kissed.

The sun sketched long shadows across the glade. "We'd better get back," Ben said. "It's almost suppertime."

"Papa probably thinks I've lost my way." As Amanda gathered her toiletries, her hand brushed the wilting bouquet. A year ago, when she was trying to be the belle of Boston, if a boy had brought her wild flowers, she would have laughed at him. But none of the boys she knew, including Joseph, ever talked to her the way Ben did, making her feel truly special, not like just an empty-headed, pretty girl.

She picked up the flowers gently. When she got back to her wagon, she would be sure to press these in her Bible, to keep always.

Chapter Nineteen

FIVE days after leaving the Bear River Valley, the wagon train arrived at Fort Hall and set up camp for the day. For Amanda it was a miserable week. Accustomed to grassy meadows and abundant waters, she thought she had seen the last of the dry prairie. But the stretch from the valley to Fort Hall passed through desert broken only by dried sagebrush and barren, black lava plains. Even the fort was a disappointment.

Located between the Portneuf and Snake rivers, Fort Hall was an ugly structure, a windowless two-story blockhouse built from hewed logs, surrounded by a wall interrupted here and there with holes that enabled the men inside to shoot out. Nothing at all like the welcoming, whitewashed façade of Fort Laramie. As Fort Hall represented the last campground shared by trains bound for

California and those headed for Oregon, circles of covered wagons were seen in every direction, with people, horses, and cattle scattered all over the valley. Amanda hated seeing those people littering the landscape. After being in a relatively small train of thirty-seven wagons, the sight of so many campsites, foraging teams, and milling people overwhelmed her. It was like a crowded city.

At least the fort meant new provisions. Members of the Compton train were already heading toward the barred gate, hoping to buy food, leather, feed for horses, dry goods, tobacco, boots, and anything else they could afford, knowing the traders who ran the fort inflated their prices, taking advantage of trail-weary travelers still hundreds of miles from their destination.

"I'm going up to the fort," Thaddeus called to Amanda.

"Wait a minute!" Amanda scrambled down from the wagon where she had been taking inventory of their food supplies. "We need flour, dried apples, and another sack of beans. And tea if you can get it. And, please, look for some material for me. I really need a new dress."

"What color?" Thaddeus removed his worn leather purse from a back pocket and checked the contents.

"Pink would be nice, but it doesn't really matter. Anything will do." The chameleon silk dress she'd been wearing was totally unsuitable for traveling. Without the required four or five starched petticoats to bell out the skirt, the hem dragged limply on the ground, getting permanently soiled. *Besides,* she reasoned as she watched her father leave, *a new dress will do wonders for my spirits.*

But when Thaddeus came back an hour later, he was empty-handed.

"No pink fabric?" Amanda asked. "I said the color didn't matter —"

Thaddeus snorted. "No material, period. Not even a scrap of burlap."

"What about the flour and other things we need?"

"The stock shelves were bare, Missy. No food, no feed, no tools, not even a twist of tobacco. Nothing. Too many trains ahead of us. If we had arrived last week . . ." He sounded disgusted, as if it were Ira Compton's fault for not getting them there sooner.

But Amanda wasn't listening. No food here meant there wouldn't be any at Fort Boise either. As the last outpost before the final lap to Oregon, Fort Boise was an important stop. How would they ever make it with so few provisions? How long could they live on a little flour, beans, and cornmeal?

"It wasn't a total loss," Thaddeus was saying, as though the lack of food supplies didn't bother him. "I met a couple of British trappers who seemed likable. Just came in from Oregon, they said. I think I'll go back there, chew the fat for a while. Maybe pick up a few pointers." For the first time in weeks, Thaddeus hummed as he dusted off his boots and reshaped his battered felt hat.

"See you later," he called to Amanda.

She was only too happy to see him go. Anything that snapped him out of his lethargy and rekindled his interest in Oregon, she was all for it. Maybe he would even eat all his supper that evening and then get a good night's rest.

When her father was an hour late for supper, Amanda left his share of beans in the pot to keep warm over the coals, believing he was probably so engrossed in conversation he had lost track of the time. But when the evening shadows deepened from purple to blue and he still had not returned, Amanda began to worry in earnest.

Slipping her shawl over her shoulders, she walked over to the Jorgenson camp. Jeb was banking the fire for the night with an iron poker. "Out for a breath of air?" he asked as Amanda approached.

"Not exactly. Jeb, is Mr. Jorgenson around? I need to talk to him."

"Well, he's in the supply wagon, talkin' to Lavinia. Is it real important?"

"My father hasn't come back from the fort. He's been there all afternoon. I was wondering if Mr. Jorgenson had seen him."

Jeb straightened, a slight frown creasing his forehead. "I don't think so. At least, he never mentioned it."

"Did Mr. Jorgenson go down to the fort?"

"Right after we got here," Jeb replied. "To see the doctor."

"Oh, that's right. Helen said there would be a doctor here. Did he see her yet?"

Jeb shook his head. "The doctor wasn't here, after all. He left yesterday, headin' up to Fort Boise to see some trapper who'd been gut-shot."

Amanda felt a sharp rush of disappointment for Helen. She had counted on seeing that doctor so much, and now she had to wait till they reached Fort Boise, four hundred miles or so from here.

"I won't bother him then," she told Jeb. "I don't want to add to your problems. Papa will probably come back any minute."

But there was still no sign of her father when she got back to camp. She banked her own fire, setting the pan of warmed-over supper to one side, casting occasional glances across the sea of white-tented wagons and the amber glow of a hundred campfires toward the gates of the fort.

Although it was late, she was too upset to go to sleep. Wrapping her shawl around her tighter, she walked across the corral, heading for the Compton wagon. She needed to see Ben, talk to him. Perhaps he had seen her father . . . but even if he hadn't, his presence reassured her.

"If you're looking for Ben, he's not there," a voice said quietly.

Amanda started, then realized she was in front of the Hawkins camp. The lone figure around the low-burning fire was Serena.

"Do you know where he is?" Amanda

asked. Serena always made her feel uncomfortable — even more so since Ben had spoken to her about his feelings for Amanda. Amanda knew the blond girl accepted the news surprisingly well, but she was not sure how Serena *really* felt.

Now Serena was shaking her head. "I'm not sure where he went. With his father someplace. Maybe down to the fort."

"Oh." Amanda stood there uncertainly, the cool air lifting the fringed ends of her shawl.

"You seem worried about something," Serena said. "Would you like to sit down?"

The offer sounded sincere, but maybe Serena was only being polite. It just was not possible that Serena would want to be friends . . . not after what had happened.

Amanda shook her head. "No, thanks. It's pretty late. I'd better get to bed or I'll never be able to move tomorrow."

Back in her wagon, she finally drifted into a fitful sleep. She awakened several times to sit up, straining to hear if her father had returned.

But when she got up the next morning, groggy and stiff, the first thing she noticed was his bedroll still in its place at the back of the wagon. He had stayed out all night.

As she was stirring the embers of coals to life, her father walked into camp. She jumped up. "Papa! Are you all right? I've been so *worried!*"

"Well, you shouldn't have," he said curtly. "I don't need looking after."

She stared at his bloodshot eyes and rumpled clothing. "I know you don't need looking after. But would it have been too much to ask if you let me know where you were going to be all night?"

Her remark hit home. Thaddeus seemed contrite. "Sorry, Missy. I should have sent word, but I got . . . tied up. Any coffee?"

"Yes. Corncakes, too? Or a little rice? We have sugar —"

He waved away her offers. "No breakfast, please. I'm not hungry. Listen, Amanda, I have to tell you something. I've changed my mind about going to Oregon."

She dropped the tin mug she used as a measuring cup. "What?" Her voice was barely above a whisper.

He paced around the fire. "I was talking to some fellows last night about California. They tell me Sacramento is a better place to settle than Oregon. The weather is milder, the trail down there not so rugged —"

"Papa! What are you *saying?*" Was he serious? Not go on to Oregon?

Thaddeus rambled on, oblivious to her horrified expression. "It'll be a relief to get out of this outfit — I never cared much for the way Ira runs things. It's not too late, you know. I heard talk of a new cutoff some people are trying. We passed it already, but we can still join up with one of the trains here and go the long way. Shouldn't take too much longer. Even if we can't join a train, the way to Sacramento is so well marked, we

245

could head there by ourselves. Imagine, Missy, in California it only rains at night and we can have bananas and oranges whenever we want."

Amanda could not bear to hear another word. Flinging down her bread pan, she fled across the corral to the Compton wagon. Ben was nowhere to be seen, but Captain Compton was hitching his team. Amanda ran in front of the lead oxen and grasped his arm.

"Mr. Compton — I need your help!"

At her urgent tone, he stopped and gave her his full attention, letting the harnesses dangle loosely from her hands. "What is it, Amanda?"

"My father wants to pull out of your train and go to Sacramento. I don't want to go to California and not with Papa babbling on about bananas and oranges —"

"Whoa!" Ira held up his hand. "Slow down. What's this about California?"

When she told him, more calmly this time, he shoved his hat back on his head, visibly concerned. "Damn! Excuse me, Amanda, but I was afraid something like this would happen. That's why I refused to stop over here more than one day."

"What do you mean?"

"I went to the fort yesterday, hoping to buy supplies. I noticed some British traders drawing people aside, telling them how strenuous the way ahead to Oregon was, how poor the land, how awful the weather and so forth."

"But *why?*"

"I'm not sure," he replied. "They're trying to head everybody off to California. My guess is that the British still want to keep Americans out of Oregon, even though it's considered American territory now, at least up to the forty-ninth parallel. Once we get some troops out here, all this confusion over who owns what should end. But for now, we have to put up with it."

Amanda was not interested in who owned Oregon. She said impatiently, "Captain Compton, can you talk to my father? He's getting ready to *leave.*"

Ira laid the harnesses on the ground. "Why don't you stay here a few minutes? I'd rather talk to Thaddeus alone."

He marched off toward the Bentley wagon. Amanda watched him, uncertainty knotting her stomach. Suppose he was unable to convince her father that pulling out of the train to strike out on his own was foolhardy? She would have to go, too, whatever her father decided, leaving Ben forever. How could she possibly leave Ben? She felt icy-numb at the thought.

"Mandy? Is something wrong?"

Ben! He crossed the ground between them in two strides, his fair hair blowing in the breeze.

Amanda ran over to him, her eyes wide. "Oh, Ben, my father wants to go to California!"

"*What?*"

"It's true. He got to talking to some men at the fort last night and now he wants to leave the train. Your father is with Papa now, trying to get him to change his mind."

Ben sighed. "Well, if anyone can turn him around, it's Pa. Sometimes I think he can ease a rattlesnake out of its skin without waking it up." He took her hand, ignoring the fact that his mother and sister were only a few feet away, packing. "Listen, Mandy, I'm sure your father just got his head filled with foolish notions. But Pa will make him see reason."

"But suppose he *doesn't* and I have to go to California . . . I'll never *see* you again!" The desperate tone in her voice revealed her feelings for him in front of the entire camp. She added hastily, "Or Helen or anybody else —"

"Try not to jump to conclusions, Mandy. You'll only get more upset."

Captain Compton came back after a while, his face grave. But when he saw Amanda, he mustered a smile.

"Papa? He's — ?"

"He's not going to California, so you can rest easy. It took a little doing, but I talked him out of it. You know that father of yours can be real stubborn when he wants to be."

Amanda nearly fainted with relief. "Oh, thank you, Captain. If you hadn't —" She stopped, suddenly aware of Ira's troubled eyes. "What is it? There's something else, isn't there?"

"I hate to be the one to break this, Amanda, but you'd find out sooner or later."

She reached for Ben's hand, the icy-numb feeling flooding back. What now?

"The reason your father stayed in the fort all last night was because he got into a poker game." Ira shifted his feet uncomfortably. "He was cleaned out."

Realization kicked Amanda in the stomach. "He lost all our money?" she whispered.

"I'm afraid so," Ira said grimly.

Amanda felt Ben's fingers tighten around her own as a multitude of emotions surged through her. Lost all their money! How could he have been so irresponsible as to let that happen?

Early in the trip, Amanda had talked to her father about his gambling.

"I'm all right as long as I stay away from a game," he had confided one night around the evening fire. "The minute I'm in the same room with a deck of cards, I'm gone." At Amanda's shocked eyes, he smiled and patted her knee. "Don't fret, Missy. That's all behind us now. Nothing ahead but a good life, I promise."

Amanda trembled with anger. He had *promised*. And now that promise was shattered, just as a sharp coyote howl shatters the peaceful dawn. Nothing but good times ahead, he had said. Would she ever be able to trust him again?

And with no money to begin a new life in Oregon, she dreaded to think what lay ahead.

Chapter Twenty

THE first day the train had left the fort, they came to the celebrated American Falls, named after a group of hapless American trappers who were sucked into the whirling waters. The falls poured over a black rock that extended over the river in a horseshoe shape, plummeting from a height of about twenty feet. Everyone was excited to see the waterfall, a sign that the formidable Snake River was not far away. Amanda refused to leave her wagon even at Helen's urging to take in the sight. Hordes of mosquitoes attacked her, nipping persistently at her hands and face until, in desperation, she drew a blanket over her head, despite the heat. *If there are mosquitoes like this in Oregon,* she thought dismally, *I'm not stopping until I'm neck-deep in the Pacific Ocean.*

Two days later the wagon party glimpsed

the Snake River for the first time, frothing wildly below through a deep gorge the water had cut between two sheer rock walls. Their trail was supposed to follow the course of the Snake, which flowed west toward Oregon for some three hundred miles. But first they had to get to the river. After hours of beating the teams and shouting till they were hoarse, the drivers managed to get the wagons through a narrow gap in the canyon walls, then up the rugged trail. Away to the south, they saw California-bound wagons struggling along the east bank of the Raft River, seeking the great Humboldt River, which would take them through the desert to their own Promised Land. Amanda watched the train diminishing in the distance, relieved that she and her father were not among them.

There was something cruel and nasty about the way the Snake River foamed and curled a thousand feet below the top of the canyon their road followed — the only water in sight, tantalizingly out of reach, tormenting people and animals alike. And there was something sinister about the black-walled gorges and bluffs that rose in every direction, as though someone had purposely thrown these obstacles in their path to further test the emigrants' already stretched endurance. *Even the Blue Mountains, which were still hundreds of miles away, couldn't be this bad,* Amanda told herself.

Thaddeus came back from talking to Henry Clay, bullwhip in hand, and announced to

Amanda and Helen, who had been talking to her, "Break's over. You girls ready to go?" Since that night at Fort Hall, Thaddeus had been quiet. He never mentioned that he had lost all his money or that he had wanted to go to California.

"Yessir." Helen climbed onto the narrow wooden seat of the Bentley wagon.

Amanda scrambled up after her, arranging her torn, dirty skirts around her feet. "You sure you feel like riding with us again?" she asked Helen as Thaddeus ordered the team to move out.

"Oh, it's grand, just you and me. And you don't harp at me to put on a shawl or go in the back and lay down. I know Mama means well, but she's always remindin' me of —" Helen's last words were lost in a fit of coughing.

Amanda nodded that she understood. Although she never mentioned it to Helen, she was secretly alarmed at Helen's appearance. She had lost so much weight her dress hung limply from her once-sturdy frame. Helen joked about it. "Look at this," she would say, gathering the folds of her long sleeves around her stick-thin wrist. "Gettin' as bony as an old cow."

Amanda tried to make light of it. "You'll gain weight when we get to Oregon." Even as she spoke those words, a nagging doubt crept in . . . *if* Helen ever got to Oregon.

For the past week, Helen had ridden most of the day with the Bentleys. Her brother

Jason walked in the dust behind the wagons now, driving the few head of cattle the Jorgensons had left. Although Helen never complained, Amanda noticed that she would suddenly sit down, her freckled face pale under the peeling sunburn, unable to finish a task she had begun. In the evenings, Helen went back to her own camp where Mrs. Jorgenson made her rest in their wagon until supper, then sending her back to bed to get out of the chilly night air. Amanda felt a rush of sympathy for her friend. Helen enjoyed working, and being sent to bed was a punishment, not a privilege.

"I wish somebody would send *me* to bed." The words slipped out before Amanda realized she had spoken aloud.

Helen seemed to know what she was thinking. "No, you don't. You may think you do because you're tired, but let me tell you, it's no fun bein' cooped up in that stuffy wagon all evenin'. I'd much rather stay up and sit around the fire talkin' with the family."

"I wish I could go to bed and wake up in Oregon," Amanda declared irritably. "I hate it here. This place gives me the creeps."

"Why? I think it's kind of pretty. At least, when we can see the river."

The elusive Snake had disappeared from view again, somewhere at the bottom of another canyon, and the area they were traveling through now was mostly desert — sand and sagebrush — with no accessible water or fuel.

"What about it gives you the willies?" Helen pressed.

"I don't know exactly. It's nothing I can put my finger on . . . but I feel like — like something is going to happen."

"You get these feelin's often?"

"No. In fact, never. I'm not a superstitious person. That's what's so odd about it." Amanda wished she could talk to Ben. If he were beside her now, he would ease her nameless doubts about the river and sinister canyons. But she had not seen him for days, and that contributed to her overall anxiety. Why didn't he come see her? Was he having second thoughts about her, avoiding her?

A few nights before, Amanda had noticed Serena coming toward her. Amanda stiffened as she always did, steeling herself for whatever Serena had to say. But then Polly had called to Amanda and Serena turned back, as though she had changed her mind. Was that why Amanda had not seen Ben . . . had he decided he cared for Serena after all?

The questions buzzed around Amanda's head like a mosquito just out of swatting range. "I'm so thirsty," she said now, wiping her forehead. "And that dry dinner we had didn't help any."

"I know," Helen agreed, tucking loose strands of hair into her sunbonnet. "We can get used to not eating, I think, because hunger pains go away eventually. But thirst seems to build until it just about makes you crazy."

254

"You should have water, more than any of us," Amanda said.

"I can wait till we make camp. Mama has some left from yesterday, but she's savin' that for the young'uns. Jason will climb down the cliff this evenin' and bring up another pail like he did yesterday."

"Jason climbs down to the river?"

"It's the only way," Helen replied. "Mama pitches a fit every time he does it, but I think Jason likes playin' hero."

Reaching behind the seat, Amanda found her father's discarded canteen. "If Jason can go down there, so can I."

"Amanda! That's a long drop! Those walls are practically straight down. You could get killed."

Amanda strapped the canteen around her waist. "If I don't get something to drink I'll die, anyway." She slid off the seat, jumping out and away from the big rolling wheels. Picking herself up, she dusted her hands on the back of her skirt and called to Helen, "Wish me luck!"

"Amanda!" Helen cried. "Come back here!" But her protests were drowned out by stomping hooves and rattling wagons.

Amanda headed away from the train toward the rock ledge that formed the rim of the gorge. Stepping up on the precipice she looked down, then gasped, nearly teetering backward. Some five hundred feet below her the Snake River rushed along, wet and delicious-looking . . . and so far down. What had she gotten herself into now? She had never really been afraid of heights, but this cliff was higher than anything she had ever seen. But the sight of water, rippling and sparkling, made it impossible to turn back now. She was thirsty enough to climb down blindfolded. She could almost taste the wonderful, cool liquid trickling down her dusty throat.

Amanda shifted her weight, assessing the situation. The hardest part would be the descent, having to climb down backward, she decided. She paced along the rim until she found a break in the rocks. Wagons were still rumbling by, but Amanda drew her voluminous skirt between her legs, tucking the end in the canteen strap. Then she dropped to her knees, facing away from the gorge, and grasped a handful of brush. Feeling with the toes of her boots, she edged over the canyon lip. Sharp rocks scraped her legs and stomach as her toes scrabbled, searching for a tiny niche. With a strange weightless feeling, as though her stomach was floating free in her middle, she let go of the brush, digging her fingers into the rockface as she inched her way down.

This was nothing like climbing Independence Rock with Ben — no gradual slope, no firm footholds. The going was painfully slow. Every muscle in her body strained with the effort; the tendons in her neck stood out as rigid as wagon bows. Her fingers were cramped into claws, every nail broken to the quick. After a few moments she dared to look up. The top of the cliff soared above her . . . she had gone farther than she thought. Beyond the ragged line of stone, the sky unfurled an endless blue banner.

Blue sky. Blue water. Blue. She was going to get water. But the world seemed reversed somehow. Which way should she climb?

Stop it, she admonished herself, facing the wall again. *Don't look up. Don't look down, either.*

Her palms bled as she continued her descent. Her cotton stockings, the last pair she owned, snagged on a pointed stone and ripped. When she thought she could not hang on another instant, she saw the bottom was within reach. She dropped the last few feet, crumpling into a heap while she struggled to catch her breath.

Gasping only made her parched throat drier, so she ran to the river's edge and swished her hands in the blessedly cool water, rinsing away blood and loose tatters of skin. Her hands stung as she cupped water and drank greedily for several moments. Nothing in her entire life had ever tasted so wonderful. At last she sat back on her heels, wiping her mouth with the back of her hand.

The walls of the gorge rose on both sides, funneling the Snake between narrow flanks. Boulders glistened blackly as the river dashed itself against them, sending up plumes of white spray. She gazed across the river, her eyes following the cliff upward.

The wall was every bit as high as the one she had climbed down but did not seem as steep. Too bad she couldn't have come down that side. Clumps of brush grew in protective ledges. Sunlight slanted across the gorge, striking shadows on the opposite wall, which indicated several level places.

Someone could be hiding there, she thought. *Watching me.* The notion was ridiculous, but it drove her into action.

She drank again, then filled the canteen. She strapped the canteen to her waist, her arms leaden. Right now she felt too weak to slip a dress over her head, much less haul herself up the wall that towered over her, taller than ever.

The water-filled canteen banged against her hip as she dug her toes into the rock and began to climb. Scaling the cliff proved to be much more difficult than going down. Although she could see ahead to pick hand and footholds, her knees and arms quivered uncontrollably. Would her strength hold out? The sun beat down upon her back, sweat ran in rivulets between her shoulder blades and off her forehead, momentarily obscuring her vision. Only a few feet from the top, her numbed hands grasped an outcropping that crumbled beneath her fingers. Her feet slipped; her body swayed uncertainly. She closed her eyes, waiting for the world to swing away from her feet, wondering how long it would take for her to fall upon the rocks below.

Suddenly strong fingers bit into her shoulders, gripping her around the upper arms, dragging her up and over the top. Amanda squirmed over the ledge on her belly and lay there, gasping as she stared unbelievingly at her rescuer.

"Ben! What are *you* doing here?"

He leaned back on his heels. "Aren't you glad I am?"

"Yes, but —" The near-fall had frightened her so badly, she could not think straight. "I haven't seen you in so long," she finished inanely.

His eyebrows lifted. "You thought I didn't care anymore, is that it?"

She fumbled with the canteen strap still fastened around her waist, embarrassed that he had read her feelings so easily. "How did you know I was down there?"

He yanked a thumb backward, indicating the end of the passing train. "I stopped by your wagon — first day I had gotten back early from scouting — and Helen was all upset. She told me where you were."

"Are you mad?"

"No. But I'm not delirious with joy, either. Mandy, do you know how I felt when I saw you crawling up that cliff? And when your feet slipped . . . suppose I hadn't been there?"

But you were, Amanda argued silently. *And you always will be, I hope.* She let his last remark go unanswered. Tapping the canteen, she said, "I had to get water. I was

259

so thirsty. And I brought some back for my fat er and Helen."

Ben rose, helping her to her feet. "I hope it was worth it, risking your neck like that. And I hope Helen realizes what a wonderful friend she has."

Days later, the wagon train halted abruptly one morning, a good two hours before the normally scheduled noon break.

"What is it?" Amanda asked her father.

Thaddeus had been called aside by Josiah Hawkins, who had ridden down the column to speak to all the drivers.

"A woman is having a baby," Thaddeus replied. "We're stopping until —" He broke off, his face reddening above his beard. A man did not discuss such a delicate topic in front of two unmarried girls.

But Helen leaned forward from the wagon seat, her face flushed with excitement. "That must be Mrs. Bell. You know, Jefferson's mother? I knew she was due in early September. Isn't it wonderful? A new member of our train."

Amanda could not imagine having a baby on the trail in a cramped wagon, with no privacy, no physician to assist. She prayed that Mrs. Bell's ordeal would be brief.

It was. Four hours later, after everyone had their midday meal and rested the teams, Captain Compton gave the signal to move out. Although the remainder of the day was uneventful, Amanda's old fears crept back.

She could not shake the feeling that something was going to happen.

"It already did," Helen said when Amanda confided in her. "Mrs. Bell had a little girl. Jefferson told me his parents named her Irene — after Captain Compton since his first name in Ira."

"I guess that's it. I had forgotten that Mrs. Bell was due to have her baby," Amanda said, hoping to end the conversation. There seemed no point in talking about vague notions.

Helen straightened beside her, listening. "What's that noise?"

Amanda had been hearing a strange rushing sound for the past hour, and wondered if it was responsible for her unexplained feelings. "You hear it, too? I don't know what it is."

The faint gushing grew louder with every mile. When Amanda jumped down to ask her father, he replied, "It's water. Shoshone Falls. We're stopping there for the night."

When they pulled into camp an hour later the roar was deafening. Shoshone Falls made the other waterfalls they had seen look like trickles by comparison. An enormous sheet of water cascaded over the lip of a semicircular rim a thousand feet wide, plunging two hundred feet into a pool below.

"Well," Amanda said, staring in awe. She had to shout to be heard over the rushing water. "At least we'll have plenty to drink for once."

After supper, Amanda wandered down to the pool, away from the noisy falls. Early twilight lay peacefully over the willow-lined clearing. Here the silvered water was so still, the trees leaning over the banks were mirrored perfectly, down to the last leaf.

Her pulse leaped suddenly. At the far end of the pool, she saw Ben bathing his pony.

She ran toward him, heedless of the loose stones that rolled under her feet. "Ben!"

He glanced up, a smile lighting his face. "Mandy! Lord, how I've missed you!" He dropped the rag he was rubbing Dancer with and waded out of the pool.

"Oh, Ben. It's been *ages* since I saw you last. Out scouting again?" He held her in his arms and, almost at once, the anxieties that had been hanging over her floated away into the lavender sky.

He nodded. "Ever since we left Fort Hall, Pa's been making me ride ahead, check out the trail. Most of the time, I don't get back to the train till after dark."

"Why do you have to be gone so long?"

He sighed, ruffling his hair with one hand. "Well, the trail through here is pretty dangerous. I have to make sure it's safe, that we're taking the best possible route."

"You know, I've had the weirdest feeling lately," Amanda admitted. "I can't describe it, but it has something to do with this area."

"Maybe it's because we're in Indian territory," he said.

Indians! The memory of that frightening

day the train was attacked leaped into her mind. She did not think she could live through another ordeal like that.

He read the fear in her eyes. "It's all right, Mandy. I know you're thinking about the time the Sioux raided our train. We are in Indian territory, but these are Shoshone. Not Sioux. Not Pawnee."

"Are the Shoshone friendly?"

"They're supposed to be. But my father doesn't believe in taking chances. We are trespassing through Shoshone land. Even though they gave us Americans permission, this is still their hunting ground. The sooner we get to the Blue Mountains, the better."

Shoshone land. That explained why Amanda felt watched the other day at the bottom of the canyon. No doubt the Shoshone were keeping a close eye on all wagons passing through. Amanda agreed with Ben's father — if they were in Indian territory, she did not want to linger any longer than necessary, either.

Ben sat down on a rock, patting the smooth surface beside him. "Tell me what you've been doing," he said. "Climbed down any cliffs lately?"

Amanda tossed her head, smiling. "One narrow escape per lifetime is enough, thank you. Helen is still riding with us. She keeps me company."

"Too bad she didn't get to see that doctor."

"She's getting worse, Ben. She can't do hardly anything without getting tired. And she coughs all the time now. I'm afraid that the doctor at Fort Boise — *if* he's there — won't be able to help her."

He picked up her hand, tracing the lines in her palm with a forefinger. "You can't think that way, Mandy. Helen is strong. She'll make it."

"But *consumption,* Ben. *Nobody* lives long with it."

"True, some people die. But some get better." He stared at her. "It's not just Helen that's bothering you, is it? Tell me."

She leaned against him. "I'm not sure. It's a lot of things . . . Helen being sick . . . not seeing you . . . and this creepy feeling that something bad is going to happen."

He was silent, waiting for her to collect her thoughts.

Amanda tossed a pebble into the pool, watching silver rings radiate in ever widening circles. "I think I've been homeless too long."

"Mandy —"

"No, really, Ben. I've been on the road longer than anyone on this train. Papa and I left Boston last October, almost a year ago. Do you realize what it's been like? A whole year of inns and endless roads, riding horses, steamboats, and now this wagon. Sometimes I think we're going to be on the trail forever. That Oregon is a dream place, like a castle in a fairy tale that the girl never gets to. I'm not even sure who I am anymore. I don't have anyplace to anchor myself to." She put her head on his shoulder.

"What kind of a home do you want?" he asked suddenly.

The question took Amanda by surprise. "I'm not sure. What do you mean?"

"Well, I know you lived in a fancy house back in Boston. Do you expect to find something like that in Oregon?"

Amanda drew her legs up under her skirt and rested her chin on her knees. A dragonfly droned low over the darkening water, its wings a blur.

"No. I was happy in that house, but only while my mother was alive. When Papa started gambling again and selling her things . . . well, if we hadn't left when we did, we couldn't have stayed there much longer." She had never told Ben about that night they had to leave Boston and he never pried.

"Would you be happy on a small farm?" Ben asked. His tone was light, but an undercurrent of something stronger throbbed in his voice. "In a cabin, not too big at first, but we could add on —" He stopped, as if he had said more than he intended.

What was he about to ask her? Amanda's heart pounded. But the moment faded as the last light in the western sky died.

"We'd better get back," he said, helping her off the rock.

They strolled slowly back to camp, leading

the pony between them, walking together but alone with their own thoughts. As they passed the Compton wagon at the head of the corral, they saw a herd of shaggy ponies tethered just outside. Fearing the worst, Amanda moved closer.

Inside the corral, dressed in buckskins and blankets, their long hair tied back with feathers, were more Indians than she had ever seen before.

Chapter
Twenty-one

AMANDA drew back in horror. Her instincts told her to run and hide. It took all the courage she could summon to whisper, "Ben, are we being attacked?"

"If we are, it's the quietest attack I've ever heard. They're just talking. I don't think Indians discuss their plans before they attack."

Amanda wanted to hit him for that, but he appeared to be right. This scene was not at all like the day when the band of Sioux tore into camp, terrorizing everyone in their path. These Indians stood in silent ranks behind one man with strands of gray woven in his long braids, who wore an elaborate headdress. The older Indian, obviously their chief, was talking to Captain Compton and gesturing with quick hands when Ira did not understand.

Bending close to Amanda's ear, Ben said in a low tone, "I think you'd better get back to your wagon, Mandy. Go around the outside of the corral." He gave her a little shove. "You'll be all right. Now hurry."

She managed to unglue her feet and stumble through the semidarkness toward her wagon. *He should have come with me,* she thought. He undoubtedly believed she had no lack of courage, but if the truth were known, she was terrified. If she came upon an Indian guard, or even a stray moccasin, she knew she would run like a scared rabbit.

She stepped over the tongue of her wagon, noting the dying embers of the fire she had left blazing merrily. Where was her father? Had something happened to him? Panic rose in her throat. Then she saw Thaddeus sitting on a log around the Lightfoot campfire, deep in conversation with Frank and Sam.

"Papa!" she cried, running over. "What's going on? Who are those Indians? Why are they here?"

In the dancing firelight, her father's face showed a glimmer of lively interest. "They are Shoshone. I think they're here paying a friendly visit."

Frank Grafius spit out a wad of tobacco, just missing Amanda's boots. "You'll find out soon enough jes' how friendly these folks really are. 'Member, we're in *their* territory and they want somethin' in exchange. I'll wager my next meal on it."

"That's no great loss," Sam said, laughing.

For weeks, everyone had been making jokes about the monotonous beans-and-bread fare.

Amanda sat down beside her father. No one seemed particularly worried that Shoshone were in their camp, but their presence made her nervous. "Well, I wish they'd go away. Why did they come here tonight?" Even at this distance, firelight flickering across so many stern faces made Amanda shiver.

"This is their country," Sam said. "I guess they can come and go whenever they please."

"You mean they'll be with us until we get off their land?" The prospect horrified Amanda.

"Mebbe," Frank replied. "But I doubt it. When they git what they come after, they'll prob'ly leave us alone."

"What *do* they want?" Amanda asked, but no one answered her.

She got up, intending to visit Polly in the Lightfoot wagon, when John Bell approached the camp. Frank and Sam stood to greet him. Thaddeus remained seated, prodding the fire with a stick.

John's first words were spoken so low, Amanda could not catch them. She moved closer to hear.

". . . negotiate for letting us cross their land," John was saying.

"What do they want?" Sam echoed Amanda's question.

John turned his hat in his hands uneasily. "I know this isn't going to be pleasant, but there isn't a whole lot we can do. We're on *their* territory. Now the chief — I forget his name — wants to sit down and have a smoke. These people set a great store by ritual, you know. We'll smoke their pipe a little, listen to the chief, then offer them presents. A few pots, knives, and so forth. Ira figures that should please them. He wants everyone to cooperate."

Thaddeus was only too anxious to comply. "Come on, Missy. Let's go through our supplies and see what we've got." He strode eagerly over to their wagon.

He acts like a little boy, Amanda thought, trying to keep up with him. *Like we're on some kind of adventure.*

"We don't have a crumb of food to spare, so stop eyeing the grub box," she told him when she entered the wagon.

"I knew I'd get a chance to use those trinkets I bought back in Independence," her father said gleefully, digging out a box from beneath Amanda's mattress. He scooped up strings of gaudy blue glass beads and coarse cambric handkerchiefs. "But maybe this isn't enough."

"Papa, we don't have a lot to give away. . . ."

He picked up one of the extra blankets folded at the bottom of her bed. "What about this? We have plenty of blankets."

"All right," she consented, even though she knew they would need every blanket they had when they reached the Blue Mountains in a few weeks.

"And this." He took Amanda's teakettle down from its hook.

"Don't get carried away, Papa. And why are there so many Shoshone? It looks like the whole tribe out there, except for the women."

Thaddeus was pawing through a box of broken tools. "Oh, I guess Indians believe in sending a large delegation to meet the wagons. Here's that hatchet. I knew it was in here." He pulled out the short-handled ax.

Amanda shivered at the sight of the gleaming blade in her father's hand, reminding her of a tomahawk. "That's the last good tool we have. Are you sure you want to give it away?"

"We don't need it anymore," he replied rashly. "And you never can tell. They might make me an honorary member of their tribe if I bring more gifts than anyone else."

With the blanket draped over one shoulder and the other offerings tucked into the box of beads and handkerchiefs, Thaddeus climbed down from the wagon. Amanda watched him hurry across the corral to join the group that was forming near the Compton wagon. There were so many men milling around, she could not find Ben. But she knew he was there — his father relied upon him more and more these days.

Since the Indians were congregated at the far end of camp, Amanda felt safe enough to walk over to the Jorgenson wagon and see Helen.

Lavinia was bundling old clothes into a sack, while Henry Clay and Jeb waited, holding a long-handled hoe and a sharp-edged pick. Jason took the bundle from his mother, then solemnly followed his father and uncle across camp to the meeting circle. Amanda could tell the boy was proud to be included in the men's activities.

Lavinia smoothed back her straggling hair, forcing a smile. "Evenin', Amanda. This is really something, isn't it?"

"I don't know. I feel kind of funny about the whole thing. I guess because I can't forget the other time." Amanda could not take her eyes off the strangers. Even though their manner was polite, she was still frightened. Stories she had half listened to came back to her: men around the campfire, talking in low voices about Indians.

"You want to see Helen? She's in the wagon, supposed to be restin', but if I know her, she's telling the little ones a story."

"Would it be all right if I visited awhile? I won't stay long," Amanda promised.

"Go right ahead. She'd love to see you."

Amanda climbed the steps, pushing aside the drawn canvas cover and calling, "It's just me."

The inside of the wagon glowed with candlelight streaming through the punched-tin lanterns. Three out of the four bunks were empty. But the bottom bunk, which

Helen shared with Ann, seemed to be overflowing. Helen was under the covers, with Martha, Ann with her doll, and Noah piled around her like pillows. Helen's face was flushed but she smiled.

"Hey there. Have a seat. There's an inch or so left at the bottom of my bed."

Amanda chose to sit on the bunk across the narrow aisle. "So that's how you've managed to keep them quiet. I wondered why they weren't outside gawking at the Indians."

"Oh, we saw 'em when they first came," Martha informed her, "but Mama made us go to bed in a hurry."

"We always have to go to bed when somethin' good happens," Noah grumbled, intent on burrowing his feet under Helen's quilt.

"Believe me, I'd rather be in here listening to one of your sister's stories than out there," Amanda told the little boy. "Indians scare me."

"Why?" Noah asked, his blue eyes round with interest.

"Because —" Amanda stopped. Why *did* Indians frighten her? Not a one had ever hurt her, and she had yet to see anyone she knew harmed by an Indian, though she had heard a lot of stories of violence. Even the Sioux that raided their wagon train that time never raised a weapon against anyone in the wagon party, even though they were being shot at. Well, then . . . what was it? "I guess because they're different," she faltered. "Not

like other people I know. They dress different, act different. . . ." Her voice died
away unconvincingly. How could she explain
feelings?

"That's no reason to be scared," Noah
announced scornfully. "*I* want to grow up
and be just like them."

"Indians scare them, too, but they'd rather
die than admit it," Helen declared. Turning her head away from the children, her
shoulders heaved as she began to cough,
unable to stop.

"Do you want some water?" Amanda hated
just sitting there helplessly.

"No. I'll be fine in a minute. It's funny. I
haven't coughed hardly at all these past few
days, but this evenin' I can't seem to quit."

"Maybe it's because the Shoshone are here.
Do you notice if you cough more when you're
upset?"

Helen looked at her with eyes that were
too bright, accented by spots of unnatural
pink high on her cheeks. "I never thought of
that. I bet you're right."

Amanda knew the bright eyes and flushed
cheeks were not a good sign. Helen was
getting worse.

Suddenly Lavinia climbed into the wagon,
her face tense.

"What is it, Mama?" Helen asked, sitting
up.

Lavinia did not reply right away but stood
there staring at her children with stricken
eyes. Amanda sensed the older woman's

fears. "Your father came back from the meetin'," she began at last. "It seems the Shoshone are chargin' a toll for crossin' their land."

"A toll!" Amanda interrupted. "What about the presents everybody's giving them? And what do Indians need with money?"

"The same thing we use it for. Buy horses, rifles, food, things from the trading posts. Evidently, they've been chargin' a fee for every train, based on how many wagons are in it. They liked the presents fine, but that chief told Captain Compton those things hardly pay for all the game we scare away."

Helen coughed again, dabbing her ever-present handkerchief to her mouth. "How much? We're kind of a small train. Shouldn't be too much."

"It is," Lavinia said. "They wanted fifty dollars a wagon at first."

Fifty dollars! Amanda's mind reeled. It might as well be a thousand. Since Thaddeus lost their savings in the poker game at Fort Hall, they did not have two coins to rub together.

Lavinia went on. "After Captain Compton convinced them that fifty dollars was an outrageous sum for poor people like us, they decided against money altogether."

No money? A tremor of apprehension rippled down Amanda's backbone. What *did* the Shoshone want?

Lavinia folded her arms tight against her body. "They're comin' into the wagons. And takin' whatever goods they need. Ira gave his permission. Wasn't anything he could do, Henry Clay said."

"Oh, Mama —" Helen gasped. Noah looked excited but Ann began to cry.

Lavinia hushed her youngest daughter. "Get dressed and we'll stand outside when . . . when they come. They won't hurt us, that's the important thing. Amanda, you're welcome to stay with us, if you want."

"I *am* scared," Amanda confessed, "but I ought to go back to my wagon."

She left, casting an anxious glance at the meeting circle on the other side of camp. It appeared to be breaking up; a number of men were on their feet.

Would her father come back and protect her while the Indians went through their belongings? she wondered, entering her wagon. She doubted it. He was probably enjoying himself too much with the novelty of smoking a pipe with them to worry about her.

What could she do? Try to hide things she did not want the Shoshone to find? Looking around her cramped wagon, she realized any attempt would be futile. Boxes could be torn open, sacks slashed, floorboards pried up. Besides, what did she own that was worth hiding? Only the clothes on her back, such as they were, and a few pots and pans.

But . . .

Opening her traveling satchel, she drew

out the enameled watch-pin that belonged to her mother, holding the small piece of jewelry in her palm. No one was going to take that from her. Next she pulled out her small leatherbound Bible and turned to the parchment page near the front headed "Family Record." Eleanor Bentley had filled in all the family history, births, deaths, and marriages, except for the final entry, which was written in Amanda's round, childish hand of four years ago: "Died, Eleanor Esther Bentley, November 13, 1842." In the back, a single pressed scarlet blossom from the bouquet Ben had given her at the hot springs still exuded its fragrant scent.

If she was going to hide these things, she had better hurry. Unfastening her bodice with trembling fingers, she pinned the watch to her chemise where it would not show, then buttoned up her dress. She could not conceal the Bible on her person, but perhaps she could bury it. She slipped out the front of her wagon, dropping to the ground on silent feet.

Hidden by the shadows of wind-tossed trees, her actions drowned out by the roar of the nearby falls, she dug a shallow hole in the sand with her hands, pressed the book into the hollow, then covered it. There . . . let anyone try to find *that*. But suppose *she* could not find it, either? It was too late to mark the spot, but she stood and judged that the Bible was buried about two and a half feet from her wagon, in line with the left front wheel.

She walked around to her camp, her heart pounding. Although she had never been successful at covering her emotions, she tried to keep her face as expressionless as possible.

Lavinia stood with Helen, who was huddled in a blanket, their arms around Martha, Ann, and Noah. On the other side of the Bentley wagon, Polly sat on the log around the fire with Sam, nervously twisting her apron strings. All around the camp, emigrants waited outside their wagons, holding onto big-eyed children. The camp was very quiet — a strained, tense silence.

The braves who had been chosen to go through the wagons came forward, while their chief and the other Indians remained with Ira.

A tall Indian, his hair tied back with dyed quills and dressed in fine deerskin leggings and a bead-spangled tunic, stalked past Amanda, not sparing her a second glance. He thrust the canvas cover aside, leaping effortlessly into her wagon. From where she stood, Amanda could see the Shoshone toss aside her mattress, rifling through the boxes underneath. Locating Amanda's travel bag, he pulled out the old riding habit she had worn to tatters on the road to Missouri, then threw the garments on the floor. He found Thaddeus's only spare shirt and tried to put it on. The shirt was far too small, but he tied it around his waist, anyway. The crate of broken tools did not interest him, nor their paltry food supplies. After giving the wagon the once-over, seeming to realize that the Bentley wagon had nothing of value, he jumped down and went to the Jorgensons' next. Two other Shoshone were already going through the supply wagon; a growing pile of goods and tools lay on the ground. The brave stormed past Lavinia and her children. Then he stopped.

Amanda's heart also stopped as the Indian stared at Ann, who tried to hide in her mother's skirts. With one swift motion, he took Ann's shabby wooden-headed doll from her. Ann's immediate reaction was to scream. Lavinia clamped her hand over her daughter's mouth, jerking her out of the Indian's reach. Ann's brown eyes were hurt and frightened as she stared at the Shoshone.

Amanda felt an unreasoning anger. Taking a doll away from a little girl just because the pickings were slim in the Bentley wagon! She guessed the Shoshone deserved compensation for having wagons rolling over their land, invading their privacy, frightening away their game. And she realized that money was not much of a substitute for having their way of life interrupted. But children should not have to pay.

Before she knew what she was doing, Amanda ran over, grabbing the brave by the arm. "Give that back! You don't want it — you're just being mean. Now give it back!" Her voice was loud and commanding, belying the terror she felt. Her bravery was hollow, temporarily buoyed up by the conviction of her feelings.

The Shoshone shook off her grasp, glaring at her with eyes like flint.

What have I done?, Amanda thought, her knees shaking. But it was too late to back down now.

"Give her back that doll," she demanded again. Did he understand English? Even if he didn't, there was no mistaking her tone.

He continued to stare at her, his unblinking gaze pinning her fast where she stood. Everyone nearby seemed to freeze. Then he looked at Ann, who was reaching for her doll. Her eyes appealed to him.

Without uttering a sound, the brave tossed the doll in the dirt at Amanda's feet and walked off, his back rigid with dignity.

The whole incident had only taken a few seconds, but it seemed an eternity to Amanda. She still could not move, but Ann broke free from her mother and picked up her doll, brushing off the dirt and crooning to it.

No one spoke for one long moment. Then Lavinia said, her voice wrung with emotion, "Lord love you, child. What a foolish thing to do. But my little girl will be grateful forever. And so will I."

Chapter Twenty-two

THE next day the entire camp was talking about Amanda's daring act. Before breakfast was finished, someone had jokingly dubbed her "Felicity's Savior" — after the name of Ann's doll. The story passed from wagon to wagon, embellished with good humor, relieving tension in the camp.

Amanda was not pleased with the attention. If anything, she wanted to shrink into anonymity, not be pointed out as "Felicity's Savior." She had not intended to grab fame for herself; she only wanted to get back Ann's doll.

Ben dropped by her camp while she was packing. "I heard about last night," he said, his blue eyes serious.

Amanda threw pans into the grub box, letting the lid slam. "I suppose you think it's funny. Everybody else does."

"Not at all. I think what you did was thoughtful . . . and stupid. Just what I'd expect from you."

She stopped to stare at him. He was the last person she thought would side against her. "I don't care what you think," she flared. "I did what I had to."

He backed away, holding his hands high in mock surrender. "Now, Mandy, don't get riled. I only meant that you acted impulsively, without considering the consequences. Like the time you climbed the cliff. Suppose something had happened to you? How do you think I'd feel?"

"Oh, Ben." She leaned against the wagon, contrite. "Sorry I snapped at you. It's just that everybody's been teasing me. There wasn't time to think about what might have happened. I know I behaved rashly . . . Sometimes I get tired of never being in control."

"What do you mean?"

She was glad of the opportunity to untangle her jumbled feelings. "Remember what we were talking about yesterday down by the falls? About not having a home for so long?"

He nodded and Amanda continued, the words rushing out.

"I was yanked across the country and never once did Papa ask my opinion about the move — like I didn't count. And on this train, we take anything that's dished out to us — awful weather, poor food, no decent clothes, wolves and mountains and rivers —"

She stopped, aware that she was rambling. "When the Shoshone took Ann's doll, it was the last straw, I guess. I couldn't let him do that. I had to get it back for her. This was a situation I could do something about, instead of standing by, watching things happen." She pushed her heavy hair off her neck. "Does any of this make sense?"

"To me it does." He flashed her an admiring smile. "You're very special, Mandy. I've always thought so, even when you used to act so bratty. But I wish you'd be more careful. Last night turned out all right, but how could you have known that?"

Amanda looked contrite. "I guess I'm just as stubborn as my father. I shouldn't complain about him."

"That's for sure. Felicity's Savior," Ben added, as if he could not resist. He ducked, laughing, when she threw a stick of wood at him.

When the train moved out again, Amanda was too busy to worry if she was the main topic of conversation. The trail moved away from the Snake River once more, down into another canyon to cross Rock Creek. The terrain was so challenging, everyone except the youngest, the oldest, and the sick, had to work, assisting fatigued teams, putting backs to wagons and pushing them up steep grades.

Amanda no longer rode in the wagon — Helen now traveled with her own family again — but walked with the lead yoke of oxen, one hand on the harness trace, ready to coax Miss Finch and Petunia when they balked at wading through boiling creeks or shied from climbing rock slides. Her arms ached from tugging the harness; her calloused palms stung from slapping Miss Finch's bony rump. At times she was even forced to grab the oxen's horns and pull them over a difficult stretch. Except for supper, meals were cold and hurried affairs, often only a hunk of dry bread washed down with leftover coffee.

How can we go on doing such hard work on so little food? she wondered one morning as she checked their dwindling supplies. *Even a piece of tough, salty bacon would taste good right now.*

They needed meat and eggs and cheese. Green vegetables and potatoes. Children on the train cried for milk, but all the cows had gone dry long ago. Amanda hoped there would be food to buy at Fort Boise. Even though they did not have any money, perhaps her father could trade for flour and beans.

"Serena still manages to hold her school," Helen observed over tea with Amanda one evening. "Martha and Ann can't wait to go over there after supper."

"I don't know how she does it," Amanda said. "I'm too tired at the end of the day to move, much less teach." She watched Serena, seated across the camp inside a circle of children, open a book and begin to read aloud.

"She must love teaching," Helen concluded.

Amanda nodded, wishing she had the nerve to go speak to Serena. Why was it she could climb cliffs and shoot a rifle, but the thought of facing those calm gray eyes turned her to jelly? Was it because the other girl had once been engaged to Ben, even if the engagement was not real? Would Amanda ever overcome feeling inferior around her?

One entire day was spent toiling out of a canyon, guided by a jagged edge of black lava like a row of sharp-pointed teeth high above. At the top, the trail crawled along the rim, while the Snake River writhed hundreds of yards below, heading south. At the steep gorge of Cedar Creek, the trail zigzagged southwest and then north, avoiding the deepest gullies and steepest cliffs, trying to find the river again.

This is worse than the long haul over the plains, Amanda decided. There they only had to contend with the heat and the monotonous road. But here, they had to struggle through strange, melancholy country from dawn to dark, up rocky embankments, down slippery slides, without a moment's rest. *No danger of falling asleep here,* Amanda thought, staring at the cindery bluffs soaring above the Snake. *I wish we could hurry out of this place. We don't belong here. . . . I get the feeling someone — or something — doesn't want us here.*

Because they were still in Indian territory, although they had not seen any Indians since the delegation visited the camp that night,

Captain Compton doubled the guards. Thaddeus grumbled that if he did not get more sleep and some food that stuck to his ribs he may as well give up, he would never last another mile. And Amanda's feeling of foreboding crept back, stronger than ever.

The Three-Island crossing gave members of the company their first break in many days. The trail wound down through a gap between the cliffs, leading them along the banks of the Snake for a mile or so, finally bringing them abreast of three sandy humps rising out of the river like the backs of whales. Captain Compton divided the company in half, ordering those in the first shift to make ready to cross, while those in the second half were told to circle and make camp as they would not cross until the next day.

Thaddeus explained the crossing to Amanda. "We can only make it over the river at this spot in early fall. Otherwise the water is too high and the currents too tricky. Between those islands is a sandy path. We start down there" — he pointed to the tip of the southernmost island — "go from that island to the head, cross the main channel to the tip of the second island, and so on till we reach the other bank."

"Why not just go right across?" Amanda wanted to know.

"We can't. The bottom shifts constantly and there are deep holes. It'll take us at least two days to get over. He's planning to hitch two wagons together and double the teams."

"Sounds complicated," Amanda said. "How come we always have to cross last?"

"For once, I'm glad," her father stated, unhitching the team. "I'm joining a hunting party as soon as I get done here. Set up camp, Missy, and have the stewpot simmering by suppertime. I'll bring us back a rabbit or else." He slapped the flanks of the cattle, sending them up the hill to graze.

"Rabbit?" Amanda could almost smell the aroma of roasting meat.

"Sam and Henry Clay and the others left a little while ago. I'll have to hurry to catch up. Mrs. Albrecht said I could borrow her mare."

Amanda hung up the chains and harnesses her father had left on the ground in his haste to get Mrs. Albrecht's horse. Meat for supper! She could hardly wait. It would not be fried chicken, but even rabbit would taste wonderful at this point.

Her father rode by the wagon, astride Mrs. Albrecht's mare, rifle in hand. "Lord, it feels good to be on horseback again!" he declared. "My feet think they've died and gone to heaven!"

Amanda smiled up at him, adjusting one of the stirrups that appeared too long. "Papa, you look just like one of those trappers we see at the forts."

And he did, with his battered felt hat face half-hidden by a bushy beard. His pulled low over his eyes, his weatherbeaten trousers, spanking new when he left Independence, were now stained and ineptly patched by Amanda, his knee-high boots mud-caked and cracked. But for all his apparent grubbiness, he had developed the keen-eyed, tough look characteristic to western men.

"A trapper!" Thaddeus echoed. "I hope not. Do I look that bad?" Above his beard, his brown eyes crinkled into a smile. "Well, I'd better get moving. See you later, Missy." He touched the brim of his hat as he clucked to the mare and rode off toward the mountains.

Amanda felt like dancing. Her father was happier than she had seen him in weeks, and she had the whole day to herself. Since she had been helping with the team lately, her own chores had piled up. She needed to air out the bedding — or better yet, find some sweet-smelling grasses to stuff her mattress.

She had dragged her mattress from the wagon and was pulling out the old corn-shuck stuffing from the muslin cover onto the ground when Lavinia strolled over, wiping her hands on her apron.

"Sure is quiet with all the men gone. Jason, too. He was tickled to death to be asked along," she said. "Changin' your beddin'? Good idea. I ought to wash sheets, but I doubt they'd be dry by tomorrow when we pull out."

"I know," Amanda agreed. "Never enough

hours in the day." She straightened, stretching to ease a kink from her back.

"I sent the youngsters berry pickin', but that leaves Helen by herself. She's not adjustin' too good to the idle life. I have to keep tellin' her to go sit, leave the work be. She's over there mopin' now." Lavinia sighed. "I don't know what I'm goin' to do with that girl sometimes."

Amanda draped her empty mattress sack over the large back wheel to air. "I'll go talk to her. I don't feel much like working, anyway."

Lavinia was right. Helen looked very despondent, sitting on a rock, bundled in a shawl cut from an old horse blanket. Her pale face lit up when she saw Amanda.

"Hey, there. Haven't seen you in a long time."

Amanda sat down beside her. "I know. I've been so busy helping Papa —"

"One thing's for sure, *I* can't make that excuse," Helen said scornfully. "Even Noah is more useful than I am."

Amanda could scarcely believe what she was hearing. What had happened to Helen's sunny nature? A twinge of guilt plucked at Amanda; she *had* been busy lately, but she should not have neglected her friend, especially since Helen had always been there when Amanda needed her.

"Come on." Amanda tugged at Helen's hand. "Let's go down to the river and watch the wagons cross."

The riverbank was humming with activity: men propping up wagon beds to ride above the water level; others chaining the wagons that were fording the narrow channel between the second and third islands, urging the doubled teams through high water. Amanda recognized Ben on Dancer, half standing in the stirrups, waving his hat to keep the lowing oxen in line.

Amanda and Helen settled in the sun and spent the afternoon watching one crossing after another and talking about their lives before they met at Indian Creek. The mountains had sketched purple shadows over the canyon before they realized how late it had become. Lavinia sent Martha down to bring them back for supper.

"Why don't you eat with us, Amanda?" Lavinia offered.

"Thanks, but Papa said he'd bring back some game. I'd better have a pot boiling before the hunting party returns."

Lavinia gave Helen a strange look before she said, "But, Amanda, the men got back over an hour ago. Jeb and Jason shot a fine brace of jackrabbit. They're skinnin' them now."

Amanda frowned, puzzled. "But where's my father? He should have come back with the others."

Lavinia called her husband. Henry Clay came from behind the wagons, a bloody skinning knife in his hand.

"This child is looking for Thaddeus,"

Lavinia said. "Did he ride out with you all?"

"Not with us," Henry Clay said firmly. "Never saw him. Are you sure he went hunting?"

"I saw him leave. He borrowed Mrs. Albrecht's horse and he went that way." Amanda pointed toward the mountains.

Now Henry Clay looked worried. "We didn't go that way. We headed downriver, to the marshes. Frank wanted to trap muskrat. When we didn't find none, we moved on to hunt rabbit."

"And you haven't seen my father all day?"

He shook his head regretfully.

Amanda raced over to her camp, in hopes that her father had come back in the past few moments and was resting in the wagon. The camp was cold and empty, the wagon just as she had left it. She ran outside the corral and up the hill to where the oxen were grazing, scanning the scattered livestock to see if he was checking on the team. Not there, either.

"Amanda." It was Henry Clay. "Come back to our camp. I'm going to ride over the river and tell Ira Compton. It's gettin' dark fast. We'd better not let this go any longer, since we're in Indian territory."

Indian territory! Amanda's blood suddenly froze. Suppose the Shoshone she had angered decided to follow the train? Suppose . . .

Henry Clay led her back to the Jorgenson wagon, then set off for the camp across the river. Amanda warmed her chilled hands at the fire, staring sightlessly into the yellow flames, refusing Lavinia's offer of rabbit stew, until Henry Clay rode up. He reined in his horse only long enough to tell her that Captain Compton had wasted no time organizing a search party. Men from both camps had volunteered and, even now, Amanda could see a line of bobbing torches, wavering toward the mountains, the direction in which Thaddeus was last seen.

It was the longest night of her life, longer than that wild and windy October night she and her father had left Boston. Then, she had no idea where her father was taking her or what would become of them. But they were still together and she knew he would take care of her, no matter what.

"Amanda." Lavinia's voice broke into her thoughts. "You can't sit outside all night. And you haven't eaten a bite of supper. Why don't you go on to bed? Take my bunk. I'll wake you the minute the search party comes back. Ben rode out with them. I'm sure he'll stop by and let you know. Now, come on."

"No." She did not look up from the leaping flames. "I'll stay here, if you don't mind. I couldn't sleep if I tried."

Lavinia sighed and left. A few moments later she dropped a thick woolen shawl over Amanda's shoulders. "Helen wanted to come sit with you, but she's coughin' so bad tonight I forbid it. But I'll stay. Reckon you could use some company."

Their vigil by the fire continued long after

frost lay thickly over the ground, bristling the trampled, cropped grass. The camp was silent, except for the unearthly howl of a wolf. Once something swooped low over the fire on huge, silent wings. Amanda was startled until Lavinia reassured her it was only an owl. *Not just an owl,* Amanda thought. *That bird was like a piece of the night . . . a warning.*

The sky was breaking in the east when Amanda, who had been dozing against Lavinia's shoulder, heard hoofbeats. She jumped up, her heart hammering, as weary riders trotted into the corral. Polly and a few other women stepped down from their wagons, their faces expectant.

Amanda forced herself to remain where she was while the searchers straggled in on lathered horses. In the pale light, the horses cast weird, long-legged shadows. The men were a decidedly grim lot. As they came closer, Amanda craned her neck, trying to find her father. Then she saw the group shift and part, making way for Ben mounted on his pony, leading another horse. A riderless horse. But no, something was draped over the saddle — something large. . . .

The ground opened beneath her feet and she was falling backward into a deep, dark pit. . . .

". . . fainted! Get some water quick!" Lavinia's voice sounded hollow, as though she were far away.

With great effort, Amanda opened her eyes. She was lying on the ground by the fire. A circle of anxious faces hovered over her.

"Papa!" She sat up, panic squeezing the life from her heart.

"Mandy." Ben put a restraining hand on her arm. "Your father —"

"He's dead, isn't he?" Her tone was flat, emotionless.

"Yes," Ben replied gently. "His neck was broken. We found the horse wandering loose near the . . . where we found your father. The horse is lame. Evidently, it stepped into a chuckhole and threw your father. We believe he died instantly."

Lavinia pressed a mug of steaming tea into Amanda's hand. "Drink this, child. It isn't much, but it'll help you feel better."

Dead . . . The word echoed in her brain. Thrown by Mrs. Albrecht's horse. She had a vague memory of shortening one of her father's stirrups . . . was it only yesterday? He never should have ridden out without adjusting the straps to fit the length of his leg. Why didn't he take five minutes to check them? As many years as he has been riding . . . *had* been riding.

She clamped her hands over her ears, dropping the cup. *Stop thinking about it!* Low voices murmured around her.

"Bury him in the morning. Keep the body in the wagon, but don't let her see. . . ."

"Tell Mrs. Albrecht her horse will have to be destroyed...."

Lavinia interrupted. "We can talk about all that later. Right now I'm putting this poor child to bed. She's been through enough for one night." She put her arm around Amanda's waist, steering her toward the Jorgenson wagon.

Amanda had a final glimpse of the blanketed bundle sagged over the saddle.

Tears blurred her vision as she whispered, "Oh, Papa. Why did you leave me?"

At the gravesite Amanda stood on wooden legs, dry-eyed, while Captain Compton solemnly intoned Scripture from the Old Testament. The words fell on her ears like raindrops. She was careful to keep her eyes averted from the body lying stiffly in the shallow grave, still wrapped in the blanket. She was glad she had not seen her father this way; she wanted to remember him as she had last seen him, sitting tall and confident in the saddle, smiling down at her, his brown eyes crinkling. An icy wind, hinting of winter and snows to come, blew her unbound hair across her face. She made no move to push the strands back.

Now everyone was bowing their heads in prayer. Across the grave, Amanda met Serena's eyes, which were soft with sympathy. In another moment, Jeb and Frank would slowly shovel clods of black dirt over the body. Amanda could not stand to see her father covered with earth, forever hidden from her sight, alone in his cold grave.

She turned to Ben, fighting panic. "I must — I have to go back to the wagon. Please come with me."

He asked no questions but walked her back to the corral, leaving her outside her wagon. "Are you going to be all right?"

"I think so. I want to be alone awhile."

"If you need anything, call me," he said, squeezing her hand.

"Thanks. I will."

She climbed into the empty wagon and sat down heavily on the boxes near the front. She never finished stuffing her mattress yesterday; the muslin sack was still airing over the back wheel.

The last thing she wanted to do now was think, but she had to. Soon the rest of the wagons would be moved across the Snake River. The company still had to push on to Oregon.

She fingered the frayed collar of Thaddeus's jacket lying beside her. Before the burial this morning, Ben had come to the Jorgenson wagon where Amanda had tried unsuccessfully to nap for a couple of hours.

"Your father had some things," he began haltingly. "I thought you'd want —"

"His jacket, please," she replied crisply. "It's warm and I — I might need it later." She had not cried and was not about to break down now.

"Certainly," Ben said. "Anything else?"

"His rifle. And hunting knife. I'll probably need those, too."

"He was wearing a nice gold watch, Mandy. Don't you want that, too?"

"No. No, leave that on — with him. He always wore it and it wouldn't be right to . . . Anyway, I don't much care what time it is."

Ben had given her a strange look, but the gun, knife, and jacket had been delivered to her wagon while she attended the brief service. Someone had piled the things neatly on top of the boxes. All that remained of Thaddeus Bentley, plus a few ragged clothes and broken tools that even the Indians had rejected.

"It's not fair!" she said aloud, pounding her fist on the crate. Her father had come into the world anonymously, a baby abandoned on the steps of the orphanage in Boston. And he went out the same way, killed in an untamed wilderness, buried in an unmarked grave, leaving behind a jacket, a knife, and a rifle. And a daughter: a girl who was not old enough to trust her own judgment yet, who missed her father so much her chest hurt with every breath she drew. Suddenly she had never felt more alone. Tears dropped unchecked into her lap.

A light knocking outside the wagon startled her. She jumped up, hastily wiping her eyes.

Ira stood by the wagon tongue, hat in

hand. "Can I talk to you, Amanda? I'm sorry to bother you. I know how you must feel, but we have to discuss arrangements."

"It's all right, Captain," she said, taking his extended hand and climbing down. "I know why you're here. It's about our wagon — my wagon — and what I'm going to do."

"Practically everyone in the train wants you to join them, including myself, but Lavinia Jorgenson put in the strongest bid, with Polly Lightfoot a close second."

"I don't understand," Amanda said. "They want me to travel with them?"

"And be a member of their family," Ira emphasized. "I can't expect you to make such a decision right off, but if you could tell me what you're thinking —"

"I've already made up my mind," she told him firmly. "I know Lavinia and Polly — and you — mean well and I appreciate the kindness, but I don't want to be a burden to anyone. I'm driving my wagon the rest of the way to Oregon."

He could not have been more surprised if she had declared she was flying to the moon. "Amanda, I don't think you realize —"

"I can do it. I drove our wagon when Pa — when my father had mountain sickness."

Ira shifted his weight from one foot to the other. "Yes, I know. Ben told me how well you managed your team. But, Amanda, we were on mostly level terrain back then. Nothing like what's around here. And up ahead, the Blue Mountains — a young girl, no matter how determined, just can't do it."

Amanda drew herself up to her full height. "I have to go on, Captain. It's what my father would want, I know. The Bentley wagon joined up with your train at Indian Creek back in Missouri and we've gotten this far. The Bentley wagon will finish this journey if I have to hitch myself to the team."

"You won't have to go that far, Mandy."

She turned to see Ben walking up."

"I warned you she'd be stubborn," Ben said to his father. "She wants to go on by herself, doesn't she?"

Ira spread his hands in a gesture of helplessness. "See if you can talk sense into her."

"Ben, I don't want —" she began.

"It's all right, Mandy. Nobody is going to take your wagon away or make you travel with another family."

"You understand," she said in obvious relief. But somehow that should not come as a surprise to her. Ben had always been on her side.

"Yes, I do." He spoke to his father again. "If some of us pitch in, we can help Mandy drive her wagon over the worst. And I'm offering my services."

Before Ira could give his consent, another voice piped. "Me, too. I want to help Amanda."

Helen stood behind the men, her arms folded defiantly. "If he gets to help, you have to let me, too, Amanda."

"Oh, no, you're not." Lavinia overheard

her daughter and came running over. "Helen, you know you're not well —"

Helen whirled on her mother, her blue eyes glistening with newfound determination. "*I am*, Mama. Amanda needs our help. She can't do everything alone. And if I'm goin' to die, what difference does it make if I lay around waitin' for it or work till it's time?"

A shocked silence followed as Helen and her mother stared at one another. At last Lavinia spoke, "All right, young lady. Have it your way. But I'm tellin' you now, you ride two hours for every hour you walk with Amanda. Understood?"

Helen hugged her mother, then Amanda.

Captain Compton clapped his hat on his head. "I've never seen such a bunch of stubborn young people in all my days. All right, you three can drive the Bentley wagon. I'll let John Bell take over the scouting. And I'm sure Frank Grafius and Jeb Jorgenson will be happy to assist from time to time."

Everyone left to hitch their teams, leaving Ben and Amanda alone.

"It'll work out," he reassured her. "I promise. We'll get to Oregon, you and me together."

Amanda was not so sure. She clung to his words like a drowning person reaching for a rope, desperately needing to hear them. He drew her to him, and his gentle kiss eased a little of the pain and renewed her strength for the difficult days ahead.

Chapter
Twenty-three

THE strength that held Amanda together after her father's funeral gave out when they hit the trail again. It was as though someone else took over her mind and body. Beset with uncertainties and anxieties, she was afraid to go on, too weak to turn back.

Although Ben and Helen were with her nearly every day, Amanda did not feel like talking. None of the emigrants socialized much; it was enough to keep up with the grueling pace Captain Compton had set in order to get to Fort Boise without further delay. Everyone was up before dawn and on the road all day, with only the briefest noon break, until they stumbled into camp long after dark.

Under lowering skies, the company finally reached the Boise River. It was some sixty yards wide, teeming with salmon. The fort was nestled in the triangle where the Boise River met the Snake River. The clouds broke away long enough to let bright sun shine on the three log buildings enclosed in a pole stockade fence. There were few supplies to be purchased at the post, as most of the emigrants had expected, but the doctor from Fort Hall was still there. He was a kind man, visiting all the wagons in turn to answer questions and treat anyone in need.

Ben was only able to buy a little beef jerky for Amanda. No flour, rice, beans, or cornmeal. "Sorry," he said, handing her the greenish-tinged meat strips. "I'll try to catch you a fish for supper."

"I don't have any money," she told him, unpinning her mother's watch from her bodice. She handed it to him. "Will this do?"

His eyebrows drew together in a flash of temper. He waved away the jewelry. "No, it won't. Mandy, will you stop playing the heroine?"

"What do you mean?"

"You act like every little thing somebody does for you is charity."

"I have to make it on my own, as much as I can. I thought you understood that." She started to walk away, confused and hurt by his sudden anger.

He caught her hands, pulling her back. "I want to help you, Mandy. Why don't you let me? And Helen, too? The other night she asked you to join her family for supper and I heard you turn her down, for no reason."

"I had to," Amanda said. "Lavinia has eight mouths to feed. She doesn't need another one."

"It's not just the food, Mandy. You've been acting strange lately. I know you're not over your father's death yet. But you aren't yourself these days. Do you want to talk about it?"

Instead of replying, Amanda made a big show of storing the beef in the grub box. Ben grabbed her arm, forcing her to look at him.

"What is the *matter* with you?" he insisted.

"I don't know!" she wailed. "I feel so . . . so *helpless*. I *hate* these mountains, they make me feel trapped —"

"We're *not* trapped. We'll be out of here in a few days."

"Then there's the Blue Mountains," she countered. "And more mountains in Oregon and heaven knows what in between. I'm so *tired*. The wagon's falling apart. Two of my oxen are lame —"

"You think you're alone?" he interrupted roughly. "What do you suppose that doctor is doing right this minute? Examining Helen? Setting the Smith boy's arm? Possibly. But he's also looking in on Mrs. Bell." Mrs. Bell's baby had died suddenly last week. The bereaved woman had refused to allow her infant girl to be buried, to the horror of her husband and the rest of the company. "Or Harrison Pilcher, who got run over by his wagon. He'll never walk again, a young man with a family. Who will till his land when he gets to Oregon? Don't you think those people want to give up? But they go on, Mandy. They have to. And so will you. Now, stop feeling sorry for yourself."

She was silent, shocked at his onslaught. Ben had never shown her anything but kindness. Was this a harsh side of him she should be wary of?

In a more gentle tone, he added, "Face facts, Mandy. The way ahead will be tough, maybe worse than what we've been through already. But it *will* come to an end. We *will* get to Oregon. Just take each day as it comes — don't borrow trouble."

When she thought it over, she realized what he said was true. There was not a living soul in the wagon party who had not endured hardships these past, long months. And some, like Lavinia and Mrs. Bell and Mrs. Albrecht, had suffered great losses. And herself. After all, she had lost her father and was alone.

Helen came over later that day, bursting with good news. "The doctor said I should get better, with lots of rest. And Oregon's mild winters."

"That's wonderful," Amanda said, but in the back of her mind she doubted Helen would make it.

The next day they left Fort Boise. The threatening skies gave way to rain, not a steady drizzle but a gullywasher that hampered the wagons as they crossed the Snake again, heading for the snowcapped line of Blue Mountains.

Ben and Amanda drove the Bentley wagon, both swathed in huge sheets of oilskin. Water dripped off the brim of Ben's hat, and his boots sucked mud with every labored step. Amanda worried that he would come down with pneumonia. The oilskin kept them relatively dry but did not keep them warm. Amanda wore her father's jacket beneath the waterproof cloth and his old traveling boots over her own shoes. But her fingers became so numb she had to blow on them to feel the reins in her hands. Helen could not walk outside in the rain but rode in the wagon, which, she commented wryly, was not much better.

By the time the rains let up, they were well into the Blue Mountains. The trail through the mountains was the worst they had ever seen, up and down, through enormous potholes, twisting around stumps, fallen trees, and boulders. They were now more than eighteen hundred miles from Independence. But winter was breathing down their necks and they had to push on.

For Amanda, the long, cold nights were the worst to endure. Often she sat up in bed, staring into the inky darkness, remembering, the blankets bundled around her, while the wind howled and rocked the wagon. She remembered how her father would come in to get his bedroll and wish her good night before he bedded down under the wagon. She remembered their talks around the campfire as he reminisced about his own past. Her memories led to Boston and her mother and her childhood.

"Amanda, you haven't said two words all day," Helen commented. "You hardly ever talk anymore. You can't go on like this."

How true, Amanda thought. *I can't.*

It was mid-September and the wagon party had spent the night at the top of a mountain. There was no grass for the animals: Only mountain laurel grew this high and that was poisonous to the cattle. No game to hunt. No water. Sometime during the freezing night an Arctic wind brought snow, dusting the camp powdery white. *Winter comes early to these parts*, Amanda remembered as she tried to find dry wood for a fire. But there was no time for a hot breakfast, everyone was so anxious to head down the mountain. They eventually left the snow behind, but the bitter cold stayed with them.

"Talk to me," Helen said again, drawing her hooded cloak tighter.

"I'm cold. I don't feel like talking."

Amanda knew she was separating herself from the rest of the wagon train, just as she had in the beginning. But the reasons were different now. She cared about them all; she didn't feel better than them; she didn't look down on them. It was just that since her father's death, she felt partly dead, too.

"Then why don't you go walk with Ben?" Helen's voice interrupted Amanda's thoughts. "He's been leading the team by himself all morning."

But Amanda did not want to face his accusing eyes, that set mouth and firm chin telling her louder than any words how disappointed he was with her.

I can't help it, she reasoned with herself. *I know what he wants me to be, but I'm not that person anymore. I'm not anything, I might as well be —*

She did not really want to be dead, but her heart and mind felt as cold and numb as her feet stumbling along the hard ground hour after hour.

"Amanda, if you don't want me here, I'm goin' back to my wagon," Helen said quietly.

When Amanda did not protest, Helen gave her a long, searching look, then walked past the plodding team, past Ben, to her own wagons up ahead. Amanda watched her, unable to call her back.

A sudden jolt jerked her around. The wagon had hit another hole, this time snapping the front axle. The front wheels collapsed at crazy angles. Ben halted the team and came back to survey the damage. His jaw tensed as he knelt, running his hand over the shattered wood.

"This is bad, Mandy. A broken axle can take all day to repair sometimes. And then it might not hold."

"You can fix it, can't you, Ben?" She

could not bear the thought of abandoning her wagon here. "I don't want to travel with other people."

"I'll try, Mandy. But I can't promise it'll work. Would it really be so bad to go with another family like the Jorgensons?"

She did not answer him. She seemed to have run out of answers. Instead, she climbed into her wagon and began unloading boxes to the ground. She had seen enough axle repairs to know the entire wagon bed had to be emptied first.

"Leave that to me, girl," Frank Grafius said, taking the box of broken tools from her. "That's too heavy for you. Let me git the rest."

"Well . . ." She stood by uncertainly.

"Whyn't you run along? Ben and me will have your rig fixed in a jiffy."

"If you're sure I can't do anything —"

"*No*, you can't," Ben said curtly, coming up behind her. "Go visit Helen. Or Polly. Or take a walk. You'll just be in the way here."

She brushed by him, tears stinging her eyes. She ran away from the train, stumbling over branches the wind had ripped from the trees the night before, the splintered end showing new wood like a fresh wound. That was exactly the way she felt, torn, confused, her thoughts as scattered as the drift of leaves the wind whirled in front of her.

She stopped running when she came to a sharp drop down the side of the mountain, spiked with evergreens. Her feet kicked a pebble that bounced over the edge, striking an outcropping far below. Amanda gulped, stepping backward hastily. If she fell down there, no one would ever find her. She climbed up on a large boulder, out of the wind, to get over her fright. When her knees stopped shaking, she found she was not ready to go back. Not yet.

A *caw-cawing* sounded overhead. Tilting her head back, she saw a large flock of crows, at least fifty, flying southward, sharply etched against the wind-spun clouds. From this viewpoint, the birds did not appear to flap their wings up and down, she observed, but rather, spread them open, then folded them close to their bodies. Open, close. Open, close. Even though the motion was very swift, Amanda wondered how the birds stayed aloft during the split second their wings were closed.

Behind her, something thrashed in the underbrush. Amanda turned, astonished to see Serena Hawkins coming toward her.

"Amanda!" Serena called as soon as she was in earshot. "I stopped by your wagon. Ben told me you went this way. Your wagon is almost fixed."

Amanda watched the slim, blond girl approach the boulder before she said, "I can't believe you'd come all the way out here to tell me that."

"You're right," Serena admitted. "I've been wanting to talk to you, but it seems like we've all been so busy lately. I see you across camp, but every time I'd go to speak to you, my mother would ask me to do something."

Amanda looked at her but said nothing. She came out here to get away from the people she had lived with continuously for over four months and she was not sure she wanted that privacy invaded.

"I was sorry to hear about your father. I know you miss him very much."

Amanda picked at some gray-green lichen growing down one side of the boulder. "Yes. I do." She was puzzled. What else did Serena want besides offering her condolences? She had just seen Ben. Did he mention to Serena how upset he was with her? Maybe Serena sensed Ben's disappointment in Amanda.

"Can I join you?" Serena asked. Amanda nodded, noting enviously how the other girl managed to climb up without showing an inch of stocking. Always the lady.

"Nice view." Serena gazed at the fir-covered mountains around them, craggy, majestic. "Did you ever think we'd see land like this? It's so beautiful here. I marvel at it every day, don't you?"

"I marvel I can get up every day," Amanda said bitterly.

"That reminds me of something else I wanted to tell you."

"You wanted to talk about getting up in the morning?"

Serena smiled. "No. Well, yes. What I mean is, I really admire what you're doing.

Going on alone. Driving your own wagon. You have so much courage."

Amanda shook her head, dismissing the compliment. "Not really. I don't know what else to do. I have no choice."

"Yes, you do," Serena contradicted. "Everyone I talk to says how much they admire that spunky Bentley girl —"

"Is that what they're calling me now?"

"— and how they'd like to have you travel with them. Amanda, when people talk about you driving your own wagon or standing up to the Shoshone, they're not gossiping. You give people hope, that we can do anything we have to. It helps them through the hard times."

Amanda could not believe it. "Why are you telling me all this?"

Serena drew her knees up under her skirt like Amanda, clasping them with her arms. "Because I wanted you to know how people feel. I thought you deserved to know. And . . . there's something else." Her blond hair, fine as cornsilk, tore loose from the netted bun, fanning across her delicate features. "I wanted you to know my feelings, too. About you and Ben."

Amanda waited, her heart quickening.

"I'm happy for you two. I truly am. You see, since I've been on this journey, I've had time to think . . . about my life. And Ben's. And what we both want. Back in Illinois, my parents were after me to get married and settle down."

"That's what Ben said."

"His parents felt the same way about him. I didn't want to get married. Not yet, anyway. I was only seventeen. And I loved teaching. But I've been raised to believe that parents know best, so Ben and I got engaged."

Amanda nodded. Ben had already told her all this.

"Since we've been on the trail," Serena went on, "I've been able to talk to my parents. Really talk, for the first time. When I began my little evening school, my mother told me she could see how much I enjoyed teaching and that if that was what I wanted to do, I should do it."

"Is that when you decided you didn't want to marry Ben?" Amanda asked.

"Oh, Amanda. Ben and I never really wanted to get married. The whole engagement was a big mistake. There was nothing between us, I promise you, but friendship. Nothing more. We were unfair to each other because we never revealed our true feelings ... until Ben met you. And I was unfair to both Ben and you, hanging on to him when I knew he didn't want to be obligated to me anymore."

Amanda felt a rush of embarrassment. A few moments ago she was worried that Serena was coming to tell her that she and Ben were going back together. She appreciated Serena's honesty.

"Thanks for telling me this, Serena. I know how hard it must be."

"Ben's always cared for you, Amanda. Ever since that day in Independence when his wagon nearly ran you down."

"He told you about that?"

Serena's smile expanded into a grin, crinkling her nose. "Oh, yes. He told me all about this silly girl standing in the middle of the road. And how her green eyes flashed fire at him. I knew then he had lost his heart."

Amanda laughed, then felt like crying for some reason. "I don't know what to say."

Serena held out her slim white hand. "Just say we can be friends."

Amanda took her hand. "You're going to be a wonderful teacher. How lucky those children are. I'd be honored to have you as my friend." Then she hugged her.

The two girls laughed as they both brushed away the tears misting their eyes.

"We'd better get back. The wagon train will be starting up," Serena said, sliding off the rock. "Coming?"

"No. I'll be along in a minute."

Amanda sat there, resting her chin on her drawn-up knees. Serena's visit had struck a chord within her. Serena was right. Feelings must be brought out in the open, no matter how much it hurt. Tears pricked her eyelids, not the gentle tears of discovering a friend but the hot tears that signaled a real cry.

"Oh, Papa!" she sobbed. The wind ripped the words from her, blowing them over the side of the mountain. Her grief, which had been pushed way down deep where she would not have to deal with it, spilled forth.

She collapsed on the rock, sobbing uncontrollably. And then, miraculously, Ben was there, holding her.

"Oh, Mandy," he said against her hair. "I was waiting for this to happen. You've been holding it back so long."

"Ben, he's *dead*. He's dead! He'll never come back. I'm *alone*," she wailed as the pain bottled up for the past weeks poured out of her.

"You're not alone, Mandy. Not while you have so many people who care about you. Not while you have me."

She sat up, her sobs subsiding. "Ben, it hurts so much. Why didn't it hurt before?"

He wiped away her tears with his fingers. "Because you didn't let it. Just like you wouldn't let Helen and me get close to you."

"Helen . . ." Amanda sniffled. "I've been so awful to her. And you, too. Will you ever —"

"It's all right, Mandy," he reassured her. "You're going to be all right now."

Before they left the clearing, Amanda looked up. The crows were gone. The sky was empty except for a few high, thin clouds. But she figured if the birds could stay aloft, so could she.

Chapter Twenty-four

AMANDA turned the sack inside out, trying to dislodge any flour caught in the seam. A small shower of the white grains sifted down, barely powdering the bottom of the bread pan. In the dimming light of dusk that fell swiftly in the Cascade Mountains, she stared unbelievingly. Not enough to make one biscuit. Without even looking, she knew the grub box was empty — no beans, no rice, no cornmeal. None of the beef jerky Ben had bought her at Fort Boise. Only a little coffee.

What had happened to the careful calculations her father had made in Independence? Two hundred pounds of flour per person and so on? She was not supposed to run out of food. But the empty sack dangling from her numb fingers told no lies. She tossed the cloth bag to one side of the trail. Then, because she was so tired of looking at other people's castoffs littering the road, she picked it up and threw it into her wagon.

Who could she blame for running out of supplies? No one but herself. After all, she had been in charge of the cooking. She remembered the early days on the trail when she would scorch a whole pan of bread, scrape out the mess and make a new batch, never giving a moment's thought to the days ahead, to the day when she would be scraping the bottom of the barrel, literally. But her food was not all wasted. Just last week she had given a half a sack of beans to Lavinia, who was also short on supplies. How could she refuse, after all the Jorgensons had done for her? And there was the sugar she let Polly have . . .

Don't think about food, she admonished herself. *It'll only make you hungrier.*

Sighing, she located the hidden cache of sea biscuits Thaddeus had purchased for emergencies. There were only four of the hard, tasteless crackers left. Gnawing on one, she hung a pot of coffee over the fire. She needed something hot to thaw her frozen blood, get it circulating again. She sat down near the blaze, grateful that they had plenty of wood at least, and held her chilled fingers as close to the flames as she could without setting her gloves on fire.

Ben had given her the gloves the week before — an old pair of his mother's, with the fingers cut out enabling Amanda to drive her wagon. The gloves helped protect a large blister on her right palm that refused to heal. He also gave her a small tin of rose salve, which she smeared on the ugly sore twice a day.

What a sight I must look! she thought, gazing ruefully at her silk dress, filthy from the hem to her knees. The sole of one of her hand-me-down boots from Helen flapped up and down like the tongue of a panting dog. The other boot had split open along the side, exposing most of her stockinged foot. On top of her dress she wore her father's jacket, a necessity in the late-October cold of the mountains. The jacket was so big, she had to roll back the sleeves into deep cuffs. On windy days like today, she wrapped her old black shawl around her neck and ears, like a monk's hood. And though there was plenty of clear-running water, it was far too icy to take a bath or wash her hair. Wistfully, she recalled the mahogany wardrobe back in Boston filled with dresses, and the little lingerie chest packed with delicate, lacy undergarments, the rows of kid boots and satin slippers lined up on the wardrobe floor, the scented box she kept her handkerchiefs in, and the cut-glass bottles of lemon verbena and lavender water on her dressing table, all left behind. How she longed to be pretty again. *What must Ben think when he looks at me?* she wondered, then consoled herself with the fact that none of the girls on the train were any better dressed or groomed than she.

The coffee was ready. She poured herself a mug, dunked the last sea biscuit in the hot liquid, and ate it slowly, thinking over the events of the past few days.

She was still hungry, but she was not alone. Everyone in the wagon party was nearly out of food. And their pinching stomachs and the hungry eyes of their children only served as a constant reminder that they were in the harsh Cascade Mountains, near Meek's Terrible Trail, where only the year before seventy-five emigrants had starved to death.

The awesome Cascade Mountains . . . Amanda could scarcely believe they were actually there. So near to Oregon City, and yet so far.

Several days ago, when the wagon train reached the Columbia River, amid much rejoicing, Ben came to Amanda. "My father is putting a vote to the drivers. If you'd like, I'll go to the meeting and cast your vote."

"What are we deciding?" Amanda hoped it was to stay here. The land was level, and there were a few crude cabins where earlier emigrants had decided to settle.

"Whether to go the rest of the way to Oregon down this river —"

"All the way?" She stared at the wildly turbulent Columbia hurtling past its banks, slamming against boulders in the riverbed in plumes of white water.

He nodded. "We'd have to build rafts. Or

knock down our wagons and float them downstream."

"How far?"

"About sixty miles. Part of the way we may be able to drive the wagons. But we couldn't get started right away. There are wagons ahead of us. Pa says it would be about a ten-day delay and he doesn't think we can hold out that long."

The beginnings of a headache pounded Amanda's temples. "What's the other choice?"

"Over the Cascades. There's a road through there now." He pointed behind him where fir-covered mountains rose above pale blue mists. One mountain dwarfed the others, soaring skyward so high, it seemed to be floating above the ground. Mount Hood.

A story she had heard around the campfire one night came back to her. "Didn't something awful happen on the road?"

"You're thinking about that trapper, Stephen Meek, who took two hundred families over the mountains last year. They were trying to use abandoned Indian trails, but they veered too far south and got lost. Some of the people died. A search party from Oregon City helped the others get through."

"*Some* of the people?" Amanda echoed. "It was seventy-five, wasn't it? Almost *half* starved. And they were in those mountains for *two months*." She pressed her hands to her throbbing temples. "Some choice. You're telling me we either have to raft down that horrible river and probably drown. Or climb over those mountains and starve!"

"You didn't let me finish." His voice held an edge of sharpness. "The road we'd take over the Cascades is not the same way Meek's people went. This one is supposed to be shorter. Just finished this year by a man from Illinois."

But she could not make a decision these days, not when she was always cold and hungry and tired. "Ben, why couldn't we have stayed at that place in the middle of the Blue Mountains? You remember, before we hit the snow? What was it, the Grande Ronde?"

The Grande Ronde was a beautiful valley some twenty miles across, an emerald cup held in the lap of the majestic Blue Mountains that tempted many of the emigrants to stop right there and go no farther.

"Amanda, you know why. Do you have money or supplies to build a home there? And where would you get any? Fort Boise was miles back and Oregon City still miles ahead. Be sensible. Now, do you want me to vote or not?"

She shook her head, tears of confusion welling. "I don't know. I hate water. And I've always despised those river crossings. Over the mountains, I guess."

"I think that's wise," he agreed. "The mountains seem the safest bet."

"Oh, Ben, how much farther to Oregon City?" She felt fragile and defenseless just then, like an egg about to be stepped on. All her inner strength seemed to have drained away.

He held her, smoothing her hair with one hand. "Only a couple hundred miles. We'll be there before you know it, Mandy."

She wiped at tears with the back of her hand. "I'm sorry, Ben. I still get scared —"

"We all do." He lifted her chin. "Can you give me a smile? Come on, bigger than that. That's my girl. I'm off to the meeting to put in the Bentley vote."

As it turned out, all the drivers opted for the land route. At first, ascending into the Cascades was not as bad as Amanda thought it would be. There was plenty of water and timber for fuel. Although game was abundant, most men had run out of ammunition and no one had the time to set traps. But the children picked the succulent fruit of black haw trees and huckleberries from the bushes lining the trail. Amanda gratefully accepted the small baskets of berries Martha gave her. The fruit was sweet and tasty, although not very filling. Still, it was better than nothing.

After crossing the John Day River, the Compton party arrived at the start of the Barlow toll road, which would lead the emigrants around the south shoulder of the mighty snow-mantled Mount Hood.

"You mean we have to pay to use this awful road?" Amanda cried indignantly when Ben informed her.

"Don't worry. My father paid for your wagon," he said.

"But —"

He put a finger to her lips, hushing her protest. "Now don't fly off the handle about accepting charity. He said it was the least he could do to help since your father died. He feels responsible, I think."

"Why? It wasn't his fault my father got thrown from his horse." Her throat constricted, but she was finally able to mention her father's death without breaking down.

"He feels responsible for everybody in the train, Mandy. You know, I was looking at him last night — he's really aged since we left Illinois. He has lines in his face I'd never noticed before. So many people depend on him to get them to Oregon. They trust him and he won't let them down, no matter what."

Some people trusted that Stephen Meek to lead them over the Cascades, and look what happened, Amanda thought, but realized the comparison was unfair. Ben's father always seemed to act in the best interest of the wagon party.

Barlow's Road — a two-wheeled track that twisted through a dense forest of pines, fir, cedar, and redwood — scarcely deserved to be called a road. The builder had slashed a narrow path barely a wagon's width around trees, rocks, and deadfall, zigzagging up the mountain. Amanda had never seen trees like these: Some had trunks as thick as the row houses back in Boston, soaring to heights that nearly blocked out the sky and gave her a crick in her neck.

On the first evening they camped near a swift-running stream, all the wagons strung out in a line as there was not enough room to circle. Ben unhitched Amanda's team, then left to see if his father needed him for anything. Amanda built a fire in the gathering darkness and set about fixing supper. That was when she discovered she had run out of food, except for the four crackers.

Ben came back to find her staring into the flames, an empty tin mug lying on the ground by her side, the bread pan with its dusting of flour still sitting on the grub box.

"Had anything to eat?" he asked.

"A few crackers." She pointed to the bread pan. "I was going to make biscuits, but I don't have enough flour. I'm all out. Did you eat?"

"My mother saved me a little rice. Barely filled the chinks in my stomach. Listen, there's no grass for your team. Can I give them this flour? If they don't get something to eat, we can forget about them pulling your wagon tomorrow."

"That little bit of flour won't feed six animals, Ben."

He went over and picked up the pan. "Four. You've only got four animals left."

"Four? What?"

"That cow died. The one that's been ailing for days. Dropped dead in the stream when it went to get water."

"And which other? Not Miss Finch?" Amanda had grown terribly fond of the lead ox.

"No," Ben said quickly. "Her yoke-mate. Actually, it's not dead yet, but it will be before morning."

"Poor Petunia." She still had difficulty dealing with her animals dying.

"Sorry, Mandy. I know how you feel about your team. I hope another cow can perform as well as Petunia did. That Miss Finch is kind of hard to get along with."

"You can train the cow, can't you, Ben? I don't know what I'd do without . . ." Her voice trailed off. Something in his face made her ask, "What's wrong?"

"I won't be able to drive your wagon for a few days, Mandy. My father wants me and John Bell to ride on ahead. Get some help."

"I don't understand. Why can't Mr. Bell go alone? And where are you riding to?"

"Oregon City. To bring back a relief party. It's too dangerous for one to go alone. If anything should happen — well, the others could still get through."

Amanda's heart plummeted. She stared at him, her green eyes wide. Words could not describe her absolute despair. No food, only four animals left to pull her wagon, and who knew how long they would last with no grass? And now Ben was leaving her in this wilderness. How could she go on?

Under the cover of darkness, he drew her to him and kissed her. "Be strong, Mandy," he said, as if reading her thoughts. "I'll be back soon. And we'll go on, as we planned, and pick out our land."

Our land. How wonderful that sounded. A real home again, one that she and Ben would build together. If only this nightmare were over and they could begin their new life.

"When are you leaving?" she asked in a small voice.

"In the morning. Before the train pulls out."

"So I won't see you?"

"No. But I'll give you this to remember me by." He kissed her again, then walked back to the Compton camp.

Amanda was unable to sleep that night, shivering in bed even though she had every blanket and rag in the wagon piled on her, even the empty flour sack. Sometime toward morning, it began to rain. She finally fell asleep, wondering if Ben had taken his oilskin with him.

The day broke gray and drizzly. Amanda got up reluctantly, every bone in her body creaking in protest. She did not want to hitch up her team, what was left of it, and endure another day forcing the exhausted animals to haul her wagon up the mountain. She wished she could stay in bed all day and dine on fried chicken and hot rolls with butter. She wished the rest of the wagon party would go away, the trees disappear, the trail dissolve.

Then she heard Jason outside her wagon, calling her to come over to their camp as soon as possible. She splashed cold water on her face from the water bucket, buttoned her boots enough to keep them from falling off her feet, then ran over to the Jorgenson camp, afraid something had happened to Helen. As it turned out, Mr. Jorgenson wanted to see her.

Henry Clay bade her a brisk good morning, then stated his business. "Ira Compton says the way ahead is goin' to be rough. He's advisin' us to pair up wagons and double-team."

"Won't that be awfully hard on the animals?"

He nodded. "But it's the only way. These mountains are worse than the Rockies. I was wonderin' if you'd like to hook up with us. Sam Lightfoot said he would join up to our supply wagon. We'll put your wagon first and your team last to give them a rest. You won't have to worry about drivin'. Jeb and me will take care of everything."

She could not believe her good fortune. Not have to drive — the answer to her prayers! Impulsively, she hugged Henry Clay. "Oh, Mr. Jorgenson. Thanks very much!"

The wagon party did not move out until thirty-six wagons were chained together — only the Compton wagon at the head of the column rode alone — and the double teams were hitched. By then it was nearly noon. Because the road wound nearly straight uphill, no one could ride in the wagons. Children had to be carried, older people helped over the rugged trail.

Amanda took Ann's hand and walked beside her wagon, which towed the Jorgenson sleeping wagon. Behind came Sam's wagon, pulling the Jorgenson supply wagon. Lavinia walked with Noah, while Helen followed with Martha. The going was indeed rough. Logs and fallen trees lay in their path. And the woods were so dense, no one dared leave sight of the road for even a moment.

"I'm hungry," Ann piped after they had hiked for an hour. "I didn't have no breakfast."

Amanda's heart tugged as she looked down into the little girl's brown eyes. What a dreadful thing to see a child go hungry. She lifted Ann over a rotted log, noting the ever-present wooden doll clutched in one hand.

"What about Felicity?" Amanda asked. "Did she have breakfast?"

"No."

"I'll bet she's hungry, too. But she can wait till noon. Then we'll eat, all right?" Actually, Amanda did not know if there was anything to eat that day or not. She hated lying to Ann, but what choice did she have? How could you tell a child to ignore her rumbling belly?

In addition to suffering from hunger pangs, Amanda was also freezing. None of the women on the train were adequately dressed for such bitter cold weather, with their worn cotton dresses and thin woolen shawls — unlike the men who had heavy trousers, boots, and coats, Amanda felt a little guilty wearing her father's warm jacket.

The rain tapered off, and the sun peered wanly through the clouds, but it was still bitterly cold. After a while, Lavinia made her husband halt the team to get extra clothing for the children. She came out of the sleeping wagon, her arms filled with odd garments that the Shoshone Indians had overlooked, and distributed them among Martha, Noah, Ann, and Helen.

"You ought to take this blanket for yourself," Amanda told Lavinia as she helped Ann slip on an old smock and drape a piece of horse blanket over that. "You'll catch your death."

"I can't let my children freeze. It's bad enough they have to go without —" Lavinia stopped herself in time, her bottom lip caught between her teeth.

"Let me fetch you one of my blankets then," Amanda offered.

"You need them for your bed."

"I'm not in bed now." Ignoring Lavinia's objections, Amanda ran to her own wagon just as Henry Clay was about to start up again.

"Wait!" she called. "I have to get something." She climbed in, yanked one of the folded blankets off her bed, then jumped down. Handing the blanket to Lavinia she instructed, "Put this around you. No sense in shivering if you don't have to."

Lavinia drew the edges of the blanket around her thin shoulders. "You're very thoughtful, child. I want you to know you're like another daughter to me."

Amanda's eyes glistened with tears. "I ought to thank *you*. If it wasn't for you and Helen when I was hurt that time, and when Papa died —"

"Are you two done bein' grateful all over the place?" Henry Clay yelled in mock anger. "I'd like to get these wagons movin' again, if it's all right with you all."

Lavinia laughed, waved at him, then picked up Noah and walked ahead.

They trudged on till long past midday. Amanda knew by the angle of the sun overhead that it was getting late, but whenever Ann asked if was noon yet so they could eat, Amanda replied, "Soon."

The giant redwoods had cast long shadows that lay across the road in stripes before Henry Clay received the signal to halt for the night. While the men broke camp, Polly came over and spoke to Lavinia in urgent tones, then burst into unexpected tears. Lavinia patted the other woman's shoulder, murmuring small words of comfort.

"We'd better get a fire started," Helen said to Amanda. "Come with me to get some kindlin'. I'm scared of these crazy woods."

As she bent to pick up a pine tag, Amanda asked, "What's wrong with Polly? I've never seen her like that."

"Same problem we all got. Food. The Lightfoots don't have enough for another meal. Mr. Grafius said he could trap, but we're too high up for game. Nothing around but birds, and you can't trap them. No more fruit trees or berry bushes neither."

The enormity of the food situation hit Amanda like a mule kick in the stomach. "Lord, Helen, what are we going to *do?*"

"Mama suggested us three families put all our food together, whatever anybody's got." The effort of climbing over a log brought on a coughing fit.

That sounded like Lavinia — always eager to share. Amanda was grateful to be included as one of the "families," even though she had nothing to contribute.

"Why not slaughter one of the cattle?" Amanda said.

"We were going to, but so many of our oxen died, we're using all of our extra cattle to pull the wagons. Pa says we can't afford to lose another animal."

The sound of underbrush crackling behind them caused both girls to whirl around.

"Serena!" Helen said. "You scared us."

"Sorry. Hello, Amanda. I see you're out picking up bark, too." Serena's apron was filled with twigs and small branches.

"I don't know why we're bothering," Amanda told her. "There's nothing to cook."

"I know." Serena grasped the corners of her apron tighter to keep the kindling from slipping out. "Mama was talking about boiling tea from pine needles. Doesn't that sound awful?"

Amanda nodded, noticing that Serena was painfully thin, more so than anyone, since she had always been tall and slender.

"Guess I'd better get back," Serena said. "See you all later."

"Everybody's in the same boat," Helen said.

After a while, Amanda stopped with a skirt full of bark scraps to let Helen rest. "I wish Ben would come back," she said wistfully. "I miss him already, and he hasn't even been gone a whole day. Do you think he's all right?"

"He's on horseback, Amanda. Mr. Bell and him will zip over these mountains lickety-split. The valley we're headin' for may only be a little way off."

"What valley? I thought we were going to Oregon City?"

"We are. But Oregon City is in the Willamette Valley. That's where my family's goin' to settle, not in town."

A thought — quick and sharp — caused Amanda to drop her skirt. Wood scraps scattered about her feet. What was the last thing Ben mentioned before he left her? Something about going to look for their land . . . Suddenly, she was filled with an unreasonable fear.

"Helen, what if he doesn't come back? Suppose he gets thrown by his horse —"

Helen grasped Amanda by the shoulders. "You know as well as I do he's too good a rider for that to happen. I'm sorry, I didn't mean to imply that your Pa wasn't. You've got to stop thinkin' this way, Amanda."

"You're right. But I can't help it." She bent and began gathering the fallen wood. "I guess we'd better get back."

Jason and Frank built a roaring fire while Lavinia and Polly heated water in Lavinia's biggest iron kettle.

"With twelve people to feed, soup goes the furthest," Lavinia said. Amanda felt if she had to provide supper for that many people with no supplies, she'd run into the woods. But Lavinia brandished her ladle as though the task was not impossible, giving directions.

"Jason, go into the woods — not too far, mind you — and dig some roots. I don't care what kind, just so they aren't poisonous. You know the difference. Helen, you and Amanda find some greens. Cress, dandelions, anything with green leaves. If we don't look out, we're goin' to get scurvy."

The soup turned out to be quite tasty, if a little watery, in spite of the odd combination of ingredients. To the pot of water seasoned with the last of Lavinia's carefully hoarded salt, Polly put in a cupful of rice. Frank contributed a handful of the cracked corn he had brought along as feed for his horse. Jason found some tubular roots, resembling half-grown yams, which had a strange but not unpleasant flavor. Helen picked some greens they could not identify but threw in, anyway, and Amanda located a windfall of acorns overlooked by the squirrels. Saving the day, Jeb shot a ruffed grouse which Polly plucked and dressed in double time. Everyone was allowed one cup of soup, saving a half pot for the next day.

Amanda greedily spooned up the tender bits of fowl from the bottom of her bowl. She could not remember when game had tasted so delicious. She wished she could have more, but at least she would not have to go to bed hungry. The group around the fire was quiet, as though contemplating hardships ahead. Amanda excused herself, reluctant to leave the warmth of the fire, to go to bed.

Her wagon was cold and dark. She fumbled to light a candle, her last, then removed her boots and jacket, blowing out the candle as soon as she was under the covers. A cold knot formed in the pit of her stomach. Unsatisfied hunger . . . or apprehension? Turning on her side, she drew her knees up and whispered one word before she fell asleep.

"Ben."

Chapter
Twenty-five

W ANT another one?" Helen asked, her hammer poised to smash an acorn.

Amanda shook her head emphatically, her lips pursed with the bitter taste of the last nut she had eaten. "No, thanks. My mouth will never be the same. I think I'd rather starve than eat squirrel food."

"I know what you mean. My stomach thinks my throat's been cut for days now." Helen sipped the acorn tea Lavinia had brewed to conserve what little coffee they had left. "Mama had to go beggin' for food this evenin'. I never thought I'd live to see her do that."

"The Smiths did give her a little rice for the children." Amanda looked over at her bed where Ann and Martha were asleep, one at each end, small shapes bundled under Lavinia's best quilt. Noah was curled up in a pallet Amanda had fixed for him on the floor next to the bed. His blond hair stuck out like straw from the blanket he had drawn around his head to keep warm.

They were sitting in the back of Amanda's wagon, talking quietly so as not to wake the children. Amanda had kept her promise, insisting that Helen and the younger children share her wagon. After tossing out the empty food boxes and barrels, there was plenty of room to make up three pallets on the floor, one for Noah, one for Helen, and one for herself.

"Rice today," Helen said scornfully. "But what about tomorrow? How much longer can we go *on* like this?"

In the flickering candlelight, Amanda observed the dark smudges under Helen's eyes. Her health had hardly improved the last few days, worrying about her family.

"I guess we'll keep going until we . . . until we get to Oregon," Amanda said with more confidence than she actually felt.

She adjusted the jacket she had wrapped around her feet for added warmth. It was the coldest night they had experienced yet. The water bucket had already frozen over and, even though Amanda had tightened the canvas cover at both ends of the wagon, icy drafts blew in as though they were sitting in an open field.

She leaned against the side of the wagon, exhausted by the day's events, her stomach rebelling against the nasty, green acorns. Beside her, Helen was silent, lost in her own thoughts.

Through her layers of blankets and clothing, Amanda felt her hipbones jutting out like hooks in a cloak room. Helen was right. How much longer could they hold out before they dropped in their tracks like the oxen? Or became unbalanced like the woman in the wagon behind the Lightfoots who cried all evening. Amanda had listened to the woman's unbroken wailing, wishing that someone would make her shut up. She felt like crying, too, but what good did it do? Tears would not put food in their stomachs. Sobbing did not get them any closer to Oregon.

Their only hope was relief from Willamette Valley. According to Captain Compton, people living in the settlements were alerted to emigrant trains struggling over the mountains this time of year and were usually in a state of readiness to rush aid. And with Ben and John Bell meeting them halfway, how long would it take? They had been gone two days already. When would she see Ben again?

There were no answers to her questions, and thinking only gave her a headache. She blew out the candle, saying, "We can talk in the dark. This is the last candle I have."

"I'm ready to go to sleep, anyway. Get this night over with." Helen slid down under her pile of blankets and rags, her cough racking her. " 'Night."

"Good night."

Amanda settled the covers around her, tucking them around her body to keep out the cold air that was seeping through the floorboards. Lying on her back, she felt every vertebra in her spine pressing uncomfortably against the hard floor. She turned on her side but that was worse. Sighing, she rolled over again. Helen had already dropped off, her breath coming in short, fluttering gasps. Amanda lay awake, staring at the canvas cover overhead until she heard the first sounds of the camp coming to life.

She could not lay on the cold, hard wooden floor any longer. Flinging back her covers, she got up, stepping over Helen, who stirred but did not awake. Outside she gathered sticks and built a blazing fire. There was no breakfast, but at least they could warm up before pulling out again.

When the morning mists burned off, the day would be clear but cold. A sharp wind chased white puffy clouds like sheep across the sky. Mount Hood, angular and ice-covered, appeared to be floating above the pale blue mists, like a mythical kingdom in a fairy tale. Amanda stared at the peak dominating the landscape. Was Ben looking up at the mountain right now, thinking about her? Would Mount Hood guide him back to her? *Ben, where are you?* But the mountain maintained its lofty silence.

It took most of the day to grind up the mountain, which was even taller than the one they had scaled the day before, but Captain Compton refused to schedule a rest stop until they were on the other side.

Papa would call him a slave driver today, Amanda thought when they finally reached the summit. She walked over to the edge, intending to flop down on a rock, then stepped back in horror. The mountain seemed sheared off, as though someone had decided that the earth should end here. Amanda could toss a pebble over the side and not have it hit anything till it reached bottom. The trail crawled down the slope, a thin vein carved into the mountainside.

"We can't drive our wagons down this!" she cried to Henry Clay.

"You're right," he replied, uncoiling a length of stout rope. "We can't. Ira ordered us to turn the teams loose and lower the wagons on ropes."

Although twilight was closing in, the men worked feverishly, attaching ropes and chains to the rear axle of their wagons, snubbing the lines around sturdy stumps, then slowly easing the wagons down, one at a time. Others drove the protesting cattle down the muddy trail. The women and children were left to scramble down the mountain as best they could.

Recent rains had made the hillside slippery. Amanda had to walk down with her knees locked, stilt-legged, to keep from falling. A stone rolled under her foot, causing her to stumble. She grabbed for a bush but missed, sliding down about fifteen feet before crashing into a log. She lay on her back, blinking up at the sky.

"Are you hurt?" Lavinia's voice sounded miles away. "Don't move. Helen's comin' to help."

Amanda managed to stand, gingerly testing her arms and legs for broken bones. Everything seemed to be intact. But the back of her dress and jacket was slick with black mud, and her left hip was sore from where she had rolled over a rock.

"That was quite a sleigh ride," Helen said when she reached Amanda.

"Next time I'll use a sleigh," Amanda said, flexing her arm, which felt raw from her shoulder past her elbow.

Helen handed her a clean rag. "Your arm is bleeding." She helped Amanda roll back her torn sleeve.

"I'm surprised that's all that's wrong from the way I feel." She dabbed at the scrape. "What else is going to happen? My dress is ruined, what's left of it. And I'm so hungry I can hardly stand it."

But Helen was not listening. She was staring beyond the camp, which was being set up down below, at something on the trail winding up the next hill.

Amanda followed Helen's wide-eyed gaze. Through the dense foliage, she saw a horse and rider come into view, edging down the trail toward them.

Ben! Her heart leaped wildly. She ran

down the mountain, skirts flying. It was Ben
— he had come back for her!

"Amanda!" Helen called. "Wait!"

But she could not stop. Joy at seeing Ben
again gave wings to her feet. She raced
through camp, ducking between oxen and
wagons, and up the hill. She could see the
horse and rider better now . . . Then she
froze, her world crumbling into little pieces.
The person advancing toward her was not
Ben but Mr. Bell.

"Howdy, Miss Amanda," he greeted, touching his hat.

She clutched his horse's bridle, halting the
animal. "Where's Ben?" she blurted ungraci-
ously. "Why are you alone?"

He rubbed his bearded jaw and Amanda
could see, even in the fading light, how
tired he looked. "We got separated."

"Separated? How?" She realized she was
behaving rudely but could not help it.

"Ben thought there was a shorter route.
We'd been riding around these mountains for
two days before I said we should go north.
Ben didn't agree. He left me this morning,
heading due south. I stumbled back onto the
trail and here I am."

"You mean you haven't seen Ben all day?
You have no idea where he is?" She made no
attempt to conceal the panic in her voice.

"I'm sorry, Amanda. I wouldn't have this
happen for all the world. It's going to kill
Rose Compton when I tell her. She thinks the
sun rises and sets in Ben." *So do I*, Amanda

thought. "But I couldn't stop him when he said he knew the way. I had to let him go."

Amanda could understand that. She knew how stubborn Ben could be when he had his mind made up to do something. "Why did you come back here? I mean, I thought you were supposed to bring us help from the settlements."

"I wanted to tell Captain Compton we're closer to the end than we thought."

Her mind was still on Ben, but she replied automatically, "Really?"

He indicated the fir-covered slope behind him. "Believe it or not, just over this mountain you can see the valley. Oregon City is probably only another three or four days away."

Three or four days! It may as well be three or four weeks. "But nobody has any *food,*" Amanda declared. "Captain Compton promised us that people from Oregon would bring food. The children just can't go on."

"I'm sure Ben will get help," Mr. Bell said. "He's very dependable. Excuse me, Miss Amanda. I have to go speak to the captain."

Helen found her there, rooted to the same spot in which Mr. Bell had left her. "Come on, Amanda. You're half-frozen. Mr. Grafius snared a couple of squirrels and Mama made a stew. We saved you some."

"I'm not hungry."

"You haven't had anything but nuts for days, Amanda. You'll get sick."

"I'm already sick. As sick as I'll ever be."

"I know about Ben. I'm sorry. But Mr. Bell didn't say he was *lost* — just that he rode off *alone*."

"He's out there somewhere, Helen. Cold. Hungry. Maybe hurt. Maybe even —"

"Quit it! Now, you're comin' with me." Helen gripped Amanda by the arm and guided her down into camp.

Lavinia offered Amanda a bowl of the pungent-smelling stew, but Amanda pushed it away.

"You have to eat," Lavinia insisted. In the leaping firelight, the older woman's face was grave.

"That's what I told her, Mama."

"Please," Amanda said to them both. "I want to go lie down."

The younger children had already been fed and put to bed in Amanda's wagon. Weary from the long climb and lack of food, they were fast asleep, breathing rhythmically. Amanda climbed into her wagon quietly, found her own pallet, and lay down, pulling the covers over her. A short while later, Helen slipped into the pallet beside Amanda.

"You awake?" she asked into the darkness.

Amanda did not reply.

"Try not to think the worst," Helen went on, as though she knew Amanda was pretending to be asleep. "Ben is as sensible as an old shoe. He knows you're waitin' for him, and he'll come back to you if he has to crawl over those mountains on his hands and knees. He loves you."

Tears dribbled down Amanda's cheeks, wetting the wad of rags she used as a pillow. "I know. I love him, too. That's why I can't stand not knowing. Helen, what if he doesn't come back? What'll I *do*?"

"You'll always have a home with us," Helen reassured her. "But you won't need to live with us because Ben will be back."

Helen had so much confidence in Ben, Amanda began to feel guilty. "I hope you're right. Good night, Helen."

"G'night."

Thoughts of Ben invaded her mind again, but even that could not keep her awake two nights in a row. She dropped into a dark and dreamless sleep, like sinking slowly to the bottom of a river.

In the still hours before dawn, something awakened her, as though she had been called. She rose, took her jacket from the bottom of the pallet, and as an afterthought, her father's rifle, and left the wagon.

The palest gray light tinted the eastern sky. The camp was cloaked in silence, except for the whinnying of the horses. Amanda slipped the jacket over her shoulders and ran through the camp, heading for the trail up the mountain. This was the last mountain, Mr. Bell had said. Over this peak you could see Willamette Valley.

A feeling she could not explain drew her up the deeply rutted trail. She felt curiously light-headed, which she attributed to not eating the past few days, and surprisingly rested, as though she had slept fourteen hours on a feather mattress. She carried the rifle crooked in her arm the way Ben had showed her. If she was alert and lucky, she might be able to get something for breakfast.

The trail wound around the top of the mountain, about fifty feet from the summit. When the ground became more level, Amanda picked up speed. Suddenly the mountain fell away, and Amanda caught her breath, but not because she was frightened.

Draped in mist, Willamette Valley spread before her, a gray-green vista flowing between two mountain ranges. A silvery river curved gently through the length of the valley. Above it all, Mount Hood commanded her gaze heavenward, so high it seemed to scrape the dawning sky, ruling the valley in all its splendor.

Oregon at last.

Amanda was filled with an awe she had never experienced before. Everything she had seen on her odyssey across the country was only an overture; this was the symphony. No wonder people risked their lives traveling two thousand miles to come here.

Then something moving drew her attention to the trail far below . . . a tiny figure rising out of the mist. As the figure came closer, Amanda recognized a horse and rider.

"Ben!" Her voice bounced off the mountain.

She ran down the slippery trail, stumbling

344

in her flapping boots, but did not stop until she was in his arms. Even before she reached him, Ben leaped off his horse and ran to meet her, swinging her off her feet. Giddy with joy, she looked down into his face, laughing and crying all at once.

"Oh, Ben! I didn't think — when Mr. Bell came back and told us — I feel so silly —"

He laughed heartily. "Don't you ever finish a sentence? I told you I'd come back. I thought you had more faith in me." He hugged her as if he would never let her go.

When he set her down again, she asked, "Ben, we're here, aren't we? This is Oregon."

"Yup. Is it everything you expected?"

"More, now that you're back. But where's Oregon City? I thought you could see it from here."

"You can't really. It's right along the river. Wait'll you see it, Mandy —"

"You've been there?" She noticed for the first time the lines around his mouth, as though he had had less sleep than she had over the past few days.

"No, but I heard about it. I stopped at the first farm I came to for help."

"You brought help? Oh, Ben, everybody's so hungry! Where are they?"

"Back down there a ways. They'll be in camp before the wagons pull out. They've all got saddle bags, extra horses, supplies. And they'll stay with us till we get to the settlements."

Ben turned her to face the rolling valley.

"Tell me where you want to live," he said.

"Me? You want me to pick our farm?"

"We're going to be married soon, aren't we? I want our place to be so special, a home you can love."

Amanda felt tears rolling down her cheeks. She could choose a place to live, choose her home. A place she would never have to leave. She knew the perfect spot. Taking a deep breath, she pointed to an area near the river where the land stretched yearningly toward Mount Hood. She always wanted to see the lordly peak that had guided her these last few days, giving her hope when she felt all was lost.

"There," she said firmly. "Near the river over there."

They stood for a moment, not speaking as they surveyed their new home. Their long journey was finally over, but their life together was just beginning.

She had left Boston a spoiled, helpless child. She had arrived in Oregon a strong young woman. She could shoot, and scrounge for food and fuel. She had lived through unbearable heat and bone-chilling cold. She had gone up mountains and across rivers. She had seen people die, and she had survived it all. And, she thought, looking at Ben, she had learned how to love.

"Think you're ready for all this, Yankee girl?" Ben asked teasingly.

"Yup," Amanda said, imitating him.

And she *was* ready.

SUNFIRE

SUNFIRE™ ROMANCES

Spirited historical romances about the lives and times of young women who boldly faced their world, and dared to be different.

From the people who brought you
WILDFIRE®...

An exciting look at a NEW romance line!

Imagine a turbulent time long ago when America was young and bursting with energy and passion...

When daring young women, defied traditions to live their own lives...

When heart stirring romance and thrilling adventure went hand in hand...

When the world was lit by *SUNFIRE*...

SUSANNAH by Candice F. Ransom $2.95

Not since young Scarlett O'Hara has there been a heroine so spirited. SUSANNAH Dellinger had lived her sixteen years as a proper Virginia girl. But when her brother and her fiancé are called on to defend the South, she must fight for her own life, for her family, and for the secret love born in the flames of war. *Coming in April 1984*

ELIZABETH by Willo Davis Roberts $2.95

The Salem witch hunts of the 1600's is the frightening setting for ELIZABETH's story. When her friend Nell is accused of being a witch, ELIZABETH has to decide whether to risk her own life and defend Nell, or to remain silent and watch her friend die. Silence will win ELIZABETH wealthy Troy and safety. Crying out will bring her reckless Johnny and love. *Coming in June 1984*

DANIELLE by Vivian Schurfranz $2.95

It is the War of 1812; the city is New Orleans. Beautiful DANIELLE is a headstrong, young girl who must choose between an exciting but frightening pirate and the quiet understanding boy she grew up with. As the war engulfs her, DANIELLE's choice is no longer a matter of the heart, but will determine her destiny. *Coming in August 1984*

An exciting excerpt from the first chapter of SUSANNAH follows.

Susannah

by Candice F. Ransom

Chapter One

ALTHOUGH no Yankees had been spotted in the area for the past two days, Susannah Dellinger scanned the woods ahead, looking for signs of the blue uniforms.

You can never be too careful, she thought.

Although it was late April, 1864, spring had been slow coming to the Shenandoah Valley in Virginia this year. But the bare-branched trees hid no enemy soldiers. Susannah was grateful for that, at least, as she clambered up the rocky hillside, the harsh words Patricia had hurled at her earlier still ringing in her ears.

Susannah had not planned on going out that evening. After supper, she had gone up to her room as usual to read. The hours between supper and bedtime were long and boring; it was still too cold to sit out on the porch. Katie would not be up for a while yet to help Susannah undress for the night, so there was nothing to do except read.

Susannah had just stretched out on her bed and opened *Wuthering Heights*, to the place she had left off the night before, when a knock sounded at her door.

Without waiting for Susannah's answer, her sister Patricia burst in. "Susannah! Where is my blue ribbon? I *know* you have it! How dare you take my things."

Susannah sat up and looked at her younger sister. "What makes you think I have your ribbon?"

"Mary Sager told me. She saw you taking it off my dressing table. Now give it back!" Patricia's brown eyes were nearly black with anger. At fifteen, Patricia was only eleven months younger than Susannah, but they were complete opposites in both appearance and temperament.

"You don't need that old ribbon," Susannah said angrily. "You've got others."

"You're just jealous that my hair is prettier than yours," Patricia returned smugly. Patricia took after their mother, who had once been a Richmond beauty, with the same doe-brown eyes and thick, lustrous hair.

Susannah *was* once envious of Patricia's

burnished curls, when they were little girls. Susannah's hair was shining auburn, always much longer — falling well below her hips — but it did not tumble into careless ringlets.

"I am not jealous of your hair," Susannah declared now, sliding off the bed and smoothing her gown. She went over to her dressing table and opened a carved rosewood box. Pulling out a packet tied with a frayed blue satin ribbon, she said, "Here, take your ribbon. I'll find something else to tie up Evan's letters." Stripping off the ribbon, she offered it to her sister.

But Patricia's face crumpled with misery. "That's right, Susannah. Flaunt your letters! Remind me that I don't have a boyfriend and probably *never* will because of this stupid war!" Snatching her ribbon, she stormed out, slamming the door.

After more than three years of war, the whole house had gone crazy, it seemed. This past winter had been long and tiresome, made even more tedious by the fact that Robert, her brother, and Evan had enlisted with the Confederate army some months before.

After Patricia's accusations, Susannah was in no mood to read. She grabbed the packet of letters, slipped on her old boots, and ran out of the house without a bonnet or shawl. No one would miss her.

She was nearly at the top of the steep hill when her long skirt snagged on a blackberry bramble. Impatiently, she yanked it free. Her dress, a rosy cotton gown the shade of peaches at the peak of ripeness, flattered Susannah's ivory skin and light brown hair, but was hardly suitable for scrambling through the woods. Besides, it was a morning dress and the chilly spring air penetrated the thin fabric as though it were cheesecloth.

Morning dress. The term made her want to laugh. As if it mattered now — after three years of war — whether she wore clothes that were supposed to be appropriate for certain times of the day.

Staring at the fabric in her hand, Susannah remembered a wonderful gown she had once. A delicate, transparent white wool, the color of dogwood blossoms, lined in eggshell satin, with a full skirt that fell in soft folds over her hoops, a stand-up collar encircled with tiny pink pearl buttons, and more buttons spilling down the creamy bodice. Susannah had worn the dress, her first party gown, at Christmas two years before. She came down the winding staircase slowly, holding her head high to show off the pearl drops at her ears, and into the central hall where neighbors were assembled around the Christmas tree. Evan Jones had watched her descend, obviously enraptured. When she reached the bottom of the steps, he told her she was prettier than the silver angel adorning the top of the tree.

At the crest of the hill, Susannah paused to catch her breath. How she loved this view. From here she could see all of Dogwood Hill:

the big white house presiding over newly tilled fields. As always, Susannah felt a surge of pride. Her home was the most beautiful in the state, she was certain. Although she had not traveled extensively in her sixteen years, she had gone to the Academy for Young Ladies in Staunton three years before. And on the long journey from Winchester to Staunton, which covered nearly the whole length of the Shenandoah Valley, Susannah had seen many grand plantations, but none so charming as Dogwood Hill.

Susannah walked through the grove, clutching her skirts in one hand. She stopped when she reached the waist-high wall made of stacked granite fieldstone. Right now her thoughts turned to the war. Three dogwood springs ago, in April of 1861, guns fired upon Fort Sumter, and the United States split into the North and the South. Susannah had not thought much about the war when it first began, being only thirteen, and she, like her parents, did not feel it would last long. Surely not three years, going on four. And who would have imagined that the war would have endured until Robert and Evan were old enough to enlist?

A snapping branch startled Susannah out of her reverie. She whirled, half expecting to see a Yankee sneaking up on her. With a sigh of relief, she recognized Patricia, struggling through the bushes.

"I want to say I'm sorry," Patricia apologized. "I shouldn't have lost my temper."

"Short tempers are a Dellinger trait," Susannah said, smiling. "Which makes it doubly hard for us to act like ladies. I'm sorry I took your ribbon. It was just lying there, but I should have asked your permission."

"And you're really pretty Susannah. Your eyes are much nicer than mine," Patricia added.

Susannah remembered one October evening before he enlisted with the army, Evan had looked into Susannah's upturned face and said, "Your eyes are like autumn smoke, did you know that? Right now they are tinged with purple, like the haze that gathers in the foothills of Big North Mountain." Susannah had lived on that compliment ever since.

Patricia was holding out the frayed, blue satin scrap. "Here. You can have it. It's really too ragged to use as a hair ribbon anymore."

Susannah accepted the peace offering in silence, recalled the harsh words she had exchanged with her sister. The war had done that to them, spinning them all out on a fine thread of anxiety and tedium, until they were in danger of breaking.

"I guess I'll have to get used to wearing worn ribbons," Patricia said wearily. "I'll probably be ninety-seven before we can afford to buy new ones."

"I know," Susannah agreed, looking at her sister in sympathy. It was difficult for Patricia, just fifteen, to have to give up pretty clothes and parties before she had ever experienced them. At least, Susannah had gotten to dress up and go to a few balls before the war had ended that, too.

"It's getting dark," she said now. "We'd better head back before Mama realizes we're gone and has a fit."

They took the long way back, skirting the red fields where winter wheat showed emerald green against the ruddy red dirt. The sudden flash of green triggered another memory — one Susannah wanted to keep buried. The boy she was remembering had eyes that exact shade of green when he tilted his blond head toward the sun. He wore the uniform of the dreaded Yankees and yet something had happened in a brief instant between the soldier and Susannah more than two years before, something she tried to forget and couldn't. Now, she concentrated on getting around the muddy field.

She loved to ramble over the vast acres of the plantation, something she was not allowed to do now that she was sixteen. Mud clung to her boots, and as she attempted to scrape off the worst of it in the grass, she could imagine what her mother would say.

"Susannah Dellinger! A young lady does not tramp the fields like a common peddler. You are no longer a tomboy."

Actually, Susannah had willingly put her rough-and-tumble days behind her, those wonderful summers when she and Robert and Evan roamed the woods between Dogwood Hill and the Jones plantation, Huntington. She accepted her new status as "young lady of the house," although she did experience a nostalgic tug now and then for the old days.

A mockingbird perched on a fence post called the same three falling notes over and over. Its song plucked a deeper, sadder chord within Susannah. This time of year, the driveway to their house should be canopied with snowy blossoms of the dogwood trees planted by old Elijah Dellinger. But now only a double row of stumps edged the drive, as blunt and ugly as tent pegs, ax scars still marking the amputated trunks.

Susannah closed her eyes briefly, trying to shut out the impression of that awful day just over two years before, when their front yard had been a sea of mud, churned by the hooves of countless Yankee cavalry horses. She did not want to relive that day, just as she didn't want to remember the soldier with the green eyes.

They were coming in sight of the house now. Susannah loved the way the driveway curved, then straightened out to dramatically reveal Dogwood Hill. The house could not be called a mansion, like Huntington, but it was nonetheless impressive. The two-story white brick structure commanded the top of a knoll, flanked by century oaks and ancient willow trees that arched gracefully over the black slate roof.

Seeing the house in this particular light, Susannah reflected, no one would suspect that Dogwood Hill had ever known anything but peace.

"Look!" Patricia cried, pointing toward the white-columned portico. "That horse! Isn't it Turner Ashby?"

Susannah squinted in the hazy twilight. There *was* a horse tied up . . . no, two horses. The black-satin horse did resemble Robert's mount, named after the Valley's dashing General Ashby, now dead. But wasn't Robert supposed to be camped somewhere along the Rapidan River, where most of Lee's cavalry had spent the winter? And who did the other horse belong to . . . ?

"Robert's home!" Patricia cried, running up the driveway.

Susannah felt a wave of dizziness. Robert was home! Then she began running, too. As she drew closer, she could see the double oak doors standing wide open, and a knot of people gathered on the porch. Sharp gravel punctured the thin soles of her boots, and her skirts and petticoats foamed about her ankles in an immodest tangle, but she never slowed. Beside her brother she recognized Evan Jones.

Seconds later, Susannah joined them. "Oh, Robert, is it really you? I thought I must be hallucinating —" She stopped, breathless, as she smiled at the dark-haired boy leaning against a slender column. "Evan! How wonderful to see you! I can't believe you both are here!"

"It really is us," Robert said. "Privates Dellinger and Jones, Fourth Virginia Cavalry, Company L." He gave her a mock salute. "Evan and I were sent out with the rest of our unit to recruit some more Valley horses . . . and men. Though there aren't many left of either."

But Susannah barely heard her brother's explanation. She walked over to Evan, her hands outstretched. "I'm so glad to see you again." Her heart was pounding like a Howitzer gun, but with her whole family watching, she could not say what she really felt.

"Evening, Susannah," Evan replied, tipping his gray felt slouch cap. His tone was formal for the benefit of Susannah's parents, but his black eyes were as caressing as ever.

"Have you been to Huntington?" Susannah inquired politely, all the while drinking in the sight of Evan's broad shoulders clothed in Confederate gray.

He brushed the road dust from the sleeve of his wool jacket. "Just came from there. Garnet threw a fit when we couldn't stay longer."

Knowing Garnet, Susannah thought, *she probably threw a fit because they didn't bring some of their comrades and stay for a party.*

At sixteen, Evan's sister loved parties and balls, any occasion that showed her dark beauty and brought her the attention she always craved.

"How did you fare the winter?" she asked Evan.

He laughed, and suddenly the sound reminded Susannah of those long-ago summers when the three of them ruled the countryside, free as larks.

"You know we spent the winter picketing the line in Madison County," he said. "Camp life wasn't what I expected. Sharing a crude hut with twelve other men, all of us freezing. Half of them without shoes or coats."

"Oh, Evan. How dreadful. To be so cold . . ." Susannah said sympathetically, thinking about the carpets her mother had cut up and sent with Robert for blankets.

He smiled, looking just as he used to when they were all younger. "Yes, it was cold, but your letters warmed me."

"Evan, it was such a long winter, stuck out here with no news," Susannah said, reaching out to take Evan's arm.

A shadow passed over Evan's face. "It was long for us, too. But we kept busy, raiding Yankee camps. The Yanks never missed the food we stole, but we would've starved without it," he said bitterly.

"General Lee asked everyone to endure," Robert added. "You know, those men would go to the ends of the earth for that man. Hungry, cold, miles from home — yet they won't give up."

"How long can you stay?" Susannah asked Robert.

"I'm afraid we've already stayed longer

than we should have. Evan, you about ready?"

Evan's eyes met Susannah's for a second. "I'll never be ready to leave this paradise, but I guess we'd better. General Lee is planning a big military move in a few days."

"Oh, Robert, do be careful," Elizabeth Dellinger pleaded, putting a hand on her son's arm. "Hannah is fixing you both some cornbread and peas. It isn't much, but if we had known you were coming . . ."

As the rest of the family clamored around Robert, Susannah used the opportunity to walk Evan to his horse. A hundred things teemed in her head, but she could not formulate a single sentence.

"Evan, I —" Her throat closed. She could not bear to say good-bye to him again. She wished she had something to give to him, a parting present.

Evan checked the girth strap, then led Susannah around the other side of his horse, where they were shielded from the others on the porch. He pulled her to him. Susannah smelled the pungent aroma of horse and worn leather and campfire smoke trapped in his wool jacket. She fingered the gold armband she had stitched herself and presented to him the day he and Robert left to enlist.

"Wait for me," Evan had whispered urgently that day. "Be my special girl, Susannah."

"I will," she replied, tears frosting her lashes and turning her eyes into violet pools.

"I'll wait forever if I have to. Do you love me?"

But Evan had mounted up, and with a jaunty wave, rode down the driveway behind Robert.

Now, seven months later, Susannah noticed the gold band was frayed and dirty, but Evan still wore it.

He held her a few second longer, then repeated the words he spoke last fall. "Wait for me, Susannah. You're my special girl. Don't think of anyone else but me."

"I won't," she promised, brushing at a stray tear. "I'll write every night. And you write to me."

She watched him climb into the saddle. Then Robert gave her a farewell hug and mounted Turner Ashby. As they trotted down the driveway, Evan waved to Susannah, though his shoulders sagged. This time, she observed, he did not look like a knight of old. He was not the same Evan Jones who pranced his horse with jingling spurs like last October, eager to beat the Yankees.

But hadn't they all changed? Ever since that terrible March day two years ago, their lives had been turned upside down. And no one would ever be the same.

The dogwood stumps disappeared into the evening mist as Susannah became lost in the memory of those unforgettable days.

WILDFIRE.

Move from one breathtaking romance to another with the #1 Teen Romance line in the country!

NEW WILDFIRES! $1.95 each

- ☐ MU32539-6   **BLIND DATE** Priscilla Maynard
- ☐ MU32541-8   **NO BOYS?** McClure Jones
- ☐ MU32538-8   **SPRING LOVE** Jennifer Sarasin
- ☐ MU31930-2   **THAT OTHER GIRL** Conrad Nowels

BEST-SELLING WILDFIRES! $1.95 each

- ☐ MU31981-7   **NANCY AND NICK** Caroline B. Cooney
- ☐ MU32313-X   **SECOND BEST** Helen Cavanagh
- ☐ MU31849-7   **YOURS TRULY, LOVE, JANIE** Ann Reit
- ☐ MU31566-8   **DREAMS CAN COME TRUE** Jane Claypool Miner
- ☐ MU32369-5   **HOMECOMING QUEEN** Winifred Madison
- ☐ MU31261-8   **I'M CHRISTY** Maud Johnson
- ☐ MU30324-4   **I'VE GOT A CRUSH ON YOU** Carol Stanley
- ☐ MU32361-X   **THE SEARCHING HEART** Barbara Steiner
- ☐ MU31710-5   **TOO YOUNG TO KNOW** Elisabeth Ogilvie
- ☐ MU32430-6   **WRITE EVERY DAY** Janet Quin-Harkin
- ☐ MU30956-0   **THE BEST OF FRIENDS** Jill Ross Klevin
